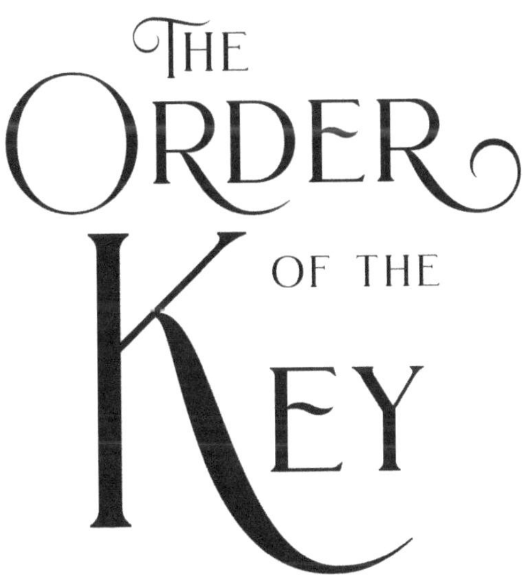

THE ORDER OF THE KEY

JUSTINE MANZANO

THE ORDER OF THE KEY

EVENTIDE BOOKS

For Ismael,
for finding the writer in me when I didn't know it was there.

For Logan,
for teaching me a little something about dreams coming true.

ONE

R U N

In my dreams, I ran with my father.

Or at least I thought it was my father. I never had the chance to meet him before he took off and kept on running, right away from Mom, from me, from kissing away boo-boos and sneaking me cookies from the cupboard when Mom wasn't looking. Or whatever it was people did with their dads. I wouldn't know.

But in the dream, we were together. His voice light and teasing with an Irish brogue, an accent unlike anyone else's in my life. He prodded me to hurry, to run faster, to keep up with him.

The air was clear, and we didn't run on a track. Our feet snagged on fallen tree limbs and slick patches of wet leaves, through the clearing in a forest I didn't recognize. We would take off so fast it was like flying.

It wasn't real. For one thing, nobody moved that way. I wasn't The Flash, though that would be awesome. For another, I'd lived in Bronx, New York my entire life, and the only stretch of open green space like that in the Boogie Down was the Botanical Garden or the Zoo. They didn't just let you blast through the trees there.

In The Bronx, there were track meets on asphalt schoolyards, or wood gym floors with bad polish jobs. Which was where I pressed my fingertips, my heels resting on the starting blocks, waiting impatiently for the whistle to blow.

Maybe that dream was why I loved running so much.

If I won this eight-hundred-meter race, I'd get the sweet spot in the first city-wide competition of the school year. I rocked up onto my toes and back down.

I could do this.

At the shrill of the whistle, I pushed off, the soles of my shoes pounding the floor as I moved across the track. Sherri Tilden, the contestant beside me, had once thrown my bookbag into the pool during a party. It was one of the rare times I'd tried fitting in at a school full of jock assholes, preppy overachievers who acted like FDR High was a one-way ticket to Harvard, and drug-peddling losers. It was also why I grinned when I pulled ahead of her.

How's my dust taste, Tilden?

I wasn't big on bragging, but beating a bully was too much fun. I might be Queen of Geekdom, and she may have destroyed my copy of *Miss Marvel, Volume 1*, but I was still the superior runner. So there was that.

I had that, but not much else. Not when the underdog, a freshman girl whose name I didn't even remember, pulled in front of me as I started my second lap.

Panic set in. I needed this race. I was a geek, not a nerd, as jocks often discovered when they asked me to do their homework and my help only managed to score them Cs. If I had any hope in hell of attending a top school, it would be because I clocked the fastest lap, not for my killer test scores.

My lungs burned and my feet stumbled. The muscles in my legs throbbed, my arms pumping as I tried to eat up the distance. We left the other competitors in the dust. But I couldn't get past her.

Sweat beaded on my forehead. I was going to lose. To a newbie baby freshman.

No way. No superhero had ever won a battle by quitting. When the odds were stacked against them, they dug deeper until they found a way out.

Dig deeper, Jacks. Come on, you got this. You are one with the speed force.

If I closed my eyes, I saw my father's laughing green eyes as he beckoned me forward, the tree trunks a gray-brown blur as we sped by.

My eyes shot open. A burst of energy flooded my veins, crackling within me like I'd grabbed hold of a live wire. The pounding of my heart drowned out the roar of the crowd in the bleachers. Blackness swam at the edges of my vision until all I saw was the lane disappearing below my feet. I went numb, inside and out. I couldn't feel my legs move anymore. But I was faster.

Faster than everybody.

And then I was done. Past the finish line, first place. The girl who had been just a drop ahead was now a good twenty meters behind me.

What the hell just happened? How? My hands shook, and my legs gave out. I hit the floor hard, pain rattling through my knees and up my thighs. Bile burned my throat as the freshman launched across the finish line.

"Jacklyn! You okay?" Coach Perl shouted as she jogged to me. She pushed my water bottle into my hand. "Drink, now."

I tipped the bottle back, emptying it in a few thirsty gulps.

"Whoa." Coach smiled, revealing a row of grody teeth. "That was insane! I don't know where that came from, but I'm gonna need you to do that again for the race." She frowned. "But drink more water first, or something. And pace yourself. You look like you died."

I blinked, and when I could manage it, nodded.

"C'mon." Coach held out her hand. "Let's get you some recognition."

Another nod, and I let her pull me back to my feet. My legs wobbled like rubber, but I stayed upright. Sherri Tilden whispered something into the ear of the freshman I'd beaten, a scornful twist to her features. Sherri looked ready to spit on me, and the freshman looked like I'd stolen her puppy.

What the hell. What's another enemy at this point?

Coach Perl announced the winners, and the crowd in the

bleachers gave the customary applause. I tuned out after my name, busy scanning the crowd. The usual mortifying extra loud whoops and shrieks of excitement had been missing during my race, and I longed for them, despite myself. Absently, I accepted the half-hearted congratulations of my competitors and praised them for a great race, all the while trying not to be disappointed.

Mom had promised she wouldn't miss this. But she wasn't there. And neither was my sister, Gana.

Coach Perl slapped me on the back and smiled. I returned it and tried to ignore the burn of disappointment eating at the bottom of my stomach. I failed.

Still, I tried to play along, chatting with the people in the bleachers about the next race and what I wanted to do after I graduated. The short answer? I had no idea, but it had better involve a track scholarship.

I killed time until the locker room emptied, then headed downstairs to get changed. I tended to be a t-shirt and jeans kinda girl, but I'd chosen a special outfit for a special day—a pink, long sleeved V-neck shirt and a brown skirt with matching knee-high leather boots.

Happy birthday to me.

I was moping, and I knew it. I hadn't really expected any of the kids at school to remember. But Gana hadn't said anything all day, and Mom had left for work before I even woke up. My eighteenth birthday, and the only person who seemed to care was me.

I released my hair from its ponytail and fluffed my long, dark curls. I applied makeup: a swipe of powder across my face, a coat of mascara, gloss on my lips. Throwing on my light jacket, I headed home.

The sky was overcast when I stepped through the heavy metal door and out into the crisp fall air. Drawing my jacket a bit tighter around me, I hurried down the steps and off in the direction of our apartment building. I needed to get home.

I was still drained and shaky from the race. Maybe if I sat and rested for a while, I'd feel better.

I barely got around the corner before a noise stopped me in my tracks.

"You think you're hot shit, don't you?"

Sherri Tilden.

I closed my eyes and allowed myself a deep breath before I faced her. The freshman and one of the other runners from the race flanked her. As they looked on, Sherri, who was model-tall and bottle-pretty, stepped forward, right into my face.

Rancid Cheeto breath. My nose wrinkled. "Can I offer you a breath mint?"

I barely got the words out before she shoved me. Stupid slippery dress boots had no traction, and down I crashed onto my ass.

A hand twisted in my jacket, and for a second my eyes didn't see fingers or glittery nails filed to a perfect point. They saw claws protruding from ink-black, moist skin. I flinched, slamming my eyes shut to clear my vision.

Monsters. Just like the ones that chased me every time that running dream with my dad went south, reminding me that in the end, I was alone.

Nightmares aren't real. Sherri's not a monster. Just a monstrous bitch.

"What's wrong?" Sherri said, with a needling whine better suited for a child. "You didn't seem scared of me before."

You didn't have claws before.

"Well, to be fair," I swatted her hand away and rose, brushing some dirt from my clothes, "it would have been tough to see me from so far behind."

"Bitch." She pulled one arm back, and I knew it was a punch on its way, but my vision seemed to slow, to blur.

"Sherri," the freshman called, and the other girl grabbed her arm, stopping her. "We should go. You'll get thrown off the team if you—"

"That's right, Sherri." I turned away to continue my walk home. "You should definitely go."

My stomach wobbled. What was going on with me?

"Hey! I ain't done with you yet." She yanked my arm, and a screeching sound echoed through my ears.

I didn't even think before the punch connected, laying Sherri out on the sidewalk.

The girls swore, dropping to their knees beside her.

As if on a delay, pain shot through my hand the minute I

moved it, the skin on my knuckles cracked and bloody.

She wasn't my first bully. Not by far. But I didn't think I'd ever hit anybody that hard.

"Fuck you, Madison," the freshie shouted up at me. I took that as my opportunity to leave.

Sherri groaned as I turned my back on the scene. I flipped her the finger and didn't look back. But I stayed alert—listening for sounds of anybody who might follow.

Mom was gonna kill me when she found out what happened, and I wanted to be wrapped up in a blanket in my room, forgetting my disaster of a birthday, when she did. *If* she did. Sherri might not have the balls to own up to her part.

It was only about ten minutes from school to my house, so I picked up the pace, pushing through my exhaustion and longing for my bed. The pounding of basketballs bouncing off the stoop in front of a nearby apartment building echoed through my head, and I squeezed my eyes shut until I stabilized. Relief fluttered through my chest when our six-story walk-up came into view.

It was constructed from graying bricks that had once been pristine. The green paint of the banister and door peeled off in sharp chips. A maze of fire escapes crisscrossed the face of the building. It may have looked like a prison, but it was our prison.

Gana's voice carried out of the apartment and froze me in place. "No, Mom. There isn't enough time for that. She'll be home any minute. I'm just gonna write 'Happy 18th Bat-Day.' If I draw Batman in icing, he'll look like a potato with bat ears."

I grinned.

"Yeah, well, drive faster. You're already later than you should have been." Gana again. Apparently on the phone with our perpetually late mother.

At least they were trying to throw something together for me.

I backed out of the apartment building. I didn't want to ruin their surprise. I'd kill time, go to the bodega, and come back, ready to be surprised.

It was strangely silent for only six in the evening. An eerie vibe settled along my shoulders, buzzing in my ears like static. Like a spider-sense.

Like before. During the fight.

Maybe I should have stayed home.

Ridiculous. The bodega wasn't far, and I could handle myself.

My boot heels echoed on the concrete. After a block, I settled into a rhythm and shed the fear. I turned the corner to go through the alleyway, my shortcut to chips and chocolate, but I wasn't alone. I jumped. Someone was there, halfway down the block, shrouded in shadows. Lurking.

Something about him looked wrong, but the dark obscured my view.

I took a step closer. Something about him *was* wrong. But what I was seeing wasn't a *him*, it was an *it*. I stepped forward again at the will of eyes that couldn't make sense of what was in front of them.

It was a monster, the kind I'd read about in my stacks of

collected comics. Except this one wasn't constructed of paper, ink, and a sprinkling of imagination.

In the dark of the alley, all that was visible was its silver, saliva-dripping teeth as they glinted in the light of a nearby streetlamp. The rest looked shapeless, undefined, like oil dumped over a sack of bones. It was broad, and the tight space of the alley slowed its stride to a shuffle.

I needed to run. My entire body tensed, but my feet remained rooted to the ground. Just a step. Just. One. Step.

My boot scuffed against the concrete. The thing shrieked, a sound piercing enough to leave my ears ringing long after the scream ended.

Disbelief numbed my senses. *Happy frickin' birthday to me.*

TWO

DO OR DIE

I tried to blink the vision away, the way I had during the fight with Sherri, but it stubbornly remained. It followed each step backward I took, its posture hunched and animalistic, with the fluid movement of a lion but on two legs. Another step and it stopped abruptly, as if it had smacked into an invisible wall. Its hiss made the hair on my arms stand on end.

I wasn't going to wait for it to start moving again. I took off the way I came, only to collide with a solid wall of muscle two steps into my escape.

Pushing with both hands, I tried to put distance between myself and what had to be a second creature. Lots of animals hunted in packs, why not these oil slick monsters?

The fingers that caught my wrists were human flesh and bone. The guy they belonged to glanced between me and the creature, a flop of black hair tumbling into his eyes. He let go of my arms and they dropped to my side. "Don't worry," he said, his deep voice short of breath. "I'm holding it back with my..." He trailed off. "Jacklyn Madison, right?"

"How do you—?" I asked. "Never mind. I don't care. Let's go!" I yanked at his leather jacket, but he planted his feet and didn't budge.

Movement over his shoulder called my attention, and I tensed, prepared for an attack.

A girl with rich brown skin stood behind the boy, carefully surveying the area surrounding us. Why was she looking so hard? She wasn't likely to miss the monster.

I yanked at the boy's arm again. He was obviously here to talk to me, and I didn't want to leave him with that thing. "Come on! Run!"

His eyes narrowed. The creature hissed and paced like a glitching video game character. When the boy's gaze returned to me, he smiled. "It's been so long I almost didn't recognize you. I'm Kyp."

I didn't even know this guy. Forget it. He could play with the monster. I was leaving.

"Stop," Kyp said, and then he pulled a freaking battle axe from a scabbard strapped to his back.

Okay. I would not be moving if he didn't want me to move. At least not until he wasn't a foot away holding Stormbreaker.

I needed to get out of the MCU right now.

Kyp widened his stance and held his hands out toward the thing as though he could stop its approach. Behind him, the girl pulled weapons from sheaths on her hips, her dark ponytail swaying with the movement—two three-pronged weapons I'd seen before. Twin sai, like Raphael from *Teenage Mutant Turtles* used to kill his enemies in the far superior original comic book.

They looked about my age but carried themselves like trained soldiers. They were all that stood between me and death by monster.

I should run, let them take care of it, since they seemed experienced in this sort of thing. I really wished I hadn't changed back into my school clothes after track.

Do or die. Maybe literally.

I ran, but I barely reached the alley's edge before another oil slick monster landed in front of me. My heart stuttered hard, and a scream ripped from my throat.

"Get down!" Kyp shouted behind me, much closer than I'd expected. I dropped to my knees, skinning them on the sidewalk, but that wasn't nearly as bad as what I'd avoided. The creature crashed to the ground, a piece of rebar protruding from its chest. Thick green liquid bubbled from the wound.

"Are you okay? It didn't hit you, did it?" Kyp's hands cupped my elbows, and he helped me to my feet.

Our eyes met, and I realized I did recognize him. I'd never met him, but I... there was something. I gasped for breath. "No, I think I'm good. Better than I would've been. Thanks."

A shriek sounded behind Kyp. He whirled to investigate, throwing an arm out and pushing me behind him. "Cass!"

I looked around him, despite really not wanting to see another one of those things. "On it!" Cass swept the oil slick's legs out from under it and thrust her sai into its jaw.

I flinched. "Where the hell are they coming from?"

"Don't worry, Jacks." Kyp used my nickname like it was perfectly natural. "Just stay" —a third creature burst from the alley with another inhuman shriek— "close." He yanked the axe free from its scabbard.

He and the creature observed each other. This wasn't a standoff between a predator and its prey, like those Discovery Channel shows my sister watched for fun. It was two predators, about to go toe-to-toe. I swallowed. That made me the prey.

The creature dove forward as Kyp readied his axe. Behind me, Cass stabbed her way through another two creatures. If I sped down the alley to the back of the buildings, I'd be able to cut behind them until I reached mine. It wouldn't be the first time I'd scaled a fence, but it would be the first time I'd done it to save my life.

No. No, I couldn't just leave them.

I stepped into the mouth of the alley and hesitated, my conscience fighting like hell against my desire to get out of danger immediately.

Clammy fingers curled around my ankles and yanked. My feet slid out from under me as the ground rushed up toward my face. Pain sparked like fireworks in my wrist and I yelped.

"Jacks!" Kyp called, but the thing that had hold of my feet

dragged me further into the alley. The yelp turned into a scream as its claws pierced my flesh, gouging my legs. My breath slammed out of my lungs, but I managed to kick the thing. Sharp slicing pain trailed along my skin.

I just wanted to go for a walk!

Booted feet crashed onto the bulky metal dumpster beside me and the claws detached with a rip. I rolled over in time to see Kyp swing, the flat end of his axe connecting with its jaw.

The monster clambered to its feet, hissing as it rose. Another ear-splitting screech sounded from inside the dumpster Kyp had landed on, and the lid rattled and thumped beneath him.

"Crap!" He struggled to maintain his balance, a surfer riding an uncontrollable wave. "Jacklyn! Run!" He tumbled off the lid and landed right in front of the waiting monster. Two more exploded from the bin, sending paper and rotting food flying everywhere.

Warm blood ran down my legs as I pushed myself to my feet. I stumbled around the corner like a newborn foal, getting away from the battle to clear my head and find something I could use as a weapon. The creature Kyp had killed earlier lay just around the corner, where Cass was now engaged in battle with two new creatures.

Ignoring the weirdly green blood, sharp teeth, and empty gaze, I wrapped my fingers around the rebar in the dead thing's chest and pulled. It came free with a wet sucking sound that made me shudder.

"Where's Kyp?" Cass slammed a sai into the side of a

creature's skull.

"Back in the alley," I said. "I'm looking for a weapon so I can help."

"Help?" Cass asked, but I was already heading back to Kyp. My legs ached and my feet tripped along.

Kyp wasn't where he'd been earlier, but low rumbles, like growls from a rabid dog, rolled down the alley toward me.

No.

I followed.

Two Oil Slicks lay dead in my path. I stepped over their bodies, refusing to look at them for longer than it took to find my footing.

In the back of the alley, a creature loomed over Kyp, illuminated by a lone emergency light over the back door of a building. It reared back and rammed Kyp in the chest with its shoulder, slamming him up against the wall. His head lolled back, and I spotted bloody claw marks along the side of his neck.

I had to do something. Kyp had already saved me multiple times in the few minutes I'd known him.

Kyp didn't have his axe. I approached with caution, but it wasn't until I was behind the thing that warning bells finally broke through the sound of my pulse beating in my ears.

I wasn't an Avenger, this wasn't a comic book, and I could die. This thing had carved holes in Kyp, and he'd been defending himself with an axe. What the hell was I doing?

Oil Slick turned toward me and there was no more time to

second guess. I clobbered it in the face with the rebar. It stumbled to the side, claws coming to its head, groaning.

"Again, Jacks!" Kyp grasped his ribs as he pulled himself back up the wall.

I swung again with the wrist I damaged earlier, but oddly it didn't hurt. This time, the monster fell. Kyp took the opportunity to kick something across the ground toward me. It skidded to my feet, metal scratching on pavement.

A dagger with a carved ivory handle. I grabbed it, the metal blade catching the light of the bare bulb hanging above us, blinding me for an instant.

"Jacks. Do it! Now!" He pressed a hand to the scratches on his neck.

The creature lunged at me and I punched the dagger into its center, sliding through sticky skin that tore like paper and scraping against bone.

It doubled over and shrieked, and my ears rang.

A thud.

A thick, wet sound.

The monster dropped to reveal Kyp's ashen face. He pressed his foot against the monster's back and yanked his axe free with a grunt.

"Good instincts." He moved to pat my shoulder, but hesitated, his brow knitted in uncertainty. "Any more?"

"Probably not." I shrugged. I didn't know where those good instincts had come from in the first place.

"He means the Gorvhans. And no, there aren't any more."

I whirled, brandishing the dagger and rebar, only to find Cass entering the alley.

"At least she learns fast." Cass frowned. "Are you okay?"

Kyp groaned and leaned against the side of the building for support. "Pretty sure I broke a rib. You?"

"Okay," Cass said. "I got a few gross bruises, my elbow is killing me, and I twisted my ankle on..."

I knew she was listing a series of injuries, but none of them registered. My pulse pounded louder in my ears. It overwhelmed everything around me, filling my head until it thumped. Both weapons slipped from my fingers. I flexed my once-damaged wrist. It cracked but was otherwise fine. I struggled to see the cuts on my legs, but the lighting obstructed my view.

"Jacks!" Kyp's shout broke through the din.

"What?" I snapped to attention.

"I asked if you were okay," Kyp said, a little more gently, his eyebrows drawing together.

"No." Duh.

"Okay." He nodded. "Okay, that probably makes sense. We should get you back to Jaina."

Jaina. "How do you know my mother?" A howl and a screech cut through the air from afar. I jumped. "More Oil Slicks?"

Cass raised her eyebrows. "Oil Slicks?"

I looked at the one we'd just killed. My stomach churned.

Kyp grinned and shook his head, dark hair tumbling into his

eyes. "Oh, them? They're Gorvhans. And we need to get you home before more arrive. I'll take point. Cass, rear."

She circled behind me and Kyp, following us as we made our way out of the alley and back through the main streets.

Kyp took two steps and swore. "Well. This hurts." He continued walking, but his jaw was clenched tight.

"Do you need help?" I asked. He opened his mouth to answer, but I didn't wait. He'd been hurt protecting me. I took his hand and looped his arm around my shoulder. "Lean on me. I've got you."

He aimed a pained grin down at me. "Thanks, but you don't have to help me."

"I know," I said. "I'm doing it anyway, so deal."

He laughed and pressed his hand to his ribs. "It's damn good to see you again. Last time, it was pigtails and cartwheels. Now... thank you for coming back for me. I wouldn't have judged you for running."

Cass tapped my shoulder, and I looked back at her.

"The dagger was your father's. You should take it with you." She held it out, a tight smile on her face.

My father. I thought about the way I'd rushed forward when I'd thought of my dream during the race. I remembered seeing something just like these Oil Slicks when I fought Sherri. The same monsters I ran from with my dad. Of course, this had to do with him. He was trouble for Mom, and now he was trouble for me.

I didn't want anything from him. I backed away from the dagger.

"It's a weapon," Cass said. "You need one."

I didn't move to take it. I didn't move to do anything. I stood there, frozen, trying to wrap my head around the strangeness spilling from everywhere around me.

"Please, Jacks," Kyp prodded. "No matter what you were told about your father, a weapon is a weapon. Don't pass up the chance to be able to defend yourself."

Reluctantly, I took it.

We headed for my apartment. Streets that normally bustled with activity were now eerily silent, like the neighborhood sensed the unnatural presence of the creatures and had shut down for the night. It was as if we were somehow operating just under the surface of reality. Our footsteps echoed. What if something heard us?

The more I replayed everything in my mind, the less sense it made. A quick glance at our bloodied and bruised troop proved I wasn't imagining things. That blood had to come from somewhere.

We passed another alley, and the now-familiar shriek heralded the arrival of another creature. It burst free from the alley, swatting Cass aside with ease before moving toward me.

It stopped short, its face lighting up as though sunlight bloomed within it. I tensed, prepared to dodge whatever it threw at me. The glow intensified, moving up the center of its face the way a flame moved along a fuse. Papery skin sizzled, then peeled away, leaving behind only a blackened, misshapen skull. It collapsed, leaving tendrils of smoke drifting around it.

Where it once stood, wearing a business suit and heels, was my mother. A ball of fire hovered over her hand.

Because yeah, of course Mom could start a campfire with her hands. That matched up with the way this day was going. Not crazy. Not at all.

I'd never been so happy to see her in my life.

"Kyp Franklin," Mom said, her lips pursed. "Why am I not surprised?"

"It's been over thirteen years. You'd think you would be, a little," he said.

She rushed over and pressed a warm hand to my cheek. "You okay, baby?"

"Yeah. Is Gana?" I asked.

She flinched. "I haven't been upstairs yet. I heard Gorvhans and I just... you must be so confused."

Confused wasn't the word. Shocked. Angry. Crazy. But not confused.

"We'll talk later. For now—" She turned her attention to Kyp. "Get her back to the apartment and check on Gana. Do you think you can manage that without getting her into any more trouble?" She barely gave him time to nod. "Good. More Gorvhans are headed this way. I saw them when I cut around the back of the buildings, so stay away from there. Hurry. I'll hold them off."

"By yourself?" I yelled. "No way! You're running with us."

"Did you see what I did to that one?" she asked. "I'll be fine. Besides, I won't be alone." She turned her attention to Kyp. "Your mother and her Guardian are here. They're still unloading their weapons."

"She followed us," Kyp grumbled.

"They'll be joining me any minute. Go. Now."

This wasn't right. Should I protect Gana, who was likely safe, or protect Mom, who was definitely fighting monsters? The others took off, but I hesitated, glancing between them and Mom.

After a couple of ambling steps, Kyp stepped in front of me, planting his hands on my shoulders. His dark eyes met mine, and when he spoke, his voice was firm but hurried. "Look, I understand how crazy this is for you, but you have to trust me. Your mother will be fine. My people will assist because it's their job. My job is to get you to safety. You understand? I need you to let us do our jobs."

His eyes were so familiar.

I grudgingly agreed. Kyp rested his arm on my shoulders and led me toward a flashy red sports car parked on the corner.

"I know it's only four blocks, but the car will keep us safer until we get there," Kyp explained.

We'd almost made it when two new people appeared from around the corner. A tall woman with long dark hair led another woman with platinum blonde ringlet curls that would have made Taylor Swift jealous.

"The Unparalleled Kyp Franklin, leaning on a civilian to keep him standing," Ringlets mocked as they caught up to us. "How the mighty have fallen."

Kyp's eyes narrowed, and he removed his arm from my shoulders to stand on his own. "Jacklyn Madison is no civilian, Gretchen. She was born a Key and remains one. Rather than escape, she chose to stay and fight."

I opened my mouth to ask how a person can be a key, but I didn't get to voice the thought. A commotion erupted behind us, and I turned to see more creatures emerging from the alley. Mom hurled fireballs in their direction.

"Go! Help Jaina," the towering woman said, and Gretchen rushed into the fray without hesitation. "I need details. What is waiting for us out there?" Her expression was stone, her tone business-like and detached.

"Unsure. We took down ten or more, but they're still coming. I haven't been able to locate the source." Kyp's voice deepened, his words clipped.

"Did you do a perimeter search?" Her gaze fell to his neck. She pushed back the lapel of his jacket, grimacing at the deep gouges underneath. "Oh, Kyp. That doesn't look good."

He shrugged off her concern, but his voice softened. "There wasn't any time."

She shook her head. "This is why I make rules, darling. You'll need medical attention for those wounds. Gretchen will handle that after battle... unless Jacklyn is already able to correctly utilize her Aegis."

My what now?

She gazed at me expectantly. I stared back.

"Gretchen, then." She turned on her heel and headed into battle, shouting over her shoulder. "Hurry, your blood supply is not endless."

He glared after her. "Come on. Let's get in the car."

We climbed in and Cass drove us out of there.

I barely waited for the engine to kick in before asking, "Okay, what's an Aegis?" I had a boatload of questions.

Kyp released a mirthless laugh. "We don't have time, Jacks. Once you're safe, we'll explain everything. Right now..." He shrugged out of his jacket with a groan. "I require your assistance with something."

Cass turned just in time to see how gruesome the claw marks in Kyp's neck were. She swore.

"It's okay, Cass. Keep driving." His eyes landed on me. "Jacklyn will help me."

"She doesn't know how," Cass argued.

"What can I do?" I asked.

"Heal me."

"Kyp, what are you doing?" Cass called back, her dark eyes flicking to the rearview mirror.

"I think you've lost too much blood," I said. Kyp's once bronze skin had lost all its color. He was starting to look downright dead.

"No, I haven't. Trust me."

"I'm trying to, but you're acting like I have magic powers, or

I'm a mutant or something!" My voice went shrill. "That's crazy. You don't need me to heal you. You need stitches!"

"Crazy like monsters?" When I didn't reply, he grabbed my hand and pulled it to his neck. I recoiled at the stickiness of his ragged wounds against my palm, but he held my hand still. "Listen, I get how it sounds. But you can do this. Just focus. Envision the cuts sewing together, the damage clearing away, the skin becoming whole." His words slurred, and he blinked hard, as if shaking it off. He squeezed my hand. "You've got this. You were born to do this."

I nearly laughed. I was born to run laps. I was born to take care of my sister. I was not born to heal random guys who rescued me from monsters. This was insane, and I'd prove it by humoring him and showing him how wrong he was.

I closed my eyes and pictured his skin drawing together, the wounds mending beneath my fingertips. A warm, pulsing sensation erupted from within, starting somewhere in my center and spreading toward my hand. I pulled back, but he kept my hand there and pressed my other hand to his side with a reassuring smile. "For my rib. You're doing great."

I returned my thoughts to where they had been. Something had stirred beneath my skin, like a live wire. On the off chance it was real, I chased the feeling. My heart vacillated between a speedy dash and an eerie calm, and I swayed. "I'm... dizzy."

"You're almost there, Jacks."

I held on for another moment before he squeezed my hands

and released them.

My eyes opened to find him running his fingers over his neck. "Thank you."

I tucked my knees under me to get a better view through the blood streaking his skin. Gently, I ran my fingers over where the wounds had been, unable to trust my eyes.

Not a single cut. Nothing. As if he'd never been hurt.

"How... did we do...? I feel weird." My tongue was heavy, and my vision wavered. Kyp caught me before I tumbled off the seat and held me upright in his arms. Tenderly, he brushed aside my dark curls.

I'd gone out for a walk, run into monsters and soldiers that fought them, and healed a handsome guy with my fingers and the power of positive thinking. This was absurd.

"*We* didn't do that. *You* did. You feel weird because that probably took a lot more energy than you're used to expending. Sorry."

My eyelids closed, and they wanted to stay that way. I slumped against Kyp. The last thing I felt was Kyp running a gentle hand over the crown of my head.

"Couldn't even get you two blocks. Your mother is going to kill me."

THREE

"*You sure you want to do this, Jacks? Because it's the dumbest thing I've ever heard." The boy sat with his back against the trunk of a tree amidst a forest of green, his legs stretched out in front of him. He wasn't any older than five but was already long and skinny—a string bean boy.*

I sat across from him and still needed to look up at him.

"Daddy says our blood is special," I said with a pout. My voice sounded tiny and slightly garbled, as if I couldn't quite pronounce everything.

"It is." He pushed a flop of black hair out of his dark eyes. "Where did you get the idea for a blood oath, anyway?"

"What's a blood oaf?" I wrinkled my nose.

He sighed. "When you make a promise and mix blood to make the promise a real *promise. It's what you were just... you asked about... ugh! Never mind." Another sigh. "I'm sorry, Jacks. Sometimes I forget you aren't... that I'm advanced."*

"*'Cause your special blood makes you smarter.*" I twisted my pudgy fingers together and dropped them on my pink corduroy pants. "*Do you think I'm stupid, Kyp?*"

"*What? No! You're smart! I'm just not... normal.*" He looked away, then gave a sharp shake of his head and smiled. "*What do you want to swear?*"

I rushed through the words. "Swear you'll be mine forever!"

His eyes widened. "Where did you even hear that? Aunt Jainey needs to reduce your TV time. And maybe pay more attention to what you're watching... Besides, that's dangerous wording for a blood oath. Do you mean I'll be your friend forever?"

That sounded okay. Or we could get married and be together forever like Mommy and Daddy. "I guess. I just haven't seen Grandpa Julian in a looong time. Everyone always goes away, and nobody tells me where. I don't ever want you to go. I want you to stay with me."

Kyp gave me his crooked smile, warm and familiar, but beneath it he looked near tears. He opened the blue backpack Daddy filled with snacks for when we roamed the grounds and removed a long silver dagger with a white swirly handle and a very pointy tip.

It was my turn to give him a dumb look. "That's huge. No little knives?"

"They put childproof locks on those. Forgot to do the display hutch." He shrugged.

"You can't open the locks?"

He rolled his eyes. "I know how to, but my fingers"—he wiggled his fingers in the air— "can't. Not strong enough. Anyway... here goes." He touched the dagger's point to the tip of his finger and hissed in pain. Blood welled up around the wound. He held out the dagger to me. "Your turn. I'm ready with my vow."

I mimicked his actions and his solemn expression. Ouch!

"Okay. Give me your hand." He pressed the tips of our fingers together. A warm glow burst from them. He brought his other hand up to block his eyes, looking around to make sure we were alone.

"Say your vow," I urged him.

"I vow never to leave you. Never. Now you say it."

I looked at our fingers and the glow coming from them. It was already done. I smirked. "I vow to always be yours, forever."

The glow grew so bright I looked away. Then it went out.

"Jacks!" Kyp's mouth hung open.

I laughed so hard I had to grab my sides with both hands. I rolled over onto my back on the grass.

Kyp joined me, reluctantly laughing too. "You're a brat. You know that?"

Rain-coated grass and leather, mixed with something I recognized but couldn't quite place, drifted to my nostrils. Whatever I was lying on lacked the warming comfort of my bed, and my head was propped up against something rigid and uncomfortable.

My eyes popped open. I was in an unfamiliar car. My

memories of how I'd gotten there made no sense. A leather jacket was draped over me like a blanket. I glanced out the window and watched as the world sped by. A highway. An exit sign read 4S: Binghamton. A long way from New York City. A spark of panic formed deep in my gut.

Where the hell am I being taken?

I strained my eyes to see the rest of the car. I needed to learn what happened after I'd passed out before announcing I was awake. Just because they'd helped me through a monster attack didn't mean these people should be trusted.

I wished I had thought of that *during* the monster attack, but I'd been a little distracted.

A peek through the space between the window and the seat in front of me revealed a messy, dirty-blonde bob that curled at the bottom. Gana. And we were in a car with strangers, heading who knew where.

That spark of panic became an inferno. This wasn't about me anymore. Somehow, Gana had gotten pulled into this mess. Which meant I needed to figure out how to get her out.

The seat across from her was empty. There had to be another row, with the driver's seat and the front passenger seat. Since I had passed out in a regular car, and this was clearly a minivan or an SUV, someone must have moved me. My view of the first two seats was blocked, but the seat beside me was definitely visible.

Kyp's head was propped against the other window, arms crossed in front of his chest. Black hair curled at his collar. His feet rested on a duffel bag on the car floor, and muddy clumps dangled from the bottom of his combat boots. One clump fell off, and my eyes followed it to discover the bag was partially unzipped. If I squinted, I could make out the ivory handle of the dagger I'd been given.

My vision swam again. I closed my eyes and pictures played behind them. Kyp convincing me to heal him, how nauseated I was once I'd done it, the obvious hallucination I'd had of his fully healed neck. When I opened my eyes, there was blood staining the collar of his gray t-shirt, but no evidence of where that blood had come from.

Maybe I was still hallucinating. That made way more sense than monsters. That meant Kyp had dosed me with something.

The inferno became a raging brush fire.

I threw the leather jacket in Kyp's direction and dropped to the car floor. The zipper on the duffel bag snagged slightly, but it opened just enough. Kyp let out a slew of curses that ended when I pulled my dagger free from the bag and pressed its point to his throat.

"Whoa, calm down." He held his hands up, but there was humor playing in his eyes.

"The next words out of your mouth better be an explanation of what the hell you did to me!" I said.

"Jaina, call your daughter off." Kyp's eyes flicked to the front. His Adam's apple bobbed beneath the tip of my dagger.

I wasn't going to be tricked into looking away from him.

"Why would I do that? This is fun to watch."

Mom was in one of the front seats. Now I really wanted to look, but I'd seen what he was capable of. The minute I looked away, he would have my dagger, and I'd be lucky to get out of the car alive.

"Why don't you talk her down, darling?" another woman in the front row said. "After all, this is your mess, and you have cleaning to do."

Kyp gritted his teeth. "Yes, Mother."

I counted the seats again. Cass and Gretchen must have taken the other car. Madisons outnumbered Kyp and his mother. Someone trying to kidnap a family would have chosen better odds.

When I risked a quick look forward, I found Gana watching me, jaw dropped.

"Okay." I lowered the dagger from Kyp's throat and backed away, returning to the seat but never releasing the dagger. "I see I may have overreacted."

Mom laughed. "Oh, honey. Don't feel bad about threatening that little shit. Hell, feel free to kill him. He'll keep coming back, anyway."

"Love you, too, Jain." Kyp sneered.

Kyp's eyes met mine. "It's okay. There's a lot going on. You must be perplexed." He leaned toward me. "But you're safer now than you were at home. You passed out because you used your abilities too fast, too soon."

"Because you told me to," I said.

"I was creatively killing two birds with one stone," Kyp said. "Your Aegis was acting like a beacon, attracting the Gorvhans. That would continue as long as you were conscious, and I was sorely in need of a healer. Hence... both problems solved. We're both safe."

"Well, you told me you would explain once we were safe," I said. "Can we start now?"

A crooked smile formed on Kyp's face. "Yes. Where do I begin?"

"Start with how you were there just in time to conveniently save me when you already knew all about me, my mother, and apparently my father," I suggested.

He nodded, lips pursed. "I am a soldier in an army called the Order of the Key. We battle interdimensional creatures, like those lovely fellows you encountered by your apartment. Our ranks have dwindled in recent years. I came to the city in search of more soldiers."

"So... how do you know me?" I wasn't sure I wanted to know.

"Because your mother used to be one of us. As was your father."

I laughed. "Um, no. That's bullshit, right, Mom? You would have told me."

But then, she hadn't told me about the firepower I'd seen her wielding during the fight.

Mom's silence answered loud and clear.

"Mom?"

She sighed. "There are two types of soldiers in the Order. Your father was a Key. I was his Guardian."

I forced down my anger. I'd save that for when I understood what the hell I'd tripped myself into. Instead, I turned to Kyp. "Which are you? Key or Guardian?"

"I'm a Key, as are you. Cass is my Guardian. Gana will be yours."

"Gana will not," Gana declared. "I'm fifteen. I'm studying for my PSATs. I am not a soldier."

"Too late," Kyp said. "It's in your blood. Jacklyn's a Key because her father, Raymond Madison, was a Key. You're a Guardian because your mother is a Guardian, as was your father, Carson Adams. You'll either get Jaina's firepower or Carson's strength."

My stepfather, Carson, died when I was seven. He hadn't liked me very much, and he hadn't treated anyone else very well either. If he was an honorable soldier, I was an Amazonian goddess... and I had to stand on tippy toes to reach the top shelves at Cosmo's Comics.

"I don't care what's in my blood," Gana snapped.

Kyp frowned, his head tilting slightly, eyes narrowed as if Gana were a peculiar insect. "But it's your duty. She's your half-sister. Why wouldn't you wish to serve as her Guardian?"

"She is my *sister*," I snapped. "I don't do family by halves."

Kyp held up his hands, a gesture of peace. "Point taken."

A sigh came from the front of the van. "Jacklyn, I don't believe we've been formally introduced. My name is Lavinia Franklin, and I am the Order's leader. For the record, I wish to expressly state that we did not authorize this retrieval mission."

Kyp shrugged. "You said we needed soldiers."

"I said we needed to recruit Guardians," Lavinia said sharply.

"And we have two more Guardians," he said. "Of course, one needs training. I assumed Jaina was a little rusty, but she's doing just fine."

"That's because I've been fighting interdimensionals pursuing my daughter." She turned to look at me. "If you don't use your Aegis, they can't find you as easily. If you aren't aware of your Aegis, you won't use it. Lavinia and I worked together so you wouldn't look for information about who you'd been. She used her abilities to make you ignore the screeches of Gorvhans, to keep you from realizing how fast you healed. We thought we were protecting you. I got you away from this life, and I kept you from using the thing that would drag you back. I don't know how so many of them found you."

"I imagine my hypnotic suggestions wore off over time. It's been thirteen years. I've never even tried to plant one for that long," Lavinia suggested.

"She used her Aegis," Kyp said. "It's how I tracked her."

"I did *not* use my Aegis, or whatever it is. I didn't heal anybody. Hell, I didn't even know I could heal anybody!"

"It's not just healing." Kyp sighed. "Your Aegis is like... the Force. But it's individually specific. Guardians have an Aegis with one specific ability. For a Key, there's a bigger umbrella. You are a Body Key. Your Aegis contains more abilities. Superhuman athleticism. Extraordinary strength. Enhanced senses. You can heal others and yourself. Also, hypersensitive pain sensors." He rushed through that last part.

"Well, there's the fine print," I said. "There's always fine print, isn't there?"

Kyp nodded sympathetically. "It's not so bad now, but it gets worse the more you use your Aegis. Every Key type has a weakness."

"What's yours?" I asked.

"Not today, newbie."

"Well, thank you for explaining in terms I can understand, anyway," I said, oddly grateful, despite the snark.

He smiled, open and warm. "Cass and I guarded Gana while she packed you a few things. I saw the Star Wars Expanded Universe book collection. Impressive."

"Mara Jade is my hero." I returned the smile. "I don't care what Disney says."

For a moment, we just smiled at each other. We weren't in this mess of a confusing situation; we were just two people with a common interest. That was when I remembered what I noticed while I was healing him. With his dark hair and eyes, strong, sharp features, and his cocky way of carrying himself, Kyp Franklin was... kinda hot.

I cleared my throat. "Um... what's your type, um... Key type?"

"I'm a Mind Key. I possess superior intelligence and have telekinesis plus an eidetic memory." He tried to say it casually, which I would have believed if I hadn't seen the flush of red overtake his face.

Returned interest confirmed!

"He's leaving off the mind control and mind reading," Mom said. "Don't forget, they can both do that. Right, Lavinia?"

"Yes," Lavinia said. "But that requires effort, and we are both aware that it is impolite. We never use it without express permission for mission-related purposes. Isn't that right, Kyp?"

It was my turn to blush. What if he knew what I'd been thinking?

Kyp nodded, but his eyes didn't leave mine. "It's true. I used it a little in the alley to stop the Gorvhans from attacking. Did you notice them forgetting how to walk forward?"

I had. The glitched video game character shuffle. I nodded.

I cycled through the list of abilities Kyp was convinced I had, then through my memories of the day. I'd helped Mom with breakfast, walked to school with Gana, vegged through all my boring classes. Nothing eventful, and then...

"I won my race."

"Oh congratulations, honey," Mom said absently.

"No, Mom, I *really* won the race. At first, I was trailing, and then, I thought about..." My father. I thought about my father.

"You let her take track?" Lavinia said in a tone that screamed her questioning my mother's intelligence level.

Mom laughed. "Well, with Jacklyn, you don't exactly *let* her do things. She signs up for them and tells you three weeks later."

"You'd have realized it yourself if you made it home before eight-thirty most days," Gana grumbled.

"Where are we going?" I struggled to keep my voice calm. "Is my father there?"

Kyp looked toward the front of the car, frowned, then sank into his seat and yanked out a pen and a notebook. No answers coming from him, then.

Lavinia cleared her throat. "Your father died shortly after your mother left with you and your sister."

"I'm sorry, baby," Mom said. Gana laid a hand on my arm, a welcome gesture of support.

So, he was dead. He'd abandoned me and then he'd died. I swallowed past a lump in my throat. It wasn't like I expected him to dance back into my life with a Band-Aid for the scratches on my knees. But knowing he was already gone... I dropped back against the car seat, resting my head against the window again.

"She's all questioned out," Gana said softly. "I think she covered mine, except for the biggest one. When can I go home?"

Nobody responded.

Kyp tapped out a drum beat on his notebook with his pen. I tried to let my eyes close, but my head was spinning. I was equally terrified and exhilarated. This was it—that moment I'd always envied, where the hero was given their calling. It was scary, sure, but I'd read about adventures all my life. It was pretty damn cool to finally get one of my own.

Kyp tapped his notebook again. I glanced over, prepared to snap at him, but he held the book out to me. He had written something on it, his handwriting blocky and precise.

Sshhh. Turn the page.

I glanced at him, and his eyebrows raised, a silent prodding to continue. I did as directed.

Three things:

1.   I'm blocking my mother's ability to read this. Speaking in your mind would grab her attention, and I can't say this out loud. Long story.

2.   I've got your back. It may not seem that way, but I've always got your back.

3.   Your father loved you. I would stake my life on that fact. Never allow yourself to forget it.

My throat tightened swiftly, and I squeezed my eyes shut, not wanting to cry in front of a stranger. Except he wasn't a complete stranger. The dream from earlier came to mind. It felt awfully real. It wasn't the first time I'd had that dream, but it wasn't until earlier that I realized the little boy from my dream was Kyp.

I held out my hand. He stared at it questioningly for a moment before passing me his pen.

I wrote on the bottom of the page in my sloppy, loop-filled script.

REALLY silly question... when we were kids, did we make a blood oath?

When I passed the book back, he smiled, lighting up even brighter than he had before. He didn't answer. Instead, he held out his finger, the same way I remembered from the dream. My cheeks heated, but I met his finger with mine.

I spent the remainder of the ride trying to sleep, but too many topics were making noise in my brain. Eventually, I settled for returning to my previous position and pretending to sleep—and this time, I purposely chose Kyp's jacket as my blanket.

FOUR

HOME SWEET PRISON

Someone poked my ribs, and I bolted upright in my seat. I didn't know when I finally managed to fall asleep, but based on the drool I swiped off the side of my face, it must have been a while ago.

"Good morning. Sleep well?" Gana laughed.

"Very graceful. She said I should wait to get out until you woke up and now I understand why."

Kyp. Awesome.

"Whose side are you on, anyway?" I growled at Gana.

"Whoever's is the most entertaining."

"Ha, ha. Screw you."

"Come on," Kyp said. "We're here."

"Where exactly is here?" I climbed out of the car, planting my feet on a grassy area where a few other cars were neatly parked. I yawned and stretched, squinting in the beaming sunlight.

"The Franklin Estate." Lavinia joined us. "The Order's

headquarters. Welcome home." She smiled fondly.

Lavinia was long—tall and thin, with endless dark hair that stretched out her precisely made-up face. Impeccably dressed, she donned clothing like the Manhattan socialites I crossed paths with whenever I journeyed to visit Midtown Comics. She was a lovely woman with a flawless and warm bronze complexion, and I understood she was where Kyp got his looks from.

"The others are preparing your rooms," Lavinia explained. "Kyp and I will take you for the grand tour."

The Order's headquarters was the size of an entire city block and stood three stories high. The dormant flower garden leading up to the stone mansion was probably striking in the spring, and even more so when covered in the red, gold, and orange hues of maple leaves from the giant trees scattered around the house.

I breathed in deeply, enjoying the fresh crispness of the air. "This place is incredible."

Gana rolled her eyes. Mom shot her the best authoritarian look she had. That wouldn't work on Gana. I'd have to talk to her later.

We walked up a hill and over a cobblestone walkway to a heavy-looking door with engravings carved in the wood. Lavinia pushed it open with a flourish, leading us into an enormous and well-lit foyer. The ceiling must have been thirty feet high, and a sparkling crystal chandelier descended from its center. Staircases led up both sides of the foyer. A decorative banister curved up and around the second and third floor balconies overlooking the entrance. The open staircases and high ceiling in the center opened up the space, making the entryway feel grand and unending.

Gana didn't look terribly impressed. I couldn't believe she was completely untouched by the beauty of our surroundings.

Kyp and Lavinia led us through a kitchen with a small seating area, into a grand dining room large enough to comfortably fit twenty-five people. All the furniture, including a hutch displaying expensive-looking china, was made of polished cherry wood. Gorgeously constructed tapestries draped the walls in images of triumphant victories and soldiers ready to face off against giant, prehistoric monsters. Another was of an insignia—a shield with a key lying diagonally across it. Over the head of the table, another depicted a man bleeding from his hands and kneeling over a glowing crack in the earth.

"He's closing a rift between dimensions," Kyp explained when he noticed me looking. "Key blood can do that."

I looked over my shoulder to find him gazing at the tapestry with as much awe as I was. It seemed heroism was still cool no matter how long you'd been doing it.

Being here was like forgetting why I walked in a room, like a name on the tip of my tongue.

We walked through the door on the other end of the dining room and through a plain room with a few bookcases, tables, and a computer station.

"This is where our younger members do research for their classes," Lavinia said.

When we emerged, we were on the other side of the foyer.

Lavinia caught my dazed look and smiled as she led us up the stairs. "Jaina, tell me, what's the average square footage of an apartment in the big city these days?"

"Our apartment was small enough to fit in your dining room," Mom said.

"How many maids and butlers does it take to run this place?" I asked.

Kyp chuckled. "None. We're the maids and butlers."

"Great. Chores," Gana grumbled.

Lavinia led us to the first room at the end of the second floor. "This is the study."

A television and sound system were set up in the room, surrounded by game systems and bean bag chairs. A girl lay on an armchair, flipping through a glossy magazine. She was pale and petite with straight blonde hair and the light bone structure of a bird.

Lavinia cleared her throat, and the girl dropped her magazine and jumped from the chair.

"Kyp?" She rushed to him, wrapping herself around him. "Never do that again! I was worried sick!"

Kyp tensed, arms floating awkwardly in the air before wrapping around her in a light embrace.

"This is Kylie Robertson," Lavinia said. "She's the Key of what we call the Light Elements, water and air, plus she's Kyp's lovely girlfriend and my future daughter-in-law."

I felt the weight of Gana's gaze and I had to force myself not to react.

Girlfriend, my ass. He doesn't want to touch her.

Kylie released Kyp and turned to greet me.

"Hel-lo." I tried to sound nice, but my tone turned cautious as she gave me a full once-over.

"Jacklyn Madison, huh?" she said, her voice like wind chimes. "Last time I saw you, you were chubbier."

I didn't let the jab bother me. "Well, it's been a few years."

"Kylie, I'm giving them a tour. Kyp will catch up with you later." Lavinia grimaced, like a long-suffering schoolteacher accustomed to being derailed.

The tour would probably be useless. I'd probably be lost for days to come.

The second and third floors were filled with bedrooms, and we were told the basement was a training area.

"This is all great," Gana said as we approached our assigned rooms. "We're never going back home, are we?"

Mom sighed. "The Order will provide protection in exchange for our return. We're part of the mission now. It's the best way to keep you safe. As you age, your Aegis will become apparent and you will be in as much danger as Jacklyn is now."

"I thought these things were after my Aegis because they were nearby and happened to sense me," I said. "You mean to tell me they can find us anywhere?"

"Yes," Lavinia said. "As little as I agree with Kyp's reckless decision to run off and bring you back here, his timing was impeccable. Had he not come, you surely would have been killed. The interdimensionals would have kept coming. You need to learn the various ways you can protect yourself."

"Why aren't they following us here?" Gana asked.

"Wards have been erected around the grounds of the estate," Mom said. "Invisible walls keeping interdimensionals out and Aegis energy in. We can pass through, if we need to, but the wards will stop the creatures from entering."

Mom's eyes were just like mine. Gana looked like Mom, and I resembled my father, but we all had the same eyes. When her gaze met mine, they did so with meaning, like she was willing me to listen. It was the same look Gana gave me when she was hammering a point home.

"The wards alert Lavinia of anything entering or exiting the grounds of the estate."

Which meant we weren't going anywhere. And we shouldn't try.

Prisoners in a cage. A useful cage, but a cage, nonetheless.

"And track? The PSATs? School?" I asked.

"Jacklyn," Mom said sternly. "We don't want to seem ungrateful, do we?"

"No, of course not!" I turned to Lavinia and Kyp. "I truly appreciate what you all did, coming to get me and taking me back into your home. But..."

"But?" Kyp said.

"It's a shock," I said. "This is your life, but it isn't ours. Can't you see how jarring this is for us?"

"I see that you'd be Gorvhan food if you weren't here," Kyp snapped.

I rolled my eyes. "Oh please, chill your man pride. You rescued me. Thank you. But it was very sudden. If someone dropped you into the city, and said you could never go back home, even if it was for your safety, you wouldn't be celebrating."

Lavinia stepped between us. "Kyp, this has been an exhausting and unsettling day for our new guests. Besides, I think it's time for you to find Cassandra and meet me in my office. We need to have a discussion about unsanctioned missions."

Kyp's jaw clenched. "Yes, Mother."

He walked away without a second glance in our direction.

I hadn't meant to get him into trouble or make him believe he'd taken a risk for an ungrateful brat, but I was rattled. Less for myself than for Gana.

We said our goodnights and headed for our separate bedrooms to wind down after the craziness of the day. My bedroom was a blank slate with a blue bedspread. Nothing much to speak of. If I was going to be stuck here, I'd have to move my shrine of collectibles.

I set to work unpacking the duffle bag Gana had packed for me, placing the clothes in the dresser and finding a place for the various toiletries and the few books she had packed. I'd only just finished when Gana came marching into my room, her eyes wild and her cheeks flushed.

She raked a hand through her hair, her short locks twisting in the wrong direction. "I tried to call Paula." She thrust her phone at me. I had to lean away from her to avoid getting hit. "It didn't work."

Paula was Gana's best friend. "What do you mean it didn't work?"

"I've roamed the entire Estate looking for an internet connection or phone reception. Nothing. Not even in the backyard."

Shit. It figured. We were now part of a secret organization. If watching far too much television taught me anything, it was that cell phones were trackable. I fully expected to receive an exhaustive, Men in Black-style identity wipe.

If I told Gana that, I'd just piss her off. "Did you ask Mom?"

"Mom's asleep." Gana plopped onto the bed beside me. "I tried to wake her, but she didn't answer when I knocked. I'm pretty sure she's decided not to talk."

Most mothers would try to talk to their children, to calm them after such a nightmare of a day. My mother did what we both did best, although often in different directions. She ran.

"Cass says it's something about the wards. Messes with airborne signals. They only have one internet connection, and it isn't Wi-Fi."

"That's not so bad," I said.

"That's not so bad?" Gana shrieked. "Your Tumblr account? Discord?"

I winced. Okay, that hurt my weird little geeker heart. "We

can use the desktop connection?"

"They're monitored," she said. "This whole place basically exists in its own cultural bubble. No emails, social networks, calls to anyone outside who isn't an Order contact who can look out for themselves. Apparently, some interdimensionals are intelligent and will use your friends to lure you out. *Meaning*" —she practically screamed that word— "not only can I never go home again, but I can't even have a best friend." She swiped angrily at the tears filling her eyes.

I didn't know what to say. "I'm sorry. I'll figure something out. We can't stay here."

"We still can't go back there! We'd just drag Paula into this mess."

She was right. Always thinking, always so much smarter than me.

"Look, we have to stay, at least for a while. We need to learn how to fight for ourselves and learn if there's any other way to avoid detection. But there is no way in hell I'm letting you go to battle with those things."

"We can't tell Mom. She was part of this before and she thinks we belong here."

"That's okay. I'm eighteen now. An adult. I can get us an apartment and stuff. We'll probably have to live somewhere else. Somewhere cheaper..."

"You have no idea what to do, do you?" Gana sighed.

I didn't. Not really. "We have until we're done training to

figure it out. You in?"

She nodded, then snuggled in beside me on the bed. When we were younger, we used to lie like that when we had nightmares. It reminded me of times when we would do anything to make each other laugh, to cheer each other up. But it also reminded me of the nightmares we recovered from together.

I had to wonder which our time here would become.

I couldn't sleep. I'd been trying since Gana had gone back to her room. All I managed to do was spin ideas around in my head and make a mental list of the questions that remained unanswered. The unknown was scary. What came next? Was this my life now? How would I get myself and Gana out of this safely? Taking care of Gana while Mom worked late nights was one thing—Gana was easy enough, ridiculously responsible for her age, despite her attitude. But being the only responsible adult?

I tossed and turned for what felt like hours, and I was jittery as hell, like I'd just guzzled down a venti cafe americano. Then something broke through my thoughts. I wasn't even sure what it was at first, only that it caught my attention, brought me out of the anxious stupor my thoughts had spiraled me into.

A cry of pain. A scream. It happened again.

My chest tightened, my breath squeezing out in a gasp. *Gana.*

I pushed the covers back and climbed out of the bed quietly, not wanting to draw any attention to myself.

Another scream.

My heart stuttered. Gana was safe. The scream came from one of the floors below ours. Not that it mattered. We were trapped in the house with whatever caused that scream. Where were all those weapons Kyp and the others used?

I took a deep breath, tried to call on whatever power was supposedly within me, and opened the door.

My eyes were used to the light from bright city streetlamps shining through my apartment windows. I wasn't used to how damn dark it was outside of the city. Still, when my eyes finally caught up, they zoomed past normal adjustment. I easily made out the shapes in the hall.

Hello, Aegis.

I tiptoed to Mom's room. As I ducked in, another scream startled me.

Mom was sound asleep, the blankets pulled up to her chin. I closed the door and knelt beside her bed.

"Mom." I shook her shoulder. "Mom, wake up!"

She took a minute, but eventually her eyes slitted open. "What, Jacklyn?"

"Mom, I heard something."

Mom sat up, rubbing her eyes. "What happened?"

I resisted an eye roll. "Mom, I heard a scream."

"It woke you up?" she asked.

"No, I couldn't sleep."

She glanced at the clock at her bedside. "It's a quarter after one in the morning. You fell asleep."

Another scream cut through the silence, this one louder than the previous ones. I gasped, my hand pressed to my heart. Mom's eyelids drooped.

"Jeez! Didn't you hear that?"

Mom blinked. "Jacklyn, making up stories about this place won't give you an excuse to leave. You need to accept that we're here now."

"I'm not making up stories."

She sighed. "It's probably your Aegis, the enhanced hearing. Whatever you think you heard, someone may have been getting treated for a wound, or having a nightmare. Nightmares sometimes get vivid here, especially after a battle."

I stared at her. "Is that supposed to comfort me?"

"Of course not. But whatever it is, I can't hear it, which means it could be as simple as Gretchen staying up to watch a scary movie." She shrugged. "I can't sugarcoat things for you. All I can give you now is the truth."

"The truth would have been nice years ago, Mom." When I considered how many times she chose not to fill me in on basic facts about my own life... It was infuriating that she blithely expected us to deal with living a completely different reality overnight.

"Look, I'm sorry, Birdie. I can't go back and change it." She used my childhood nickname, something she only did when she was worried or genuinely apologizing. I'd heard it far too often. "Just go back to sleep, Jacks. You'll feel better in the morning."

I highly doubted that. "Good night, Mom."

"Good night, Jacks." She rearranged her covers. I waited until she was tucked back in before leaving the room as cautiously as I had entered. I still wasn't sure where those screams had come from, but it damn well wasn't a dream.

Back out in the hall, the creaking of floorboards down the hall made me still. Someone started up the shower in the bathroom. It had to be whoever I'd heard.

The hallway was pitch black. If I stayed very still, I would be invisible. The shower cut out in ten minutes, and the door opened in another five. Illuminated in the doorway for just a moment, Kyp stepped out of the bathroom and walked toward me, his steps sluggish.

I held my breath and struggled to quiet my thoughts. Where was his room again? Would he have to pass me to get to it?

He stopped in front of the room beside mine and reached for the doorknob. His head jerked up. He stopped and stared at the door. He caught me.

But I wasn't guilty of anything. I'd gotten up to ask my mother something. Nothing wrong with that.

And then I had stood in the hall, creepily waiting for Kyp to leave the bathroom. Nothing weird about that at all.

My heart pounded as his head pivoted in my direction. His eyes softened when they landed on me, and his hand raised to his face. He pressed one finger to his lips, eyes locked on mine. Then he stepped closer until he was standing a breath away, reached around me, and turned my doorknob.

My pulse pounded in my neck when he moved to walk through the doorway with me still standing in front of it. His body brushed against mine before I realized I was supposed to be following his lead.

I'd never had a strange boy in my bedroom before, or any unrelated boy, for that matter. I stopped short and shook my head. His eyes were still locked on mine, and this time they smiled with his lips. He leaned in and my throat went dry.

"I just want to talk. Remember, you can kick my ass," he whispered into my ear.

He had a point. But, more importantly, I trusted the boy from the dream, the one who'd taken a blood oath to never leave me, only to have my mother yank me away. My once best friend.

I stepped back and allowed him into my room, closing the door behind him.

"Are you okay?" we asked in unison, then stared at each other, waiting for a response.

"I'm okay," I said, but as I spoke, I saw Kyp more clearly, and it was a shock. He looked ill, almost gray in tone. "I heard something. Screaming. And don't tell me I was dreaming, because I was wide awake when I heard it. As wide awake as I am now."

He swallowed hard, his eyes drifting shut. "You weren't trying to leave, were you?"

"No." Not yet.

"Good, because you c-can't," he stammered. His attention

dropped to the string on his sweatpants, which he promptly began twirling and untwirling. "You can't leave, not without getting hurt. Killed. You shouldn't... you can't..."

My eyes narrowed and my stomach sank. "What's going on with you?"

He huffed a humorless laugh. "Nothing you have to worry about."

I tried again, more forcefully. "Kyp, you don't look good."

A weak smile crossed his lips, and he plowed his hand through his hair. "Thanks, Jacks."

I rolled my eyes. "You look good. You just don't look well." *What?* "I mean, you look... like..."

"Stop talking." He laughed. Then he closed his eyes and breathed deep. When they reopened, he seemed more composed. "It was me. I fell asleep downstairs in the sitting room and I had a nightmare. A bad memory from a past mission."

"Really?" I said.

"Look, I'm already embarrassed you heard me, okay? Can I skip the details? It was me, but everything is fine."

Except I'd seen embarrassed from him in the car. He blushed. This was twitchy, fidgety. He was lying to me and I wasn't sure why, but I didn't know him well enough to butt in and figure it out.

Besides, he had Kylie for that.

"Fine, I'll accept your explanation, but I won't accept that you look ready to fall over."

"I do?" He forced his shoulders back. "Sorry. The nightmare

has me rattled."

"Is there any way I can help?" I asked. "Use my healing thing?"

He chewed on his lower lip for a moment. "Yes, but I don't want to knock you out. Mother will expect you up bright and early tomorrow for training. There's one possibility. Remember that blood oath we took?"

"It's about the only thing I *do* remember. Why?"

"Well... if it worked the way I think it did, it was like, it should have connected us. We may be able to use the bond it created to do things you can't do with your average Aegis."

"How would I know? I haven't even learned what an average Aegis can do."

He offered me a shaky grin. "We might be able to trade energy. If we can, you won't lose anything, and I can heal myself with your ability. Just give me your hand."

I lifted my hand up, palm facing outward, and waited. His trembling hand pressed against mine.

"Imagine it," he whispered. "Like in the car. Guide the energy away from you."

I envisioned giving him some of my healing. My hand warmed, and the warmth traveled out of me as his traveled back through my palm and up my arm. His eyes closed, and he slid his fingers between mine, holding my hand. As he sighed deeply, the color returned to his cheeks, and his shaking slowed to a stop. My heart banged against my ribs.

When his eyes reopened, they stared back into mine. "Thank you." He didn't let go of my hand.

I had to force myself to speak. "I... um... Like you said, I should be getting to sleep."

He smiled. "I suppose." He didn't move.

"Goodnight, Kyp." I let his hand drop. I'd just met him. And he had a girlfriend.

"Goodnight, Jacks." He headed for the door, but turned as he touched the knob. "Kylie."

"What about Kylie?" I really didn't want to hear about her.

"She's not... Mother introduced her..." He ran another hand through his dark hair, making it completely unruly.

I bet it's soft. Shut up, Jacklyn!

"It's politically motivated," he said. "An arranged thing. I'm not interested."

"Why are you telling me this?" I knew exactly why he was telling me.

"No reason. I... you said if you took me away from here and dropped me in the city without any of this, I wouldn't exactly celebrate. Well, I would. I'd dance in the damn streets." His voice got wobbly on that last statement, and it stabbed at my heart.

"I'm sorry. I shouldn't have said that. I don't know you."

He smiled. "Oh, you do. You just have to remember. Welcome home, Jacks. Sleep well."

He left the room. I would have liked to talk to him more.

And if he hated it here, when it was time for me and Gana to hit the road, maybe I'd take him with me.

FIVE

The following morning, I was immediately summoned to Lavinia's office. It didn't help the jittery nerves that remained from the night before.

When I arrived, she was quick to welcome me, and invited me to have a seat.

Lavinia's office was as meticulously plotted as her appearance. Thick burgundy curtains hung over the windows, denying entry to the sunlight. Lavinia sat at a large wooden oval-shaped desk. Vines and leaves were engraved along its edges, as well as those of the bookcase and hutch behind her. She sat in a high-backed leather chair, beckoning me to a similar one across from her. I settled into it, nervous despite myself. I tried not to let her see me wiping my palms on my jeans.

She greeted me with a warm smile. "Jacklyn, how are you this morning? Did you sleep well?"

I couldn't tell her about last night. "I woke up for a minute.

Nothing important, just nightmares. Yesterday was... rough. I'm still adjusting."

She nodded, steepling her fingers in front of her. "I owe you an apology. I wasn't very welcoming yesterday. I tried—"

"No, you were fine." I didn't want to sound like I didn't appreciate being saved from monsters. "I never once felt unwelcome."

"Good," she said. "I was a bit out of sorts. It's been a long time since I've seen you and our parting wasn't under the best of circumstances. Couple that with Kyp's purposeful flouting of the rules, and I fear I may not have been a proper hostess."

I understood. The Madisons weren't the only family whose lives were thrown into upheaval last night. I wanted to say that, but something else Lavinia had said caught my attention. "How did we part on bad terms? I was five!"

Lavinia's warm demeanor wavered momentarily, her smile dropping into something like a grimace, although she was far too elegant to ever truly make a face like that. "Dear, it's a long, unpleasant story. But one you'll need to hear, sooner or later. Do I have your word that you'll hear me out before rushing to judgment?"

"Oh God, what did I do?" I groaned. I wasn't really responsible for the actions of five-year-old me, but this didn't sound good.

Lavinia laughed, a throaty chuckle. "Of course, the issue wasn't with you. It was with your father."

Yeah, what else is new. "What did he do then?"

"That's where the somewhat long story comes in."

"I'm listening." Really, I clenched up against the idea.

"Long ago, your father and I were quite close. He was a cherished friend, practically a second father to Kyp. But then, something happened. I can't begin to comprehend what, to be honest. He became very ill... mentally. Paranoid. And with me as the leader of the Order, I became the perfect place to direct that paranoia. He started an internal war within the Order because he managed to persuade others I was a monster, working against their interests. It was disastrous and even resulted in him attempting to assassinate me."

My stomach seized. My father had tried to kill someone? Was that better or worse than abandoning me? My mind scrambled to catch on to something that made sense, but most of my previous framework was dissolving.

"It was just a difficult time. I understand he was ill, but it was difficult to see his actions as anything but betrayal. It stings, even now."

"I'm sorry," I said. "I didn't mean to bring up such a sore subject. I know almost nothing about Raymond Madison except that he's my father. I've seen a picture or two of him and that's it." It seemed like a bad idea to mention the dreams.

"You favor him," she said. "Same dark brown, curly hair, although he kept his considerably shorter. You have his smile as well in the roundness of your cheeks, the way it takes over your face, the arch of your eyebrows. You have probably been told your entire life that you have your mother's eyes, but there is a mischievous glint quite like his. It was a bit hard to take for a moment. But I can't hold the sins of your father against you."

Her voice was soft and sad. Why would she speak that way about someone who betrayed her unless... "You were in love with him." It slipped through my lips before my brain had time to process it.

She flinched, and I felt even worse. "That obvious, is it? It was a long time ago, before your mother arrived. But yes, I cared for him dearly. Which made things much more difficult when he fell apart."

"And Kyp..." How Raymond Madison became "like a second father" to him suddenly became an urgent question.

Again she chuckled. "When you live in a communal atmosphere such as this, parentage doesn't matter. We discover attachments to people as we grow. As a child, I latched onto Raymond's father, Julian. We had many things in common, so he helped raise me. He taught me much about leadership. Kyp got rather attached to Raymond and eventually to you."

My heart ached, and I wished there was a way to ask Kyp about Ray without hurting him.

"Now, Cassandra informed me you jumped into the fray yesterday, grabbed a weapon, and assisted my son. You seem to have taken to these changes in yourself quite well, despite your shock." She walked around the desk and settled onto the edge nearest me. "You have potential, Jacklyn. I want to grow that potential. In his early days, your father was an outstanding Key, a leader, a trusted figure among his people. You can become greater than he ever was. His mistakes need not be yours. I want to see you shed his shadow and step into the light. Work with me, and you will."

"Thank you, Lavinia. I'll do my best to earn that."

"You are very welcome." She smiled. "If you ever find yourself plagued by paranoia, please speak to me. I am a Mind Key. I may be able to help. If your father had done so, he may not have been so troubled." She breathed in deeply, as if steeling herself. "Promise me you will tell me if you need me."

"Of course." It was already clear how this lifestyle could break a person.

She nodded, an eyebrow raised. "Wonderful. Shall we head to training now? The others should already be getting to work."

As we headed to the training room in the basement, guilt weighed heavily on my chest. If I left her, would it upset her in the same way?

The training room was a massive open space, split into activity quadrants. Lavinia walked me to the one closest to the stairs where Gana was set up, working with Mom and Cass. As she alternated between lifting weights and trying to light a candle with her Aegis, she looked absolutely miserable.

"Aegis training," Lavinia said, waiting a beat while I offered a wan smile and a wave to my adorably angry kid sister. She all but hissed at me. "You, too, will train for that today."

She nodded at Mom and Cass before moving on to the next quadrant, where Kyp fought with a bo staff against a man I didn't recognize, who wielded a pair of batons. They put on an amazing show, dodging in and out of close combat, moving with a fluidity I'd only ever seen in choreographed fight scenes.

"Time out!" Lavinia clapped her hands once, and both fighters stopped and turned to face her. She strode past Kyp toward the other man. Dressed in all-black clothing and studded jewelry, along with stringy hair and pocked pallid skin, he resembled an aging punk rocker. He looked less like a warrior for good and more like someone I would find passed out on a subway bench with a beer bottle dangling from his fingertips.

"Jacklyn Madison, this is Hector Moretti."

He shook my hand, and I resisted the urge to wipe it off on my sweatpants.

"It's a pleasure to see you again, Jacklyn," he said, in a gruffer version of Kyp's deep voice.

"I'm sure my son is overjoyed to have you around. You two were good friends, once upon a time." He clapped Kyp on the back, hard. Kyp grimaced.

"Hector is Ross's Guardian. He has increased agility..." Kyp trailed off. "Wait, have you met Ross?"

I hadn't, but I assumed he was the frowny-faced dude sidling up to us now. Short and stocky, he looked as if he had once been tall and thin and somebody had stuck him in a vise, turning the lever until he looked like he did now. An incomplete straw-yellow beard dusted his peach chin.

"Welcome back, asshole," Frowny Face said, bumping Kyp aside with a shoulder check. Kyp's lips twitched into a snarl, but his face was blank again within seconds.

"I see you brought back some hot souvenirs with you. Gonna introduce us?"

"Yeah, try again, but with a lower creep factor," I said, nose wrinkling in disgust.

"Nope," he said. "But now I know exactly who you are. Jacklyn, it's been a while. You probably don't remember me. You were tiny when you left here."

"She was a year younger than you." Kyp rolled his eyes.

"I'm Ross. Ross Ebell. Dark Element Key. I control the earth, but I can heat things up, too." He waggled his eyebrows.

I rolled my eyes. "How many times have you used that?"

His smile was insincere. "Nothing impresses you, huh?"

"Show me something impressive," I said.

"And who's she?" His chin tilted toward Gana, a predatory glint in his eyes.

"That's my sister, Gana," I said. "Mess with her and I'll detach your favorite body part."

Ross cracked a smile, glancing over at Kyp. "She's fun, huh?"

"Yeah. Fun." Kyp's smile was devious. I kinda loved it.

From another training quadrant, Kylie cleared her throat obnoxiously and tapped her foot. "Hello, we were working over here."

"She *is* right about that." Lavinia placed a hand on my shoulder. "Hector, please take over hand-to-hand combat training with Kylie and Ross. Gretchen, I'd like you and Kyp to come assist me in Aegis training for Jacklyn."

Gretchen was the pale woman with porcelain skin and platinum ringlets who had mocked Kyp for needing my help. She hadn't made a very good first impression. And, based on her face when she approached, the feeling was mutual. Her mouth stretched into something that was supposed to represent a smile but was actually a tooth-baring snarl. Then she returned to looking bored by my presence.

Lavinia led us to a fourth portion of unused training space and waved at the others to continue their work. A low buzz of conversation picked up as they did.

"Just to be clear, you have never utilized your Aegis intentionally before the events that led you here?" Lavinia asked.

"If I had, wouldn't I be creature-chow?" I shrugged. "Even when I did use it, it definitely wasn't intentional."

"Okay then!" She clapped hands together in a flurry of excitement, a sweet break from her normally rigid behavior. "I am going to walk you through channeling your Aegis. Ready?"

I nodded.

"Close your eyes and focus on your breathing."

I did as she requested. But with my eyes closed, it was like everyone's gaze gained weight and pressed down on me. I couldn't forget that they were watching.

"In through your nose, out through your mouth."

Nervous laughter escaped me, and my eyes shot open. "Sorry."

"Clear dedication." Gretchen strutted over to me, her ringlets bouncing with each step.

She sized me up for a moment. Then she punched me dead in the nose.

Pain erupted in my head, and my hands shot up to my face. I struggled to blink away the haze. I'd been punched by bullies more than a few times, but never by a battle-trained adult. As it turned out, there was a difference, and that difference was a whole lot of pain.

"Hey!" Kyp snapped.

"Gretchen!" Lavinia shouted.

"What the hell?" I groaned.

"What? I bet she'll be more dedicated now!" Gretchen said.

I swiped the back of my hand across my nose and found streaks of blood left behind. My resolve strengthened, along with my anger. Closing my eyes again, I worked to center myself, breathing in and out through my mouth because my nose wouldn't cooperate. This time, I ignored the presence of the others.

Lavinia continued speaking as Kyp projected the words into my head in perfect unison. A well-rehearsed lesson.

"Reach deep within. You'll find it, this center part of yourself, a part pulsing with light, with power. Pull from it. Let it spread through you. From your core through to your limbs."

It quivered through me, then thickened into a quake. My eyes cracked open, Gretchen coming into view, a smug smile on her face.

I wanted to punch it off.

Kyp added in an oddly casual tone, "Go ahead. Punch her back."

My fist shot out and hit Gretchen's jaw with a crack. She dropped to the floor in a heap, like someone had tugged out her skeleton.

Lavinia looked from Gretchen on the floor to me with humor in her eyes. "I suppose she deserved that. Can you find it in your heart to try healing her?"

I could.

My first chore was post-lunch dishwashing with Kyp. We worked silently for about ten minutes, once I'd declared that I would wash and he would dry.

Kyp broke the silence with a thoughtful noise. "Jaina looked pissed when she saw your nose." He leaned in, eyes tracking over my face. "Healed up quick, though. If only it had been a minute sooner, she may not have seen it." He grinned.

I sponged off a plate. "Today I learned that getting punched in the nose makes you feel like your brain will dribble out of your eyes. See! I learned something!"

"Don't sell yourself short." He placed a dish into the cabinet overhead. "You learned how to harness your Aegis."

I smiled serenely. "I wish I'd learned it in a way that didn't leave bruises, even if it *was* only a few minutes."

"You expected to learn battle techniques without getting a bruise?" The look he sent my way told me he thought I was nuts.

"Of course not, but she sucker punched me!"

"Yes. It was highly unorthodox."

I handed him another clean plate. "Any idea why she did it?"

"Aside from Gretchen being sadistic?" He shrugged. "Mother wants you trained and ready for missions as soon as possible. To do so, you need to pass your first Key test. Mother may have put pressure on Gretchen and she acted out."

"What's on the Key test? Advanced wound healing and the art of nose punching?" I asked.

He grinned. "It's an obstacle course to test our skills and how we think on the field. As we pass the tests, we increase our rankings. If I pass mine, I'll be considered a full Key and a teacher."

I waggled my eyebrows at him, handing him a dish. "Impressive, Mr. Franklin."

His cheeks reddened, and he gingerly placed the dish on the rack. "Kylie's next in line, then Ross, and now you."

I dropped my voice to a whisper, turning my attention to the mug I was washing. "Speaking of Kylie... what you told me was true?"

His eyes cut over to me. "Yes. But we keep up appearances. I do it for Mother. She does it for the power that comes with Mother's approval. Kylie seems to think she has something to worry about with you. She got on my case last night. I'm trying to avoid her causing you any trouble with Mother."

I nodded. "And, uh, is there any reason for Kylie's concern?"

He stared at the dishwater.

"In that case, you probably shouldn't have reacted the way you did when I got hurt."

Kyp took the washed mug from me, fingers brushing mine as he did. He met my gaze steadily. "Pretending not to care will be harder than I expected. We were best friends once. And with my memory, it's still kinda like yesterday. But... different." His eyes lingered on mine for a moment, and I wondered...

He cleared his throat, snatching the pea green dishtowel from the counter and drying the mug as though it was the most important thing. "When I'm in charge, I'll get an electrician in here and completely rewire the house so the circuit doesn't blow at the sight of a dishwasher."

He muttered it so angrily I had to laugh.

"I hate doing dishes," Kyp said. "It's my least favorite chore."

"Is it weird that it's my favorite? Back home, I used my time in the kitchen to daydream. Mom was always working, and on most days, it was my responsibility to look after Gana. But when I cleaned up after dinner, she'd go off to read and I'd have time to think, or dream up fantastic adventures, and not be responsible for a few minutes. Be... free." I blushed. "Now, it's just nice to chat with you without Kylie trying to bore holes in my head."

"Ah, so that's why you asked about Kylie." My shoulders sagged under the weight of his eyes on me. I scrubbed at a crustedon lump of pasta sauce. It was something like forever before he spoke again.

"We can talk other times."

My heart stuttered. "Like when?"

"We share a wall." He smiled. "When we were kids, you would put your hand to the wall and I would put mine there, too, and we'd transfer thoughts. It's one of those things we gained when we did the blood oath. It's like talking, but a little more immediate. And nobody else will hear us because it's a semi-direct connection. Difficult to intercept."

"I'd like to test that out." I handed him the last dish to dry and unplugged the sink. "Okay, all done here."

"Cool. I'll knock later. You knock back if you can talk." He placed the dish in the cabinet and left the room. I followed closely behind.

Kylie and Ross approached from the hallway as we left.

"Honey!" Kylie cooed. "We were just going to go bake snacks for everyone." She stepped in close to him and brushed her fingers across his chest. "Want a cookie?" Her eyebrow rose.

I fought the sudden urge to vomit.

"Sorry, I can't. Probably shouldn't have had seconds at lunch." He shrugged. "I've got to play tutor to Gana in about" — he glanced at his watch— "ten minutes. Can't stick around. But maybe Jacklyn will join you guys." He patted her arm twice in quick succession before jetting off down the hall like his tail was on fire.

Kylie and I watched him go. Ross was already in the kitchen, grabbing ingredients from the refrigerator.

"I can tell what you're doing," Kylie said, not even looking in my direction.

"What am I doing?"

She leaned toward me, blue eyes alight with a vicious glow. "If you think you're going to come in here and become top girl, you are sorely mistaken. It's better you understand now, before you embarrass yourself by trying." Her head tipped in the direction Kyp had headed. "And stay away from him. He's taken."

"Huh. And here I thought I left high school behind when I came here," I said. "Turns out, things aren't much different."

"Watch your step, Jacklyn." She stormed back into the kitchen.

As she left, my eyes caught Ross', and I was surprised to find them round with anguish.

Shaking my head, I headed back to my room and flopped onto my bed to read. I chose a book Gana had packed for me, my last bit of fun reading before I had to start learning from the books in the library. Apparently, I needed to learn Key and Guard history. And here I thought I'd been close to done with school.

I read for nearly an hour before I heard the scrape of knuckles against the wall I shared with Kyp.

Smiling, I knocked back, then pressed my palm to the wall. Energy passed through our connection, warming the wall.

"Kylie is a horrible person," he said.

His words swirled in my head, more of a thought than a voice.

It was a bit uncomfortable, having an unfamiliar person's voice floating around in my head, but I had welcomed him there, and it was fun to have a secret way to talk.

"Jacks? You have to think your thoughts back at me. I could read them, but I don't think you want me having access to everything rolling around in your brain." His laughter filled my head.

I gave it a try. "What do you mean? Kylie is delightful. She seems to think I'm not allowed to speak to you."

"Sorry I left you behind," he said. "The act makes my skin crawl, and she knows it! It's all the touching..."

I didn't expect to be able to feel him grimace, but it came through the connection.

"It *is* pretty gross."

"You know how I hate washing dishes?" he asked.

"Yeah?"

"Well, I met this really cool girl who happens to love it. And I dunno, maybe she's on to something."

I was grateful for the wall between us, blocking my lame blushing. "Maybe she is."

He paused. "I have a bunch of stuff I want to talk to you about. Important things, but... can we save that for another day? I really want to get to learn everything I've missed while you were gone."

My heart swelled. "Kyp, a lot has happened in thirteen years."

He laughed. "Okay, I know to you it sounds crazy. But... you were my closest friend."

My heart gave a little squeeze. "Where do I start?"

"Anywhere."

"Okay. My earliest memory is me reading a book to Gana..."

Six

HARD LESSONS

"That's not a smooth cut. You're letting the sword wobble." Mom reached from behind me, positioning my hands on the wooden sword. One by the guard and one further down the handle. It was the Korean form. I kept using the Japanese way of holding the sword, my hands together in the middle of the handle. She said it left more leverage if someone tried to snatch my sword away. She probably just liked the Korean method better, but fine, I'd take it. What did I know about sword fighting?

A lot more than I had last week.

"I want a body cut that doesn't wobble. Hold the sword steady. Stay focused."

I nodded, narrowed my eyes, breathed in deeply, and cut right through the newspaper page hanging in front of me. I also managed to send the severed edge floating across the room, but that was better than just wrinkling it. That was progress.

"I can't do this!" Hector shouted from another quadrant in the training room.

Mom and I shared an exhausted look before she turned. I sheathed my sword.

We didn't even have to look to guess what caused the ruckus.

Hector marched away from the table where Gana sat, frustration making his steps rigid. "She's impossible."

"I'm impossible," Gana parroted, smug as hell. "Guess I should go home."

Mom dropped her head back and sighed dramatically. "Take five." She marched over to where Gana was sitting.

I walked past where Lavinia and Kylie were getting in some hand-to-hand combat, toward where Gretchen and Ross were watching with their arms crossed.

"She can't lift a weight or strike a spark," Gretchen commented, smiling and waving when she realized I was listening. "Maybe she doesn't have it."

Ross' jaw worked. "She has it. She just wishes she didn't."

I settled on a nearby bench to watch Mom talk Gana into making herself useful somewhere she didn't want to be. I mentally wished her luck with that and focused my Aegis so I could listen.

"Sorry, kiddo," she said. "Hector and Gretchen totally got forced into this teaching gig. We're low on teachers these days. Doesn't mean they're good at it."

Gana adjusted the blue tapered candle in its crystal candle holder. Her foot kicked at the metal table. The defiance on her face was chilling.

I glanced around the room and winced. Mom was right. We were seriously low on soldiers. Most of our team was down here in the training room, except Cass and Kyp. Ten people. Not a considerable force against a dimension of creatures that wanted to eat us.

It seemed like a lofty goal for such a tiny team.

As I watched, Gretchen slid into place beside Mom, bumping her out of the way and sliding into the seat across the table from Gana. "Why don't we start with you telling us why you don't want to use your Aegis."

"This isn't a frickin' therapy session," Gana grumbled.

"She gets in her own way." The voice came from so close I jumped.

Lavinia smiled. "You can't focus your Aegis so hard; you lose track of what's beside you. That could get you killed one day. Moderation in all things." She ran a towel across her forehead, then slung it over her shoulders.

"I'm still getting used to having to worry about that." I turned my attention to her.

"That's why we wait before putting you on missions." She sat on the bench beside me. "You worry about her."

"Of course I do," I said. "She's my sister."

"I understand," Lavinia said. "But you needn't worry. She's got a fierce soul. You both show a tremendous amount of promise. Gana just needs to accept what she is. Gretchen is prepared to assist."

"Yeah?" Gana's response was bound to be entertaining.

"Don't laugh, I'm serious." Lavinia raised an eyebrow. "We discussed it. Many of us have something in common with her."

"A stunning sense of style?" I teased.

She ignored me. "We didn't always want to be here."

"You? Somehow I can't picture that."

"Oh, I hated it here." She leaned forward, stretching her back. "I had this unique gift. I would read books about these scholarly adventurers, see a movie like Indiana Jones, and think, 'that should be me.' Instead, I was here, sharing my family home with generations of people who didn't understand me. Ask Kyp. When you're a child who is smarter than most of the adults around you, it makes people nervous. People don't know what to make of you."

"That sucks." The idea of Lavinia or Kyp searching in vain for understanding sent a pang through my heart.

As Gretchen spoke to Gana, Gana's cheeks reddened.

"What is she telling her?" I wanted to listen in, but that was the Aegis equivalent of ignoring Lavinia to play with my phone.

"The truth," Lavinia said. "It's not the nicest tactic, but it will work."

"Not the nicest—" I was quick to respond.

"No harm will come to her," Lavinia said. "Once she harnesses it, it will become simple for her. As it has largely become for you. She just needs the trigger. And that trigger is what we overheard Ross and Kylie snickering about earlier."

My eyes cut over to her expectantly.

"They asked why Jaina insisted on a metal table instead of a wooden one when there was zero chance of her lighting the candle, let alone burning the house down."

Across the room, Gana gasped. A tiny burning flame danced along the edge of the candle's wick.

"Holy crap," I slipped.

Cass let out a whoop from nearby. I hadn't noticed her come in. Hadn't noticed Kyp, either. He leaned on the doorframe, arms crossed over his chest, a satisfied smile on his face. Our eyes met, and for a moment, I couldn't glance away.

Lavinia bumped me with her shoulder, grinning. She patted my back the way Coach Perl did after a particularly good run. "You see, my girl, she just needed proper motivation."

Watching us celebrate, Gana blushed, and the flame on the edge of the candle shot up a couple of inches.

"Alright, alright. Don't burn the house down."

Gretchen blew the candle out. Maybe she wasn't as bad a teacher as Mom thought.

A huge textbook rested on my lap and yet I'd been unable to read for a solid hour. It was hard to read over so much bickering.

The entire younger generation of the Order was sitting around the couch playing a fighting game, just like I should be. But I hadn't finished the reading Hector had assigned because I kept staying up at night, talking to Kyp.

Bad girl. Very bad girl.

Meanwhile, Gana had finished the reading in a snap. Little showoff.

And just like the showoff she was, she quickly took Ross down in the game they were playing.

"Whoa! How the hell did you do that?" Cass asked.

"What, like it's hard?" Gana shrugged. "You told me what buttons did what, and I used them."

There were words on the page in front of me. I knew that. But none of them were being processed by my brain.

"You cheesed me!"

"You kept running into that kick. Why wouldn't I just keep doing it?"

"That's it!" Ross shouted. "First chance I get, I'm feeding her to a Gorvhan."

Now I wasn't trying to read at all. "I didn't hear that right, did I?" I started to rise from my chair, but Kyp laid a hand on my shoulder and pressed down until my butt was back in the seat.

"Relax," he said. "Ross is harmless. Don't get yourself all worked up."

He didn't seem harmless to me.

"I'll show you harmless, you little pr—" Ross said.

"Ross, enough," Kylie snapped.

Ross sat back in his chair, arms crossed.

Cass scoffed. "He wasn't serious, anyway." She leaned forward, mock-whispering in Gana's ear. "Don't worry. If he kills you, I'll channel you and we'll haunt him together."

"Channel?" I asked.

"Oh right," Kyp said. "That's Cass' Aegis. She can summon spirits."

My eyebrows rose. "Spirits?"

"Yes," Kyp said. "It's not enough that we've sprung all of this on you. But now, ghosts." He wiggled his fingers in the air playfully.

I let my head fall back on the couch just as another fight erupted over the game, this time between Cass and Kylie.

I groaned and snapped the book shut. "I've had enough." I stomped off toward my bedroom. I may have slammed the door too hard, but I didn't care, which meant this truly was becoming home. That was dangerous.

The other night, Mom had taken Cass and Hector to pick up the rest of my things. My room was now decorated with my usual mix of geeky posters, figures, and bits of memorabilia. It was an even better, more ambitious shrine to everything I loved.

I collapsed onto my bed and started reading about the rifts between our dimension and the Dusk, aka what the Order called the place interdimensionals came from because they were uber-dramatic.

In the Dusk, there were several types of creatures, and a whole hierarchy. Some were like Gorvhans, animalistic in nature. Others were sentient, like Sirins or Arvokians. And just like sentient beings in our dimension, some of the beings were utter dicks. In their dimension, Arvokians were fragile so Sirins, the dicks, enslaved them and treated them downright horribly.

The Arvokians discovered weak entrances into pockets between the two dimensions and accidentally tore rifts between the two. They hid in the pockets and found they were actually stronger there. However, Sirins and several other kinds of creatures like them started coming here, looking for them, and developed a taste, even an addiction, for our fluids.

I threw up in my mouth. Just a little. The description was... detailed.

To make up for accidentally making us a gourmet delicacy for creatures who shouldn't even be on this side of the rift, Arvokians offered their help. We became allies, and they provided us with Rituals we could perform to do things that were outside our given abilities, like Rituals to protect us from the abilities of other interdimensionals. They also maintained our wards and acted as a sort of governing body when there were issues within the Order.

Our Arvokian Liaison was named Cxarana, and we needed a Ritual to get to her.

The writing in the book was as dry as my eyes after reading the dusty old tome for a few hours. It was a miracle I was still awake by the time I'd completed the three chapters we'd been assigned. There was an entire section dedicated to every Arvokian and founding Order member involved in the initial treaty.

My eyelids were drooping closed when Mom slammed through the door.

"Jacks! An emergency! We need you!"

I was already moving. I'd been here less than two weeks, and it was becoming routine to be woken from sleep to heal some injury or another. Still, this was the first time anyone had said the word "emergency."

"What's going on?" I tried to fight away my sleepiness with activity. "What should I expect?"

"Liv sent a team to destroy a nest of interdimensionals discovered in a patch of woods ten miles from the local high school," Mom said. "They were met with unexpected difficulty."

"Unexpected difficulty?" I asked.

A mess of activity fired off downstairs. Voices shouting. Weapons clanging to the floor.

I ran down the stairs, Mom close behind. Our team had returned, covered in blood and gore, some in colors and consistencies that made sense, others that didn't. Some on their feet, others carried in. The odor of blood filled the air, and the taste of iron was thick on my tongue; I had to fight for control of my stomach.

I stopped in front of Lavinia, waiting for an assignment.

"Talkers. Sirins." Kyp clutched his head, blood leaking between his fingers. "They were ready for us. Weren't we looking for a Gorvhan nest? Not Sirins?"

Lavinia pursed her lips. "There were only supposed to be Gorvhans. That's not good."

Kyp's look was a nonverbal "No freaking kidding."

"How can we help?" Gana asked.

I hadn't heard her come downstairs.

"Gana help me get Hector on this table!" Lavinia shouted. She glanced at me. "Heal Kyp."

Gana complied with her request while I took stock of the damage. Kylie was cleaning out an ugly looking wound in Cass' calf. Mom worked on Gretchen, who was covered in bruises, while blood gushed from her arm and nose. Ross was in the worst shape—blood poured from a deep gash across his midsection.

"Jacklyn." Lavinia was calm as she tore Hector's shirt to get it clear of his wound. "We have Guardians bleeding out. We need medics. You heal Kyp. If you can heal Gretchen before your Aegis drains, do it."

"But Ross... I think he's actually dying." Blood pooled on the floor, surrounding him. My legs shook.

Lavinia tore her attention away from the task at hand, anger flashing in her eyes. I flinched and immediately hated myself for it.

"Mother, go easy on her." Kyp swiped at the blood dripping into his eyes. "She's never seen post-battle triage like this before."

"People are dying." Her tone was razor-tipped. "You take orders. You don't need to understand them." She yanked the lid from a bottle. The sharp smell of antiseptic filled the air, mingling with the iron tang. "You fail to listen, more people die. I'll take Hector. You take Kyp. *Now*, Jacklyn." Gana handed her bandages and a needle and thread, and she returned her full attention to Hector.

She was right. Questioning her now was dangerous. "Okay."

My voice shook. I closed my eyes and breathed, channeling my Aegis. My feet moved away from Ross dying on the floor, away from the boy my instincts urged me to save.

Kyp was propped up against a decorative table, hands coated in his own blood. I pressed my fingers to the puckered gash on his forehead. Blood spurted from it and hit me on the cheek.

He swore. "I'm—"

"Yes, I know. You're sorry for bleeding so much."

"You're right. That's ridiculous." His lips turned up at the corners, barely a smile, and he winced. "Don't worry. Ross won't die. Not permanently, anyway."

"I don't understand." My fingers warmed, and my energy drained into the wound.

"Keys are bound by the Arvokians at birth to complete our mission. It's a kind of baptism. We've all gone through it. In being bound to the mission, we are also bound to our lives. We die, we return." He grimaced as he shifted. "The only permanent death for us involves an Arvokian Ritual that breaks that binding. Sirins, the inter-dimensionals we faced today, are more dangerous to Keys than Gorvhans because they aren't animals. They are intelligent creatures. Some have learned the Ritual, which means they can kill us. Permanently."

"And if we don't do the Ritual? We live forever?" That took some of the pressure off being on the battlefield.

"Not unless you want to start falling apart." His smile grew. "Eventually, you choose your time. Eventually, you want to."

"You said Keys. What about Guardians?" I asked, as fresh skin formed over his wound. I ran a finger over my work. *Perfect.*

"They are bound by no such contract." Kyp's eyes met mine. "Go to Cass. I'm good."

Now it made sense why Lavinia wanted me to ignore Ross and save the Guardians. My stomach flip-flopped. I may be slightly safer, but Gana and Mom were not, and they were supposed to protect me.

Kyp squeezed my hand as he passed. "Thank you."

Drained and already dizzy, I moved on to Cass.

It was nearly a week before we made it back to the training room, and even then, it was only for a low-impact lesson on battle formations.

"Jaina and Kylie are out meeting with a friendly contact for information on a Gorvhan sighting," Lavinia said. "However, such small missions are rather rare. Typically, the size of the threat dictates the number of soldiers deployed."

"You've learned how to use your Aegis to fight more effectively," Gretchen said. "Your hand-to-hand sessions have started to teach you how to land a punch or a kick. But you need to learn battle formations. You need to learn style. The most important thing is to remember it's the Guardian's job to protect you. You have to let us do our job."

"Meaning you stay in formation," Hector said. "Kyp, Liv."

They fell in, the two of them back-to-back, weapons at the

ready, while the Guardians created a barrier around them, a cocoon.

"Anything attempting to attack will deal with the Guardians," Cass explained. "The Keys are always protected."

I tried to imagine standing safe and protected, watching Gana battle interdimensionals on my behalf, and it felt completely wrong. "Isn't there a better way to do this?"

Everyone turned to face me, as if I had suggested we drop everything and learn to fight from a Matrix movie marathon. Which would be fun, but not a realistic approach.

"You'll still be in the fight, Jacks," Kyp snapped. "You'll still get to play superhero."

I flinched at his tone. Just because he had to pretend we weren't friends in public didn't mean he had to be such a jerk.

"That's not the issue." I fed his own attitude back to him.

"This is the way things have always been done, Jacklyn," Hector said. "What makes you think you know better?"

"Probably read it in a comic book," Kyp said with a smirk.

"I think we should hear our lost Key out," Cass said. "She may have a fresh perspective from her time on the mean streets of New York City."

I grimaced. "Thank you, Cass, for somehow agreeing with me and making me sound like a bargain basement hooker in the same sentence."

"What is your idea, Jacklyn?" Lavinia's lips tightened.

Beside her, Kyp shook his head, ever so slightly, more of a

tick than anything.

He was probably trying to tell me not to argue with her, but I didn't see the harm in it. If she listened, I'd keep Mom and Gana a bit safer. If she didn't, she'd lecture me. I still planned to leave. That wouldn't change.

"I think we should reverse positions."

"This doesn't make any sense," Lavinia said.

"It makes so much sense," I countered. "Guardians die permanently. Keys come back. I understand the original formation if a Key dies and needs to be protected from Talkers. But normally? A Guardian's life is much more fragile. We should be protecting them."

"You don't understand," Hector said. "There are only five living Keys. The number of potential Guardians is in the hundreds."

"How are there only five living Keys?" Gana asked. "That's oddly unbalanced for an international system of rifts."

"Are Guardians expendable to you?" I looked from face to face. Not a single person seemed to accept my version of reality. Not even Kyp or Cass. They viewed Gana and my mother, as expendable. Cass viewed *herself* as expendable.

"Jacks," Cass said with a sigh. "Nobody is here against their will. We pledged to protect the Keys. I met Kyp and knew I would give my life to keep him safe."

"You are willing participants in your own oppression," I said. "How can you not see that?"

Kyp stepped forward, but Lavinia grabbed him by the elbow,

stopping him. Her words were a whisper, but they came in loud and clear to me.

"You brought her here. She's your responsibility. If you can't keep her under control, you will both bear the punishment for her behavior."

Kyp shrugged her arm off and took a step closer to me, his eyes cold with fury. "God, Jacklyn, please shut up! You think you have the right to come here and question everything we've ever done? You don't even know anything."

His words were smacks across my face. I grasped for a response.

"Kyp, there is no need to yell." Lavinia pushed past him, and he glared at her as she passed. "Gana, to answer your question, there were once many Keys. But that was before paranoia divided us. This left us vulnerable to the interdimensionals and swaths of our people were led to their demise. You see, Jacklyn, the last time a Madison decided things should be done differently, he nearly wiped out the entire Order. Do you want that on your conscience?"

My stomach clenched. Nobody would make eye contact with me, not even Gana. I couldn't be part of this. I turned to leave.

"You cannot simply leave training," Lavinia said.

I faced her. Chaotic rage built within my veins. "Is my family expendable?"

"This is how it has always been done."

"Then I think I'm done training. You keep hiding behind the cannon fodder. I will *not* be doing the same. I won't sit back and let you train me to put my family in danger." I turned on my heel and left.

Kyp called after me, grabbing my arm as I passed. His pulse beat wildly beneath his skin. I pulled away.

As I left, Lavinia spoke, her voice almost chipper. "We'll need to teach her about speaking out of turn."

I stormed up to my room, slammed the door, and threw myself onto the bed.

Knuckles scraped against the other side of the wall, a tentative knock. When I didn't answer, Kyp spoke anyway.

"Jacks, I agree with you, but what you did was insubordination. This isn't a game. She's raising warriors. She can't afford to allow room for interpretation. Jacks? Jacks, please."

I had nothing to say.

SEVEN

The following morning, I woke to find a note tacked to my door when I left for my morning jog. A test had been scheduled for noon. Kyp warned me I'd have to take a test to rise in the ranks, but I thought I had another couple of weeks, at least. Either he was messing with me, or Lavinia was punishing me for yesterday's outburst.

She was totally punishing me for the outburst.

I didn't like what I'd seen from her in that training room. I'd believed her when she said she expected me to do well and that she cared what happened to me. I thought that included my family.

Silly me.

I didn't know where Kyp and I stood now, but if there was any chance of sharing information that would get us all out of here, I'd take it. The idea that my family might be on borrowed time churned my stomach.

The morning progressed as usual, and nobody discussed

the test. In fact, nobody spoke much at all. They stayed in their respective zones, athletes with a training regimen. That was familiar, like before a track meet.

When I made it down to the basement training room in my workout clothes, my jaw dropped. Laid out in the center training space was a huge obstacle course.

"Don't freak. You've got this." Gana gave me a quick squeeze. "Kick ass out there."

"It seems daunting, but don't worry," Mom said. "You are bright, capable, strong, and beautiful."

My mom with the helpful motivational speeches.

"I hate to break it to you, but beauty ain't gonna help me here."

"You never know." She winked. "One should be prepared to use all assets in battle."

Kylie and Ross laughed.

There was something endearing about how misguided she was. "Thanks, Mom, for always giving the worst possible advice."

She stuck her tongue out. "Good luck, Birdie." Her hazel eyes twinkled with laughter, and she pressed a kiss to my cheek before heading off to sit on the bench.

"Jacks can use her *assets* on me whenever she likes," Ross said.

Charming.

I flipped him the middle finger. "Never gonna happen."

The training room doors slammed open, and the time for socializing was over. Lavinia, impeccably dressed in a black pinstripe suit and heels, stood in the doorway, flanked by her Guardians, who commanded only slightly less attention than their Key. Hector was all dark hair and clothes, Gretchen all platinum hair and a white dress. Together, the trio was striking and far too coordinated for it to be a coincidence. Whether they were trying to present a united front or trying to make me roll my eyes, they were succeeding.

"Good afternoon, all," Lavinia greeted.

A muscle in Kyp's jaw jumped.

"As you all know, this testing period is particularly important. Kylie and Ross stand to make a step forward, Kyp is poised on the edge of completing his training, and Jacklyn has the chance to move forward to her first mission."

Beside her, Gretchen smiled widely.

"Due to the importance of this event," Lavinia continued, "we've decided to add a feature to shake things up a bit."

"Competition." Kyp mouthed the word as she said it, a grave look in his eyes.

"We will have two races through the obstacle course we have constructed," Lavinia said. "You will be allowed to use the entirety of your Aegis as needed. The second match-up will pit Kylie against Ross. But first—"

"No," Kyp said.

Lavinia's eyes cut over to him sharply. "Excuse me?"

"That's not a fair challenge. Jacklyn is a novice. Below me. I'm testing for expert status. I refuse to earn my full Key status by default.”

Below him? I may not be at his level, but to act as if I wasn't worth his time... I hadn't expected it, especially not in a room full of people who were looking for me to show weakness.

“Kyp.” Lavinia shook her head. “You yourself claimed she was more powerful than anticipated.”

“An intelligent newborn is not necessarily the next Stephen Hawking,” he said.

“Kyp,” Lavinia scolded, “don't you think that's a bit harsh?”

I thought it was. Kyp had always treated me and my abilities with respect. Until I'd dared challenge his mother.

“I can't tell,” I said. “Are you serious?”

If I let him change the match-up, it implied I agreed with him. That wasn't going to happen.

Kyp whirled on me. “Yes, I'm serious, Jacklyn.” He took a step forward and loomed over me. “We've been doing this all our lives. You've just started. How well do you think you can possibly stand up to a lifetime of training?” He turned back to his mother. “Let me race Ross or Kylie, but don't make me waste my talent and energy on *her*.”

I didn't bother deciphering the murmur rippling through the others. It wouldn't do any good. This went beyond feigning disinterest. This was cruel.

“I accept your challenge,” I blurted. If this was a purely physical training ground, Kyp wouldn't be so cocky. There had to be a surprise waiting for me. I shouldn't have accepted. Kyp was right—he had far more experience than I did. But I had something to prove.

Kyp barely suppressed a growl. "Goddammit, Jacks!"

Lavinia shook her head and placed a hand on his shoulder. "It's okay, dear. She needs to see what she can accomplish." She turned an eye on me, and determination burned within me.

If I didn't want to face Kyp, I looked weak. If I faced him and lost, I looked weak. Defeating him was the only way to come out strong.

"Fine," Kyp spat. His jaw was still locked tight, eyes narrowed.

I glanced back at Mom, whose eyes glowed a flickering orange. Gana whispered into her ear, a hand on her shoulder. Was that for restraint or comfort?

Hector called us over to our starting points. Gretchen counted to three, and the race began.

Kyp and I bolted toward the first obstacle, a rope with a hook at the end and a rock-climbing wall. I had a choice: use my enhanced hand-eye coordination to throw the hook over the wall and snag it or scale the wall without the hook. Either way, I had to be careful of the drain the selection had on my Aegis, which was why I couldn't just speed through the race from beginning to end.

While I contemplated, Kyp pitched the grappling hook over the wall. He misdirected, and it sailed off to the right. I did better. Once the rope latched on, I quickly climbed it. Kyp used his telekinesis to lift him up and over the wall, and I followed closely behind.

Once over the top, I let myself drop; my enhanced strength spared my knees.

The acrid stench of smoke filled the air. Someone must have started a fire somewhere further along my path. I would have to find out when I got to whatever obstacle required fire. First, there were hurdles. Warmth burned through my legs, and I jumped.

No, no, no, too far! I overshot, hitting the floor with a bang and the clatter of the third hurdle I'd almost cleared. *Shit.* I still needed to work on controlling my Aegis abilities.

Kyp's head whirled in my direction, his foot catching on his own hurdle. He barely managed to right himself, avoiding his own nasty fall.

I pushed myself to my feet. Pain flared, burning along my hip and down my leg in sharp bursts. It hurt worse than it should. Kyp had said something about overactive pain sensors. What a great time for that to start.

Kyp was already at the next obstacle, and if I stopped to heal, he'd get too far ahead of me. I'd rest my hip when this was over.

One hurdle. Two. Then I spotted the next obstacle. Ahead, in two orderly rows, was a series of low hanging wires, a foot off the floor. We were obviously meant to army crawl beneath them, but there was a catch. Flames danced along the wires in licks of red, orange, and blue.

From a hurdle away, I focused on the flames, hoping I'd inherited Mom's Aegis as well. I was told it was a possibility in Key/Guardian pairings. I used what I remembered the Guardians telling Gana in training. The flames suddenly flared higher. I hadn't meant to do that, but at least I had an effect on them. I tried again, imagining suffocating the flames as I focused on the thrum of power deep inside. After a moment, the flames dulled, flickered, and went out.

Kyp was so close I could smell his deodorant.

I focused on his flames next. As he knelt to climb under them, I made them flare. He shouted and swore. A brief twinge of regret was quickly eclipsed by my desire to best the competition in any race.

I dropped and army crawled under the wires. My body ached when I reached the end, and I rose to my feet with a wince. The next obstacle was a series of stands positioned into patterns. I needed to make my way across, leaping from one to another.

I landed on the third and it wobbled precariously beneath my feet. I leapt to the next just in time for it to drop out from under me. Continuing on, I checked each as I crossed, careful to keep my balance. Adrenaline concealed the throbbing pain in my hip.

My feet touched the ground, and I realized I was at the straightaway. I had come full circle. The finish line was in sight, and I didn't hear Kyp behind me. I pumped harder anyway, wanting as much of a lead as—

I was running in a field. No, not a field. The backyard of the estate. But it seemed much larger than normal.

No, my legs were smaller. I was smaller. I emitted a high-pitched giggle. In front of me was the boy from my blood oath dream. Kyp shushed me, even as he stifled a laugh of his own. He pushed his black hair back from his forehead, his dark eyes twinkling with mischief as he reached for me, snagging my chubby hand in his. Even then, he filled my world. It didn't matter what the problem was; Kyp would solve it. Kyp would explain any confusion. Kyp was always there for me.

He pulled me along, laughing and stumbling, his legs already a bit too long for his body.

"The tree! Climb the tree!" I pointed up at a towering willow tree, hopping in place.

Kyp turned back to face me, his hands on my shoulders, his expression earnest. "We can't. You won't be able to get back down."

"I can climb it! Kylie and Ross are gonna catch us." My lip quivered.

"So what? It's just a stupid game." His eyes shadowed. "It's not worth the trouble we'll get into when we get caught."

Tears tumbled over my cheeks. "You never, ever, let me have any fun." I stomped. "You're mean. I don't like you!"

The determination in his eyes wavered, and he looked as if he might cry, too. But that wasn't behavior fit for a hero. He took a deep breath. "I'm older. You should listen to me."

"Kyp?" a squeaky voice called through the forest. "Ross, I think I heard Kyp!"

Kylie.

Fear jolted through me. Kyp grinned, back in the game. "We

gotta hide," he mouthed before tiptoeing farther down the path, assuming I followed him because he commanded.

Instead, I put all my energy into a lunge for the lowest branch on the tree. I grabbed it and shimmied up. The rustle of leaves finally caught Kyp's attention.

"Jacks, no!" It was a hushed shout, a mockery of a whisper.

I kept moving up the branches and didn't look back until I was higher in the air than I'd ever been. It wasn't until I stopped climbing that I noticed Kyp, two branches behind me, struggling to catch up.

"See," I whispered down at him. "I told you this was a good idea."

He glared as he moved toward my perch. "This was a terrible idea. We're gonna get in so much trouble."

When he finally caught up with me, he cuddled close, making us as small as possible so nobody would see us. He whispered in my ear, "The minute we're sure Kylie and Ross are gone, we gotta start climbing down. We do not want to be caught here."

I nodded. We listened closely for any approaching noises, but heard nothing. After a few minutes, Kyp nudged me, and we headed down.

The bark bit into my fingertips. I got down one branch, then looked for the next. My heart pounded as I stared at the long drop to the ground. I reached with my foot, pointing the toe as if I could grab the branch with it and climb down the rest of the way.

"Kyyyyyp." A drawn out, teary whimper.

"What?" He dropped down onto the branch beside me and looked from me to the branch I was feebly reaching for. "Just drop yourself onto it. It'll hold you."

I removed one shaky hand from the branch for all of two seconds before screaming and throwing my arms around Kyp, nearly knocking us both from the tree. He shouted one of those words five-year-olds are not supposed to say, but held on, stumbling only a little before righting his balance on the tree limb, one hand grasping the tree branch above, the other wrapped around my waist.

"Ha!" Kylie did a victory dance at the base of the tree with Ross scowling beside her, his arms crossed over his chest. "You owe me a whole dollar." She grinned at Ross. "I knew they were in there!"

"Guys, come down now." Ross's voice was a hesitant whine. "You're gonna get in trouble."

Kyp made a move to step down to the next limb, and I squealed, burying my face in his shoulder like a damsel in distress.

Gross.

He made another attempt. His foot slipped, and he grabbed onto the tree trunk and leaned against it. "We can't get down."

"I'm gonna go get Auntie Liv." Kylie laughed. "She's gonna be so mad." She raced off toward the estate. Ross looked up at us helplessly, hesitated, then ran after her.

"She's stupid." Kyp's tone held genuine disdain. "The rule is *no going into the forest.* If she tells them we're here, she's ratting herself out too. Dummy."

"Climb down," I said. "Run away and hide."

His arm tightened around my waist. "Not without you."

I thought of the last time I'd seen Lavinia mad at him and shuddered. "Go. Leave me. I climbed the tree all by myself."

Something flashed behind Kyp's eyes. He looked down. He was going to do it. He *should* do it. He should leave before his mother found us. Carefully, he sat me down on the tree limb against the trunk. Then he sat beside me.

"What are you doing?"

He wrapped his arm around my shoulders. "Uncle Ray says I'm supposed to keep you safe. Protect you, no matter what. When you're older, we can look after each other, but for now, it's my job. You know, 'cause I'm a big boy."

Tears filled my eyes. "I don't want you to take care of me. Leave! Now! Go away!"

He studied me for a second. "That's why I can't." He hugged me tighter.

I had no idea what that meant, but I was sure it made sense to him. Kyp never ran into a puzzle he couldn't figure out.

The grown-ups arrived in a chorus of rustling leaves and snapped branches. When Lavinia came into view, Kyp tensed, rigid as the tree trunk we leaned against. The scowl on her face made my eyes refill with tears.

"You get a boo-boo now?" I asked.

A tear slid down his cheek. "Yeah. Probably." Then he called out, "Mother? Aunt Jainey! We're up here!"

A pair of fingers snapped in front of my eyes.

"I made him climb it," I blurted before looking around. I was indoors now.

Mom knelt on the floor in front of me. She turned to glare at a fully grown Kyp, who leaned against the wall, cavalier. "I swear on all that is holy, Kyp, if you damaged her brain in some way, I will tear out your intestines and feed them to you. Cooked."

Kyp's eyebrows rose. "Colorful threat. Don't worry, she's fine."

"The race!" I jumped to my feet. "What happened?"

"You lost." Lavinia placed a comforting hand on my shoulder.

"*Kyp* happened," Mom said through gritted teeth.

I flew at him, but the image of the boy in my daydream flashed in front of my eyes and I stopped short, poking my finger hard against his chest instead. "You! You... used your Aegis on me!"

He held up his hands as if to toss off his blame. "Don't go taking the moral high ground with me. You messed with the fire. You sabotaged my race, too. At least there was no chance of me physically harming you with my method."

He was right. My throat tightened. I'd cheated, and I hadn't cared.

I walked out of the training room amidst the concerned looks of the Guardians. I tried to keep my head high, but tears stung my eyes and my lower lip quivered.

Once out of the training room, I raced up the stairs. I prayed the footsteps behind me weren't Kyp's. I couldn't face him. Not now.

I didn't look back until I was in my room and ready to slam the door in whoever's face followed.

It wasn't Kyp. It was Mom, her eyes troubled.

I turned away but didn't slam the door, so she followed. Gingerly, because of the injury in my thigh and the weighted pain in my heart, I lowered myself to the edge of the bed.

Mom watched me, her face soft, eyes pleading. "Jacks."

"Please just—" *Stop. Leave me alone. Stop looking at me like I screwed up. Like you pity me. Let me break down in peace.*

She pulled me into her arms, and I buried my face in her shoulder. Her familiar powdery scent, always a source of comfort, pulled the tears from me.

"Oh, Birdie," Mom whispered into my hair. "I thought you didn't want this."

I hadn't. But at some point, that had changed. I had started to enjoy myself. I'd become attached to the people here. I *did* want this. I wanted to help people. I wanted to be strong. I just didn't want this for Gana.

Which made it that much worse that it had been Kyp who'd made me look like a fool and violated my trust by rooting around in my brain. I'd flirted with requesting his assistance in getting Gana out of here. He'd dashed both of my conflicting hopes at the same time. It took skill to do something that shitty to a person.

"You're already crying a ton, so I'll take this as an opportunity to tell you I owe you an apology."

My head whipped up. "Really, Mom?"

She offered me a wry smile. Despite myself, I laughed through my tears.

"Oh, come on!" she said. "You know I'm not good at this. That's why Gana only listens to you."

I couldn't argue with that.

"I'm not saying it's okay. I'm just..." She sighed. "Look, I grew up in an awful family before I joined as a Guardian. I've mentioned before that there was a reason we had no extended family, but I'm not sure you grasped how serious I was." She brushed my hair out of my eyes. "And then I came here and... well, I never expected to do this alone. I never wanted to need to handle it all by myself again. Before I knew it, I was trying to juggle a job and two kids and protect you from this huge secret. I had no idea how to do that. And I certainly wasn't prepared." She shrugged. "I made shitty choices. Several shitty choices. A lot of them involving that very secret."

"You mean all the lies?" I said, because I could. But in reality, a knot loosened in my chest.

"All the lies." She nodded, her lips quirking up at the edges. "And a lot of stuff involving men." She made a face, and it pulled another laugh out of me. "I relied on you too much, and I wasn't around as much as I intended. I mean... I hope you know, between the jobs and the killing to protect you, that wasn't the plan."

I nodded and my eyes blurred with tears again.

"But I didn't really make a mistake trusting you. Because you are and have always been an amazing person." She swiped at the tear tracks on my cheeks with her thumbs. "And you helped me raise Gana, and she's smarter than both of us." She tilted her head as if in thought. "All of our sass and not an ounce of our sense of humor. We're gonna have to work on that."

"And we will." My voice came out thick and watery and I grimaced.

"Are we good? Because I love you, and I want us to be good."

"Yeah, we're good." And maybe we were. I wasn't happy with how things had gone, but her choices were limited. And she did apologize.

She leaned over and pressed a kiss to my forehead.

A knock sounded on the door. Mom glared at it, but didn't budge.

"It's me!" Gana called from the other side.

Mom and I shared a look, and she got up to let her in.

"Jacks, are you okay?" Gana practically ran Mom over to get into the room.

"I tried to get here sooner, but Lavinia wouldn't let me leave until the second race was over." Gana sat beside me on the bed and wrapped her arms around my waist. "Seems like you really pissed her off the other day."

Mom knelt, so she was eye-level with me. "Pissed her off how?"

I didn't answer. Her gaze hardened.

"Jacklyn told Lavinia the combat formations are wrong," Gana said. "The fact that she's right doesn't matter, apparently."

"You told Lavinia what exactly?" Mom spoke so fast the words slurred together.

"That the balance of power was wrong. Keys are stronger and return from the dead, and she has Guardians protecting us like we're weak. It's ridiculous!" I said.

Mom shook her head. "It's the way—"

"—things have always been done," I said. "I know. It doesn't make it right. Their priorities are wrong."

"You don't understand how she'll take that." Mom's voice was colored with panic. "She'll be offended. She offers her home to you, and you—"

"—tell her how not to get my mother and sister killed? Hell yeah, I did."

"This is where that got you. Are you too blind to see that?"

"I see fine. I just didn't realize I wasn't allowed to question."

"Think of this as the military. You don't question. You follow orders."

"Yeah, you guys keep telling me that, but it seems the number of soldiers you have are shrinking," I snapped. "Maybe you need my advice."

"Enough!" She grabbed me by my upper arms, her eyes wild. She had never handled me that way, maybe had never dared, but the look on her face was meant to scare me.

It was such a complete shift from our earlier conversation, my insides rattled. I forced myself to remain calm. "Get your hands off me."

She shook her head. "You don't understand what you're doing."

"Then tell us! What did Jacklyn do?" Gana asked. "What bear did she poke by questioning authority?"

Mom stiffened, but she dropped my arms. "I'll talk to Lavinia and see what I can do. From now on, keep your mouth shut during training. Lavinia is trying to accomplish something, and she needs soldiers that follow orders. Soldiers who fall out of line are a problem and you need to keep yourself from being a problem. Understood?"

I didn't reply.

"She understands, Mom." Gana's eyes bounced from me to her and back again.

"I don't think she does." Mom glared at me.

I rolled my eyes, stood, and fixed her bra strap, which had slid off her shoulder and was now hanging around the middle of her upper arm. "I'll behave."

"I'm sure." Her tone lightened slightly. "Lie low today. Both of you." She walked out the door and closed it lightly behind her.

"What the hell?" Gana said. "What got her so pissed?"

No. Not pissed. Scared. Maybe even terrified.

I shrugged. I didn't want to worry her.

"Are you okay?" Gana rose from the bed and paced around my room. She stopped to scan the bookshelves.

"I will be." I wasn't going to let this setback stop me. I had a plan. And if Kyp couldn't help, I'd find another way. A better way.

She pulled out a book and lowered herself onto the mattress beside me. "Can I keep you company for a while?"

I forced a smile and grabbed my book from the bedside table. "Thanks."

I tried to read, but as my eyes drifted across the words on the page, my mind was preoccupied. The vision Kyp had given me replayed in my mind. It felt like a memory. Maybe it was. It didn't matter.

Kyp may push back against the rules, but if what he'd shown me was true, he was terrified of his mother. I wouldn't have believed it a couple of days ago. She had welcomed me with open arms, had shown me nothing but kindness. But this had revealed a different side of her, and Mom's reaction hadn't lessened my concerns.

If Mom and Kyp were afraid of Lavinia, I definitely needed to find out why.

EIGHT

HIGH STAKES

I'm being watched.

I felt it through the fog of my sleep, the idea that eyes were on me. Dimly, I remembered I'd fallen asleep with Gana in the room and relaxed, sinking back into sleep.

A wet, snuffling sound woke me right back up.

I tensed. That was not Gana. That sounded like something else... something more animalistic.

My eyes flew open to find a shadow moving over the foot of my bed. It took a moment for my eyes to focus and for my Aegis to kick in, but that sound was unmistakable. A Gorvhan climbed over my footboard and onto my bed.

I bolted upright, but managed to keep myself from screaming. Gorvhans hunted in packs and I wasn't eager to draw more my way.

Weren't there wards to prevent this? It didn't matter, because like it or not, a Gorvhan sniffed up my leg like I was a four-course meal ready for consumption, and that needed to stop.

I inched up the bed. The oil slick, with its misshapen skull and empty eye sockets, stared back at me, silver teeth dripping with saliva. Like a cat, it batted at my leg, muscles bunched, prepared to leap forward.

I gulped and flattened myself against the headboard, heart hammering, entire body convulsing against the idea of any saliva dripping onto me. It leaned forward and growled, rancid breath wafting into my face. I had to swallow the bile before it escaped.

My eyes darted around the room in search of a weapon. I hadn't been allowed to keep my dagger, or any other weapon, because Lavinia said I needed to earn weapons by training with them. I didn't necessarily disagree, but right now, I really needed something to kill this thing.

It growled again and gnashed its teeth just as my eyes landed on the heavy Batman bust on my dresser. I worked an entire summer at an ice cream shop to get that damn thing and I didn't relish the idea of denting it on a Gorvhan's skull, but it was likely the heaviest thing in the room. Unfortunately, the Gorvhan stood between me and my weapon.

Sharp silver nails scratched across the bedding as it pulled itself closer. When saliva dripped onto my arm, instinct took over. I swung my fist into its head hard, ignoring the crack and flash of hot pain in my hand as the punch connected. It crumpled under the blow, and I managed an uncoordinated kick to its side. Once it rolled off me, there was plenty of space to leap to my feet and run for the Batman statue.

I hefted it up and swung it down on the Gorvhan's head once, twice, three times, cringing with every crunch, every splash of green ichor that erupted from its body. Every crack of its skull was another crack in my skillfully crafted collector's item. The Gorvhan deserved it for entering my room uninvited, but Batman did not.

The door slammed open, and I whirled, new weapon at the ready.

It wasn't another Gorvhan seeking its dinner. It was Kyp, barefoot, in a t-shirt and flannel pants, eyes wide, hair messy. A spot of green blood marred the pure white of his t-shirt. That spot meant there was another Gorvhan in the estate.

He rushed to close the door behind him. His eyes traveled over me, blinking, lingering on my legs for a moment before moving back up to my face. His hand gripped the doorknob hard enough to turn his knuckles white. Then the anxiety in his expression melted away, a crooked smile forming in its wake. "The Dark Knight has seen better days. Are you okay?"

I nodded, looking at the Gorvhan blood splattered across the long red Wonder Woman t-shirt I wore as a nightgown.

I had killed something. Not helped kill something, but killed it without a second thought. I'd known I would have to eventually, but the reality of it had been hazy, an unformed thought. My vision blurred with tears.

Kyp wrapped me up in his arms, my cheek pressed to his chest. I tensed for a moment, confused by his constant seesawing between hot and cold.

"You're okay. You did great." His next words came as a prayer. "I knew you'd be okay."

I relaxed into the hug. He was as scared as I was, the embrace a moment of comfort for both of us. And hell if I didn't need comfort.

It was there, snuggled against the chest of a guy I was harboring a massively complicated crush on, that I realized I wasn't wearing any pants. I tensed, and so did he.

He pulled back, his hands dropping to his sides, and he rocked on his heels. "So, um. We need to check on the others."

The others. Gana!

My face must have reflected my panic because he stepped forward again, taking my face in his hands. "Don't be afraid. Remember the alley. You can do this."

"No." I pulled away, my eyes frantically searching the room for her, as if I would find pieces of her scattered in blood-soaked chunks left by the creature. My heart seized. "You don't understand. Gana. She was here when I fell asleep and—"

"She left earlier," he said. "I saw her in the hall."

"That doesn't mean she's okay. Everyone could have been woken by a Gorvhan of their very own!" I babbled, my anxiety taking over.

"We won't find out unless we get out of this room." Kyp

leveled a weighty gaze on me.

I tried to shake off my nervousness. "Okay, what's happening? How'd they get past the wards?" I needed to do something. My family was out there.

"I'm not sure," he said. "I tried to contact Mother, but she went out with Gretchen earlier for a low-level mission. I don't think she's returned yet. I'll try Jaina and Gana."

"Yes, please."

His eyes closed, his brow furrowed, and energy radiated warmth from him as he sought them out.

Something battered the door, breaking Kyp's concentration. One hand shot toward the door, palm out. "I'm holding the door closed. I can't reach anyone while I'm doing this. Go out the window, now."

"Like hell!" I brandished Batman.

Kyp's eyes jumped from the door to me. "I can't figure out if you're brave or insane."

"I don't think this is an either-or situation."

The door jerked again.

"Wakey, wakey, little Keys. We're hungry." The grating voice sounded moist.

"Starving." Another gurgling voice joined the first.

I wrinkled my nose. "How cliché."

"Sirins. They don't just kill you. They reenact horror movies before they do," Kyp whispered. "They get more off the kill if you're petrified." His skin was chalky, and his focus remained on the door, even as he backed away from it. "Don't argue. Get down to the next floor. Find somebody else. I'll hold them off."

I wasn't leaving without him. Besides, I had an idea. "Step back."

"What? No." He didn't even look at me.

"If you plan to hold that door until I run away, you'll be disappointed." Ducking under his arm, I slid between him and the door. There wasn't much space, but I needed his attention. I ignored the warmth of him so close to me and the way he gulped as his eyes darted manically between me and the door.

"Are you trying to get us killed?" A hoarse whisper.

"I need you to trust me," I whispered back.

"That's hilarious. I trust you with a lot of things, but combat isn't one of them."

I glared. "You talking to *me* about trust is even more hilarious, brain invader. I'm barricading the door. Get out of the way. Now."

He searched my eyes for a moment, then nodded. One small step back. Another. I channeled my Aegis, upping my body strength, then walked to the vanity table beside the door and shoved. The legs of the vanity scraped the hardwood floor as I wedged it beneath the doorknob. My pink ceramic bear wobbled, then tipped, tumbling to the floor in an explosion of jagged bits. I swore.

It was silly to be so emotionally attached to it, but Gana had painted it for me at her sixth birthday party. It was special.

"I'll buy you a new one." Kyp took his cue from me, levitating my mattress and guiding it to the door.

I stepped around the shattered memory dusting the floor. "It's irreplaceable." I shifted the mattress slightly, so it pushed against the vanity, adding weight to our barricade.

"What now?" he asked, and I was surprised he wanted my opinion this time.

"Now, out the window."

The door rattled again. I didn't need a Sirin-to-English dictionary to understand they weren't pleased.

I threw the window open. "You first. I'll lower you down to the second floor."

"No way."

"I'm stronger. I lower you down by your arms, then you use your abilities to break the glass. I can swing through easily once you clear the way."

He looked back over his shoulder, hesitating.

"If I was a Guardian, I'd be *expected* to stay behind while you ran," I said.

"If you were a Guardian, I'd still... I told you, I agreed—" He shook his head sharply. "Now is not the time for this."

"Go." I held his gaze.

He broke his focus from the door and raced toward the window, straddling it before he had time to think it through. "Really wishing I'd grabbed shoes. Or thicker pants."

"Why didn't you?"

He looked at me as if the question was absurd. "You were

in danger." He lowered himself as far off the ledge as he could. His fingertips gripped the edge until I took over, lowering him further toward the second-floor window by his wrists. Using his telekinesis, he shattered the window just as the door behind me splintered under the pressure of the Sirin's pounding.

Kyp's head shot up. "Jacks!"

With no other acceptable options, I threw him through the window and turned to face my fate. Five Sirins with mottled blue skin, bony ridges protruding from their foreheads, and burning red eyes pushed their way over my dresser and into my room, brutishly crushing anything in their way.

Great. Now I'll never have time to grab some pants.

"Tasty Key. Nowhere to run now." The nearest one smirked, several rows of needle-like teeth revealing themselves. "It was nice of you to wait around for us."

I stared in open-mouthed surprise, my brain oddly focused on the human clothes they wore, as though they could blend in seamlessly with the population. The one who'd spoken came complete with a fedora and a pair of round-framed, hippie-style sunglasses perched precariously on the bridge of his nose. I couldn't make this up if I tried. Either I was actually seeing this, or my mind had finally, and decisively, snapped.

It tossed the mattress aside. It fell at my feet with a resounding thump. Dust flew into my nostrils and my sneeze was almost enough to drown out the sound of the door crashing against the vanity, the only remaining piece of furniture between me and five interdimensionals who wanted me dead.

I had to get out of there. And to do that, I needed a distraction.

They stalked toward me. With every step backward, I focused my Aegis, channeling it into my hand. I refused to take my eyes off the Sirins.

My heart pounded in my throat. When my back hit the window frame, I released the building warmth in the tips of my fingers. Flames shot from my hand, and the bottom of the creature's trench coat became an inferno.

It shrieked, yanking at the jacket, trying to get it off. The others scrambled backwards, avoiding the flames, and I didn't waste another minute.

I climbed out onto the ledge with my bare feet. The icy cold wind whipped through my hair, pulling several strands loose from my ponytail. I closed my eyes and channeled my Aegis to strengthen the muscles in my legs to absorb the impact.

I jumped, but only fell for a moment before my body abruptly changed direction, as if yanked by an invisible rope. I hurtled toward the window of the floor below. Kyp's shouts broke through the whipping wind in my ears as my head hit the window frame and my vision exploded in reds and yellows and whites.

I dimly realized what had Kyp so upset.

Time slipped along with the sound of muffled voices. The faint outline of people around me showed they were much closer than their voices seemed, but the world was wrapped in cotton fuzz. The floor was stiff against my back. My head throbbed.

"I misjudged the velocity of her descent." Kyp groaned. "I can't believe I did that."

"You couldn't let her die where the Sirins could get her," Kylie said. "You did what you had to."

"Those weren't her only options." Kyp sounded miserable.

"Whatever. If it weren't for me, she would have fallen to her death after what you did."

A door creaked open. "This argument is still happening?" Ross sighed. "Kylie, yes, your air control saved her, but in a house full of heroes, nobody's giving you a medal for acting like one."

Kylie made a haughty little noise. "Oh, hey, you found the brat."

"I'm not a brat," Gana snapped. "I was headed to the bathroom, but I ducked into the closest room once I heard them."

My head rattled with each footstep as they pounded across the floor.

My eyes peeled open slowly. Kyp was hovering over me. Gana had dropped to her knees beside him.

"Cass found her and sent her my way," Ross said. "The Guardians said she wasn't trained nearly long enough to face the threat. Told us to stay undetected."

Mom was out there with Hector and Cass fighting those things when we had five people in here who could help? It made no sense, but when I pondered it, my head felt like an elephant was sitting on it. I groaned.

"She's waking up," Gana said.

"Hey, champ," Kylie said, speaking to me like a two-year-old who fell off the swings. "You okay there?"

I pushed myself up on my elbows, but the world shifted, and I fell back against the floor. "The Guardians. They need us." My throat was dry, my tongue like sandpaper.

"They're keeping them bottle-necked." Still, Gana looked worried.

"Gorvhans and Sirins together. Like that last spoiled mission," Ross said. "Something isn't right."

"Kyp," I croaked, "what's the plan?"

Kyp stared off somewhere over Gana's head. His lips moved soundlessly, his fingers twitching, eyes narrowed as he worked to solve an invisible problem.

"Earth to Kyp?" Gana snapped her fingers in front of his face, and I winced at her obnoxiousness.

When his focus shifted to her, the look on his face made me wonder what Aegis you needed to shoot lasers out of your eyes. "What?"

"Kyp, I seem to have a head injury," I said, attempting to diffuse his anger. "Do you think you can try to listen to me when I talk?" My words came out slow and clumsy.

He turned his attention to me, his eyes softening. "You're right. Sorry." Then, to the others, "We need to find a safe room. Jacks is still broadcasting like a beacon, and it will draw them to us. Jacks, I'll teach you to hide your energy signature. Then we'll need to move very quickly and very quietly."

"Okay." I sat up, but it made my nausea worse.

"I need you to start by channeling your Aegis." His voice was more of a hum.

I closed my eyes, channeled my Aegis... and promptly puked all over the floor, luckily in the opposite direction of Kyp.

He muttered a soft curse. "This isn't going to work. I'll take care of both of ours. Ross, take the lead. Jacklyn and I will follow, with Kylie and Gana bringing up the rear. Are we good?"

Various murmurs of assent circled us.

Kyp looked at me. "Can you walk?"

I tried, but my feet touched the floor and the floor ran away. I stumbled, and he swept me into his arms, cradling me close to his chest.

"What are you doing?" A fragile protest. No movement was vastly preferable to movement.

Kyp smiled crookedly. "Gotta survive somehow, right?"

"Or we could leave her here," Kylie said. "They'll eat her up while we sneak out the back."

"I'm sure no Sirins thought to use the back entrance," Gana said, and I practically *heard* her rolling her eyes. "You're stupid *and* heartless. Can we throw Kylie in front of them as a distraction?"

Kyp didn't hide his smile well enough. "No." He tilted his head towards the door. "Onward."

We slinked through the darkness, Ross using his fire to create a dim glow in the hallway. The flames cast their light on Kyp's face, shimmering in oranges and purples. His lips moved, his eyes focused outward. He muttered something about gravity and the rate of acceleration and physics. He was redoing the formula for the velocity of my descent, the one he'd mentioned earlier, and my heart clenched at his guilt.

I drowsily leaned my head against his shoulder, my fingertips splayed across the muscles of his chest, palm resting over the *pound-pound-pound* of his racing heart, which beat in time with the *pound-pound-pound* of my throbbing head. I'd hated him when I'd fallen asleep, but that hatred was difficult to maintain.

"Mistakes happen," I whispered in his ear.

His breath caught, but he recovered. "Not to me." His eyes darted around the hallway, searching for the next attack.

I was too tired to fight him. Thoughts moved thickly around my mind. How Kyp's fingers dug into my thighs as he carried me around in my long, flimsy Wonder Woman shirt. Embarrassment at him seeing me vomit.

I probably had a concussion. That was the only good explanation. My brain was scrambled.

Once we'd made it halfway down the hall, I decided to try walking again. If he was carrying me, how would he be ready if things got bad again? I pushed back against his chest, but his arms tightened around me. I looked him in the eye, trying my best to look forceful.

"Fine," he whispered, his breath hot in my ear. "Just stay close."

I slid from his arms, my feet sinking into the carpet, and

finally, blessedly, the ground didn't shift and tilt. My Aegis must have been doing its thing.

Ross motioned toward the door at the end of the hall. I hadn't noticed it before, on account of my fried brain, but the firelight glinted off the battle axe in his other hand. I hoped the others were armed as well, because Kyp and I certainly weren't.

Kyp nodded at Ross, then motioned for Kylie to move to the front to back him up if necessary. The air picked up a chill and Kylie's hair moved on the unnatural draft she created. The fire hovering over Ross' hands flared, and the resulting glare pushed a knife into my brain. My eyes slammed shut for a moment while I steadied myself.

When I reopened them, I tried to focus my Aegis in case of a further attack. My vision blackened around the edges, my limbs went numb and, though Kylie's wind chilled me, sweat broke out along my forehead.

"Save it," Kyp advised. "You've got us."

"But—"

"Please. Don't argue."

Ross glanced back at us one more time to make sure we were ready. Then he threw the door open and let out a string of profanities that would've made a trucker blush.

Several Gorvhan shrieks pierced the silence. Black cut over my eyes again and this time I couldn't blink it clear.

A crash of glass startled me awake. My lips tasted of iron, and when I swiped at my nose with the back of my hand, it came away bloody. It took me a moment to figure out where I was, and my location did nothing to alleviate my confusion. I was lying in the fetal position under a crescent-shaped table positioned against the wall between two bedrooms. My eyes zeroed in on a familiar pair of worn brown leather boots, hastily pulled on, laces ignored.

Mom.

Relief came as a wave that threatened to drown me. I took a deep breath to stem the tide and tried to look beyond Mom for the others. Through the commotion, I spotted Cass and Hector locked in battle.

A pained grunt ripped my attention from my search. Flesh tore and bones crunched, and Kyp hit the floor in front of me with a jarring crash. His skin was pale, his face bloodied, and he was struggling with his arm. The bone jutted from the skin.

I swallowed back vomit. He was so close I'd throw up on him, and he really didn't need that right now.

His head lolled to the side, as if he was barely conscious, but his eyes betrayed his alarm.

A tear escaped my eye to sink into the carpet. I would not cower while everyone fought. I took a deep breath and channeled my Aegis. My muscles tensed, prepared to throw me into the commotion unfolding around me.

"No," Kyp mouthed. "Save it. Please."

A shadow fell over Kyp in the now well-lit hallway. I hoped it was one of us, but a clawed hand reached down and gripped the front of his t-shirt.

I exploded from the floor, throwing the table outward. It whizzed straight into the head of the Sirin. He dropped to one knee, momentarily stalled by the blow to his face.

Blinking back a wave of dizziness, I hopped over Kyp and landed on the table, snapping the wooden legs free with little effort. I slammed one hard into the Sirin's throat, then whipped the other across the room to where Mom was fighting a Gorvhan on her own. The wood sank into the creature's chest and it collapsed. Mom's look of shock morphed into a proud smile as she moved on to her next attacker.

My speedy healing had kept me fighting long enough to protect Kyp, but the ache in my head came crashing back, and I dropped to my knees beside him.

"Wow." He stared up at the ceiling past me, a dopey smile on his face. "That was astounding." A closer look revealed the blood wasn't only coming from his arm. Several deep, meaty slashes cut across his legs and stomach.

"Cass!" I called. Keys may come back from the dead, but my instincts, born in the normal everyday world where death was permanent, wouldn't let Kyp die.

Cass cried out when she spotted Kyp, but she got dragged right back into the action, only getting a brief reprieve. Hector and Mom closed ranks around us, a protective wall of Guardians.

A fireball whizzed past the side of my head and took down a Gorvhan I hadn't noticed approaching. Gana followed behind it, sliding down to help me.

"He's bleeding out. We've got to heal him while we still can." I patted Kyp's face when his eyes narrowed to slits.

They flicked to me, surprisingly lucid. "Waste of resources," he grunted through the pain.

"Come on, drag him into that room." I pointed at the nearest empty one. Gana and I grabbed Kyp and, careful not to make his arm any worse, started moving him.

I gingerly set Kyp to the floor while Gana locked up behind us, as if a Sirin hadn't taken the hinges off my bedroom door just a little while before

"I need to heal him so he can rejoin the battle," I said.

"Healing me takes you out of the battle," Kyp argued, his voice shaking.

"You're a better fighter."

"Your head... you couldn't use your Aegis without puking."

"Rapid healing comes in handy, and the only thing making me want to puke right now is looking at your arm."

"Same," Gana said, carefully examining the bone. Gana had once wanted to be a doctor. Thank goodness for that, because I wasn't sure how much help I'd be with the bone... not where the bone should be.

"I thought you said you wouldn't risk Guardian lives for a Key," Kyp said.

He was right; I was being a hypocrite. "I did. But will dying hurt?"

For a moment, Kyp didn't answer. "Yes. And it messes with

your head. Especially the first time."

"Have you?" I asked.

"Once." The tears in Kyp's eyes proved pain was the great equalizer. "They need your strength out there."

"Says the guy who destroyed me in my qualifying race," I said. "We're healing you, then we'll rejoin the battle."

"Jacks," Kyp said, resigned. "Don't you ever just listen?"

I laughed, a high-pitched hysterical sound. "Hi, I'm Jacklyn. Have we met?"

I pressed my hand to the side of Kyp's face. His skin was burning, his cheeks flushed red, and the rest of his face was ghostly white. He stared blankly at the ceiling, his mouth moving soundlessly for a moment before he finally pushed something through his lips. An apology.

I scrunched my nose. "You're apologizing for bleeding on me again?"

He barked a laugh that morphed into a groan of pain. His hand moved to grab his broken arm, then recoiled in horror.

"Keep him still," Gana warned. "I need to see what I'm doing here."

Kyp tugged on my hand, knocking me off balance. I sprawled against his chest, my hand on his blood-soaked shirt. His breath was hot against my face, leaving his lungs in rapid-fire bursts. "She is going to push my ulna back into my body without the benefit of anesthesia. Are you sure you don't want to just let me die?"

I struggled for an answer. "We're right here for you." I took his other hand in mine, eyes locked on his. "How can I help?"

His eyes were wild. "Sometimes... sometimes when I'm with you, I wish... I want to—" A horrible pained cry ripped through him, his face contorted in agony, and his eyes rolled back in his head.

I tore my eyes away to find Gana holding Kyp's arm in place, the bone back inside. The taste of bile coated my tongue, and I clapped my hand over my mouth. When I finally got control, I glared at her.

Her shoulders slumped. "He's delirious. Did you really want to have to unhear whatever foolish thing was about to tumble out of his mouth? Heal him."

I channeled my Aegis and got to work. My head throbbed, but I pushed through the pain, healing until a surge of vertigo slowed my progress.

"I don't think I can manage much more. I healed the arm completely, but only closed up most of the wounds. I need to save energy for the battle. And for, like, consciousness."

Kyp's eyes fluttered open, but he remained mostly still.

"Do you have a plan?" Gana glanced between me and Kyp.

"Besides trying not to die?" I tried building energy, but it was slow-going.

"That's not much of a plan." Kyp groaned. "I've got an idea."

"Please," I said.

"Antithetical Aegis use." He pulled himself up to a seated

position. "Anything your Aegis provides, you can also take," Kyp explained. "You have enhanced hearing, you can block people's hearing. You have strength—"

"I can take people's strength?" That would have been good information to have had earlier.

The shattering of glass and the thump of bodies hitting the floor somewhere outside the door interrupted Kyp's answer. His eyes darted around the room. "Mother's room. She'll likely bless the spot where I nearly bled to death on her floor."

The confidence in his delivery was chilling. I recalled the memory of how terrified he'd looked when his mother came to get him and my throat tightened. Was this how he really felt?

"Grab the swords." Kyp motioned to a longsword and samurai sword displayed on the far wall.

Gana tossed the samurai sword to me and kept the longsword for herself.

"Help me to my feet," Kyp said.

"Have you forgotten you nearly died a few minutes ago? Shouldn't you rest?" I still helped.

"I've rested enough." His voice was firm again, but his body was still a bit wobbly.

I tried to build the ball of energy at my center as we approached the doorway. Gana yanked the door open, and we all braced ourselves for an attack that never came.

The battle had moved to the bottom floor, stretching out through the foyer. Crushed glass, broken furniture, and torn works of art littered the floor, interspersed with Gorvhans and Sirins lying in bloody lumps. The Order had beaten the interdimensionals back toward the door. On the other side of the battle, Lavinia and Gretchen stood their ground, having apparently returned from their late-night mission.

Gana jutted his chin out in their direction. "Talk about coming home to a messy house after a long day on the job."

"Yeah, my heart bleeds for them," Kyp murmured.

Gana's eyes cut my way. "I'm going back out there. You guys rest while you can."

Kyp and I watched from the railing overlooking the foyer. Our warriors fought, broken and bloody. We wouldn't hold out for much longer. We were stronger than the interdimensionals, but their numbers seemed endless. If they kept coming like this, they would eventually exhaust us.

When did I start thinking of the Order as "we"?

I scanned for Mom and Gana, finding them going blow for blow with monsters.

"I can try the energy drain, but I barely have the strength," I whispered to Kyp. "I wouldn't have anything left to heal them with. Is it worth trying if I'm not sure I'll succeed?"

Kyp's voice was sorrowful. "What use would healing be if everyone is dead? You have to try."

Shakily, I stepped out further, leaning against the railing. I inhaled deeply and closed my eyes, building what little energy I managed to summon and drawing it to my center. I started when

Kyp's long, thin fingers threaded with mine. Squeezing his hand, I shot him a questioning look.

"We'll be stronger together." His energy traveled across our clasped hands, feeding my Aegis through our connection.

A familiar scream broke my concentration, and I shot forward, dragging Kyp with me.

Mom. A Gorvhan had latched onto her leg and pulled her down. She seared its flesh, but it had locked its jaw and wouldn't let go. A Sirin crept forward, and Gana followed with a mess of Gorvhans on her tail. She launched a fireball at the Sirin standing over Mom but was immediately jumped by a Gorvhan biting into her shoulder, as another leapt over them and onto my mother.

My Aegis flared within me, luminous. It wasn't just mine; I'd yanked Kyp's from him as well.

The first creatures to drop were the ones attacking Mom and Gana. Their energy fed mine, gnarled and sinister enough to make me reel, even as I redirected that power toward the next creature. A deep sense of chaos fed into my soul, darkening with each life I extinguished, but I couldn't stop, or I wouldn't save them. One by one, each creature's energy increased my ability to drain the next until they all laid on the floor, emaciated husks. Drained of whatever force gave them life. Drained by me.

Every depleted creature lying still on the floor was a life I had ended. I wanted to cry, to scream in anguish at the atrocity I had committed despite my reasons, but starting the chain reaction and keeping it going ensured I had nothing left when it worked its way to the end. I slid to the floor.

Kyp caught me on the way down, but I had drained him, too, so he fell with me.

The voices of the others were a dull echo. The last thing I heard was Mom's voice calling for me before I lost consciousness.

NINE

PEELING BACK THE LAYERS

My eyes fluttered open to stare at a light blue wall. Not my wall, Mom's. A comforter encased me like a cocoon, and my face was pressed to a pillow. Every muscle was stiff and achy, and I rolled over and stretched.

"Hey! You're awake," Gana greeted from the doorway. An image of her killing interdimensionals like it was routine popped into my mind. She looked pretty damn chipper, all things considered.

Meanwhile, something dark, like a bruise, bloomed in my heart. I had massacred an army. "How long was I out?" Talking was like swallowing glass shards.

"A day and a half." She made her way in on crutches. Each time they hit the floor, my achy bones rattled.

Mom followed her in, cuts and bruises peppering the skin exposed by her tank top. "I had to bring you into my room while yours was repaired. What a mess you guys caused in there."

I smiled weakly, and she returned it.

They were exhausted, banged and bandaged up, but they were, thankfully, alive.

"I'm sorry I couldn't help heal everyone," I said. "Our medic team patched you up?"

"All but Kyp." Gana plopped into a chair that had been moved to my bedside. "He woke up late yesterday. Hasn't been out of his room much since then."

I took him down with me.

"But he's gonna be okay?" I asked.

Mom's eyes landed on me, scrutinizing. "He'll be fine. Just needs to recover." She smiled. "You did well. It was a brilliant idea."

I scrambled to figure out what she thought we did. "Yup, brilliant."

"No wonder you're both so exhausted," Mom muttered. "Holding them still while you drained their power. It's remarkable you both managed to hold out as long as you did."

I smiled. My face hurt a little, but the achiness eased the longer I was awake. I needed to avoid wasting my Aegis again. The recovery sucked.

A knock sounded at the door, and Mom answered.

"How is she?" Lavinia's voice drifted in from the doorway. "Is she still asleep?"

"She just woke up, actually." Mom stepped aside, allowing Lavinia space to enter.

She swept in, tension in her gait. Her eyes landed on me, and her shoulders relaxed. She managed a weak smile. Her eyes were heavy-lidded, the skin around them bruised. For the first time, she looked slightly disheveled, her hair tugged back into a messy ponytail, her face makeup-free, in gym clothes she never wore outside of training sessions. "There's our girl. How are you?"

"Unsure." I returned her smile and probably looked just as exhausted doing it. "You know me, figuring it out as I go along."

"You are quite good at that, aren't you?" She lowered herself to the edge of my bed. "I was impressed by what you managed to pull off. Not a single interdimensional left standing." She shook her head. "Remarkable."

"Everybody played a role," I said. "How did so many of them get past the wards?"

"We lowered them to bring you through," she said. "There must have been an error in our efforts to reinstate them."

"Have they tried getting on the grounds before now?" Gana asked. "Or did they happen to try their luck and hit the lottery?"

"Who knows how their minds work?" Lavinia sighed. "The important thing is that I met with our Arvokian liaison, and our wards have been reinstated and fortified. It will not happen again, I assure you. Anyway, if I may, I wish for a moment alone with Jacklyn."

"Why?" Gana asked.

Lavinia smiled, but there was a hard edge to it. "To discuss her progress. That's all."

Mom's eyes narrowed, assessing. In the end, she must have decided it was safe enough. "Okay, we're going to dinner. You hungry? Want me to get you something?"

I hadn't been, but now that she mentioned it... "Yeah, that would be great."

My family left, and Lavinia waited for the door to close before speaking.

"What you did out there was risky."

I considered her words. "I don't see how it was. If I had failed, we wouldn't have been any worse off. If I had done even half of what I did, it would have weakened their side."

"And left you and my son vulnerable to attack," she said sharply.

"I didn't really see an option where we weren't vulnerable," I countered. "We were all in danger and things were getting worse. Kyp and I made a decision."

"Yes." She nodded, thoughtful. "Why were you, Kyp, and Gana away from the battle?"

Because I'd broken protocol by healing a Key. *Crap.*

"It's my understanding you were healing Kyp," she said, "and while my first instinct is to thank you for caring for him enough to protect him, my rules state that as long as Keys are safe from a Ritual, they are healed post-battle. How was this situation different?"

I scrambled for an answer that wouldn't say more than I wanted to reveal. "I thought he was a greater asset to the battle than I was. I was wounded, and my concussion was taking its time to heal."

"You made the decision to rescue a Key rather than the Guardians outside?" She tilted her head, a feigned look of wonder on her face. "I don't understand. After your astonishing speech on not using Guardians as cannon fodder, you decided that didn't count when the Key was somebody you cared about?"

I couldn't argue. I'd known it was hypocritical when I did it.

Lavinia rose. "I would love to allow personal attachments to dictate my choices, but I have an army to run. I'm sure you're starting to understand why the rules must be made and followed *before* the battle. Your split-second decision may have worked this time, but it may not work the next."

I had to make this right if I planned to stick around. "Look, I screwed up in training. I get that. I'm not used to the rules here. Even if I disagree, I shouldn't publicly argue. Nothing gets accomplished that way."

Lavinia hummed thoughtfully. "From now on, I expect you to be a model student. This is not how you shed the reputation your father created for himself. Are we clear?"

"Yes," I forced out.

"Good, because I want you to think about the overwhelming numbers of interdimensionals we had here." Her expression hardened. She took a step forward, looming over me. "It would be a shame if you were to find yourself without the protection of our well-trained Order or the safety of our wards. Such a shame if you and your family were to violate the rules enough to find yourselves out in the woods, alone, with interdimensionals closing in. Wouldn't it?"

She walked through the door, leaving nothing behind but the chill that slithered down my spine.

I sagged back in the bed. My head ached. I wanted to take my family and run out the door, but I still hadn't learned how to hide my energy signature. Which meant it would take time. More time.

I closed my eyes in frustration and allowed myself to rest. I wouldn't be able to act until I rebuilt my strength.

I spent the next few hours fading in and out of sleep until Gana crutched her way into the room. She stopped to hand me a brown paper bag before making her way to the bed. Dropping onto it, she curled up like a cat in front of the footboard. "I'm exhausted."

"It's been a rough few days." I placed the paper bag on the nightstand.

"It's only going to get worse." Gana lazily untangled herself, sitting up and stretching. "I've got something to tell you. You're not going to like it."

A knot formed in my stomach, and Gana pursed her lips.

"You know how I wasn't here when you woke up to that Gorvhan?"

"Yes."

"I broke into Lavinia's office."

"You what? Why?" Panic welled within me. "What the hell were you thinking? Are you trying to get us thrown out of here?"

"No, *Jacklyn*, I was trying to figure out a way to protect you." Gana scowled. "A way to keep the mind readers out of your head. Out of *our* heads. And to try to understand why Mom was acting so weird about your argument with Lavinia."

"I am going to kill you! Do you realize what could have happened if you were caught?"

"She hasn't figured it out yet," Gana said. "It's been a couple of days."

"Of chaos!" I argued. "Of worrying about her son. What happens when that's over?"

"Nothing. Only Cass saw me, and I told her I was hiding in there from the interdimensionals. She believed me."

"And if an attack didn't happen? What would your excuse have been then?"

"I wouldn't have been caught."

I sighed. What was done was done. "And what did you find out?"

She brightened. "That the computer in the library isn't the only computer here. There's a laptop in her office. Our phones may be useless here, but they can still act as hard drives. I filled my phone with the contents of her computer. A cursory glance shows bank records, passwords, e-mails, phone records, contacts, and Arvokian Rituals. We'll need to dig through it. Maybe something in there can help."

"This is insane. Do you have any idea of the risk you've taken?" Images of the three of us surrounded by Gorvhans flashed through my mind.

Gana sucked her teeth. "If I'm stuck training as a soldier, I'm gonna have to start taking risks."

She was right. Our world was filled with risks now. At least, if we attacked this as a team, we had a better chance of survival. And to survive, we needed to know *all* the risks.

"I hand-copied this Arvokian Ritual from what I found on Liv's computer." Gana tugged a folded piece of paper from the back pocket of her jeans. "It's a Mind Block. Prevents mind reading and control." I looked it over as she spoke. "It could ensure that what happened during the race never happens again."

"Good find." I would need several Arvokian herbs to perform it, and I had no idea where to find them. I leaned over and tucked the paper into my bedside table drawer, inside a Red Hood comic Mom had procured for me.

I lowered myself back onto my pillow. "We'll figure out a way to go through what you found in Lavinia's computer tomorrow. For now, I think I'm gonna crash."

Gana nodded and rose from the bed, motioning to the paper bag with her crutch. "Kyp asked me to bring that here. Not sure what it is."

We said our goodnights, and when she was gone, I snatched the paper bag up. Maybe he was trying to apologize for being an emotional pinball. Maybe it was baked goods or candy, or perhaps a geeky surprise. I reached in and my heart clenched. My bear. The pink ceramic bear that had broken during the attack. It looked awful, held together with tape and glue, but somehow, the shattered remains of it had become whole once again. A red ribbon was tied around its neck, strung through a hole punched in a small piece of paper folded like a card. I opened the note.

Wait until midnight and meet me by the tree. You know the one. I'll be waiting.

~ Kyp

You know the one. I did. The willow tree we'd hidden in to avoid Ross and Kylie all those years ago. I set the alarm on my phone for eleven-thirty. When it buzzed, I was already wide awake.

TEN

I left through the back door and glanced around to make sure nobody was watching before I took off to find Kyp. An expansive field of grass turned yellowish brown in the chilly autumn air spread before me, marred only by a sycamore tree on one side of the yard and a covered above-ground pool with wood decking on the other. The sycamore had lost its leaves, and they had been raked into a large pile near the pool. In the distance, the yard opened to a densely wooded area. No fences contained the yard or the forest. It all belonged to the estate.

A sharp chill cut through the air. The tip of my nose grew numb and my cheeks were wind-bitten by the time I made it to the tree line. I tried to use my Aegis to warm myself, but smoke seeped from my fingers, so I stopped. I'd gotten lucky during the race. I still didn't have a handle on that aspect of my Aegis. The last thing I needed was to set myself or the entire forest on fire. Actually, that was pretty much the last thing *anybody* needed.

I came to a stop in front of the willow tree.

"I was beginning to think you wouldn't come."

My breath stuttered, and my body jolted with fear. I whirled around and nearly collided with Kyp. I smacked him hard on the arm.

He offered me a perplexed smile. "How could I scare you if you knew I'd be here?"

The unexpected warmth in his eyes hit me like a stab to the chest. I was sick of being jerked around. "Yes, I'm hilarious. But I'm not here to laugh with you. I'm not sure what I'm here to do. You treat me like you did at the race, and then you treat me like you did during the attack. You snap at me, then you rebuild my bear. I don't know anymore, Kyp. How am I supposed to take you? Friend, foe, or what?"

The warmth drained from his eyes, and he lowered himself to sit against the tree. The moon provided a spotlight, and he was center stage. He stretched his long legs out in front of him. "Sit. I'll explain everything."

I sat on the grass facing him, far enough away to keep it impersonal.

He leaned forward, lowering his voice to a whisper. "I get that you're angry at me, but I need your hand. This will get stronger with practice, but for now." He wiggled his fingers at me.

I narrowed my eyes at him.

"Remember what I wrote to you in the car."

I may not seem like it, but I've always got your back.

With a gulp, I pressed my hand into his.

"Thank you," he said, but this time it was in my mind, like our conversations through the wall. "I understand how difficult it must be to choose to trust me. I can explain. But before I do, I'll speak to you with action."

He leaned forward and tugged something from the back pocket of his jeans. It was a thin book with a worn brown leather cover, and he tossed it onto the ground in front of me. "Only full Keys get one of these. Fifth page."

The Arvokian Mind Block Ritual was on the fifth page. I'd have to do a direct comparison with the one Gana obtained from Lavinia's personal files, but at a glance, they looked identical. He was giving me a way to protect myself from him. I wasn't sure what that meant.

He plucked at blades of grass as I looked the book over. "May we proceed?"

I nodded. He'd won a bit more trust from me.

"Good!" He squeezed my hand, and my cheeks heated.

"I have the herbs for the Ritual. I'd understand if you didn't trust them, but there is no way you'll manage that without drawing negative attention to yourself. Not at this stage of the game. The Ritual would protect you from Mother and—"

I spoke over him. "Was what I saw during the race a real memory?"

He swallowed hard, letting my hand slip from his. "Yes. It was locked in your subconscious. I simply unlocked it."

"Why did you show me that memory?" I asked.

"Why did you try to burn me alive?" His eyebrows rose.

Because I needed to win the race. "Did *you* really need to win the race that badly?"

"Why did I show you *that* memory?" He folded his arms across his chest and leaned back against the tree trunk.

I wanted to be annoyed that he wasn't answering me, but in his weird Kyp way, he was. The memory had one main idea—Kyp would protect me, no matter what fresh hell I brought down on his head. "You're saying you thought you were protecting me?"

"I'm saying I *knew* I was protecting you." He looked away. "Jacklyn, I can explain every perplexing thing I've done, but it will open a whole other can of worms I'm not sure you're ready for."

"If the truth is that your mom is secretly awful, I've been picking up on that."

He blinked an exceedingly long blink, and his surprise drifted through our connection. "Well, yes. That's the root of it. You're probably wondering why I go along with Kylie's power grab. Like, what's in it for me?"

"I hadn't thought about it. Not even once."

The corners of his lips lifted slightly, but dropped again, all the way down into a frown. "If I don't follow along, there will be grave consequences. Experience has illustrated that if I act out or act up, Mother finds unique ways to punish me and the people I care about."

An image of the way he'd reacted in the tree when we were children flashed through my mind, and I swallowed hard. "I'm guessing you don't mean the way she punished me by making me test early."

"I actually mean the way she lowered the wards and let the interdimensionals in so you would listen to her without further question." He said it calmly, but when his eyes met mine, they burned with intensity. "You really shouldn't have argued with her in the training room that day."

My stomach churned. "And she'd do that? Risk everyone to teach me a lesson? Why?"

He gave my hand another squeeze. "You're probably terrified to step out of line again. We were fine, as it turned out, and you were taught a lesson. Besides, having a blindly compliant soldier with enhanced physical combat skills that comes back from the dead would be worth the loss of a Guardian or two, wouldn't it?"

My doubt must have traveled through the connection to him. "No, she wouldn't do that. It's not like she threatened you with something just like it."

His eyebrow rose again.

I swore, loudly and colorfully, my blood running cold.

"Exactly," he said. "*That* is the kind of woman my mother is. That is what you need to navigate if you plan to stay here. I've been dealing with her my entire life. So I only step out of line when it's worth the risk."

"Like bringing me here." The pieces fell into place.

"Yes, and Cass and I paid for it."

The screaming on the night I arrived. A chill ran down my spine.

He gave himself a shake. His nervousness was a wavy jolt skittering through our connection. "I'll be blunt. Raymond Madison wasn't crazy. He wasn't paranoid. He was right."

My heart stuttered hard.

He took a deep breath. "Our abilities feed on the energy from the rifts. If they close, we lose them. Mother is not interested in losing her Aegis and will do anything to keep the rifts open. She has somehow managed to keep the interdimensionals coming at such a rate that we haven't been able to close a rift in years. Ray tried to stop her. You know how that turned out."

My breath caught. "She... she told me she loved my—"

"She did. Just as she loves me. Until we became inconvenient to her plans." His eyes dropped to the grass, and he plucked at it.

I breathed deeply, panic building in my chest. "She kills Keys."

"And Guardians. And whoever the hell gets in her way." He paused to let it sink in. "But I will change that. Intellectually, Mother and I are matched, but she has experience. If I intend to wage war against her and her supporters, I need more firepower." He paused, his eyes meeting mine. "I need you."

My throat went dry, nervousness hitting me from two directions. "Why me?"

"Who else is strong enough? You have tremendous potential."

He placed his free hand on my knee and brushed his thumb across it. "We have to unseat her from her place of power. I'm not sure how, but that's the center of it. If we can, for long enough to close the rifts, our problem goes away. The interdimensionals that also feed off the energy from the rifts will die. You'd have had your adventure but get to go back home to your city and live a perfectly normal life. And I'll finally get to live a normal life." His face tilted up, his eyes closed, face serene.

"You have this amazing gift and... you don't want it?"

"I hate it. I was trained to kill things before I understood what killing meant. First the whys, then the hows, then the actual practice of it. I want out." He swallowed and looked away.

"Yeah." A dry laugh escaped. "All we have to do is what the Order has been trying to accomplish for generations."

He smirked. "I'm not promising you a cake walk. Just direction. Something to work toward besides your plan to run away."

Damn it. "You're sure you're not reading me?"

"Emotions sneak through the link at times." He shrugged, leaning back against the tree again.

What emotions? "How are we going to unseat Lavinia?" I changed the subject, but that wasn't an easy thing to discuss either.

"I have an idea for a rebellion. Not a plan, as yet. But if you work with me, I'll look out for you. We can work together, and I can train you on some of the things you may need against her in advance. Like the Ritual. And how to avoid ending up in her cross hairs. I will protect you and them. No harm will come to you."

"You can't guarantee that," I said. "And I don't need you to protect me."

He smiled. "But I want to."

"But you don't *need* to."

He leaned forward, and I blushed again. "I know you don't need to be protected. But I need to protect you." His eyes met mine with enough intensity to drive the point home. He might never need to save me, but he would never stop trying.

My heart clenched. He wanted me to understand, and now I did, more than I'd ever believed I could.

I leaned forward, watching his eyes for any signs I should stop. He gave me none, just watched me until my nose brushed his. His eyes closed, the inky black of his eyelashes brushing his bronze skin, and I let myself stop worrying about the leap I was about to take.

My lips pressed against his. They were warm and soft, and his breath carried a hint of peppermint toothpaste. It was barely a kiss, more like a taste, much less than I wanted, but he pulled away, my name a whisper on his lips.

I opened my eyes to find his still closed. His jaw clenched, a look I'd seen on him in anger, but also in frustration.

"What is it?" An edge of sarcasm infected my words. "Did something you didn't like?"

His eyes finally opened to glare at me. Beggars couldn't choose. "Jacklyn, we don't have time to go down this path. It's dangerous." But our hands were still linked, and regret weighed his words.

"For whom?" I asked. "More dangerous than living with someone who has you killed if you step out of line? More dangerous than purposely stepping out of line to rebel against that person? I mean, if you're scared of something, why not let it be this?"

He stared back at me, his breath coming quicker, but our connection was a jumble of more thoughts and feelings than my brain could handle.

I pulled my hand from his. "Okay, I shouldn't have done that. I'm sorry. I misjudged and—"

"Shut up."

"What?"

"Just, you know, shut up for a second. Okay?" That crooked smile flashed my way. He grabbed my hand and tugged me close enough that I felt his breath on my lips. "You're a very difficult person, you know that?"

I raised my eyebrows. "You want to rebel? Rebel."

He took my face in his hands. "I'm in so much trouble with you." He kissed me, and at first the kiss was gentle, but it deepened quickly, his mouth moving urgently over mine. I returned the kiss until my knees went weak and he pulled me closer, breathing me in. No guy had ever kissed me that way. When he pulled away, he was gasping. "So much trouble."

"Says the guy who just recruited me as a soldier in the

revolution," I teased, nudging him in the arm.

He let his forehead rest against mine. "Not *a* soldier. *The* weapon."

"That's intimidating."

"It won't be. We won't act right away. We need time to train."

"And this?"

"This?" His lips found mine again, this time in another lingering kiss. "This I hadn't planned on. But I'll admit, I've been wanting to kiss you since you got here."

"Me too."

"Now," —he leaned back and tapped the book— "let me teach you a few things. I'd like to keep kissing you and to do that, I need to keep you alive."

"So romantic."

"I suck at romance." He smiled shyly. "This, I'm good at. I brought something for you." He pulled two vials from his pocket. "These are the herbs you need to perform a Mind Block Ritual. Want to learn how?"

Yes. Yes, I did.

ELEVEN

COMING CLEAN

Arvokian Rituals were very different from the thought-based casting we used regularly. Way more chants and herbs, way less channeling your own inner power. And any of us could perform any Ritual we chose. Still, the process was familiar, and I found myself thinking back to the day Kyp and I had made our blood oath, that sense of a forgotten word on the tip of my tongue that came with a lot of the things I did on a regular basis here.

The Ritual had been relatively simple to perform, and I was grateful for that, since I had to repeat it with Gana later that night. That hadn't been a fun conversation, but she'd mostly accepted the rebellion when I pitched it as a means to eventually get her out of this place. Which meant there was no involving Mom—she didn't want to go, and we'd never convince her without building a case first.

Kyp said the Ritual helped cover anything you actively didn't want others to know. Somehow, it would still allow Liv to read me, but when I thought of anything secretive, she'd be redirected to my surface thoughts. I'd probably seem like a vapid idiot to her, and she may even come to suspect I'd done something to cause that, but she had no reason to ask without sounding suspicious—and proving to everyone that she was eavesdropping in our heads. Something Kyp said she openly claimed to be against.

It wasn't foolproof, but it was something, and it had been working for Kyp so far.

I was reading a new book for my Order required learning. This one was just as stale. A book on Arvokian botany, assigned by Kyp, who was now a full Key and could do that without raising any eyebrows.

I was on a chapter about Dreviara, an herb used in the Death-Bringer Ritual all Keys hid from. It turned out the Ritual wasn't actually named that—some edgy Key in the 1600s had given it that nickname and it had caught on. In actuality, it was called the "Ritual of the Unburdening." I liked that better, the idea that permanent death was an unburdening of the soul.

The Ritual had found its way into the hands of the interdimensionals, and now it was a constantly looming threat. It had been leaked by a member of the Order. The suspected party had been brought to trial by the Arvokians.

The Arvokians. An idea bloomed within me, and it brought a smile to my face. I had forgotten the Keys weren't alone in this.

I knocked lightly on the wall Kyp and I shared, hoping to get his attention. No response.

I tried again. Nothing. Odd. Kyp should have been back from weapons training with Gana by now. Today was my weekly free day, and I had been intending to bother him when he got back. We needed to find a way to get Gana and Cass in a room with us so we could plot out our next moves together. After all, Keys and Guardians always worked as a team.

I did what anyone did when someone didn't answer the door. I listened for voices. Except, with my Aegis, that was full-blown eavesdropping. I wasn't really worried. He probably wasn't in there. Training had probably run late.

"I don't know what this is about, but these little meetings between us are completely unnecessary." Kyp's voice. So he *was* there.

Who he was speaking with?

"You haven't decided to be a father to me before, why push to be one now?"

Shit. Hector.

"This has nothing to do with that. I'm here because you clearly aren't aware of the nightly patrol your mother set up in case more interdimensionals find a way through the wards."

"Okay," Kyp said. "So, what? You want me to take a patrol slot?" But it was bullshit, and the pitch of his voice betrayed a spike of anxiety.

I slid off my bed and made my way to the door while I listened, ready to break into the conversation at any moment.

"No," Hector said. "I want you to avoid it better."

"I don't know what—"

"I saw you. Both of you. Yesterday."

No way was our luck this bad.

I left my room and headed to Kyp's, knocking on the door like it was no big deal.

"Not now," Kyp growled.

"Yes now," I answered. I wasn't certain of the effect my presence would have on the discussion, but I couldn't let Kyp face this alone. Not when we were both responsible.

Hector yanked open the door. "Quick. Get in." He carefully closed the door.

Kyp immediately spoke up. "We were just—"

"I saw exactly what you were doing. Don't lie to me." Hector sighed.

"Hector, please. You can't tell Mother—" Kyp tried.

He cut him off with a wave of his hand. "Whatever it is, I don't want to see it again. I warned you to be careful. Now get it out of my head."

Realization dawned on me. "You said you wanted him to avoid it better." Hector nodded, but Kyp seemed equal parts confused and ready to crawl out of his skin. "Replay this conversation, Mr. Perfect Memory. Hector said he wanted you to avoid the patrol better. He wasn't trying to rat us out. He was trying to protect us."

"Yes. Now take it out. The memory of what I saw. You need to remove it." Hector's eyes widened. "I warned you and now I want it out before it can do any of us more damage."

Kyp reached out, but I stopped him with a hand on his chest. "Or you could help us."

"I can't. Not with your relationship, and not with whatever else you're planning. No matter how much I want to see her fall, I won't help you. I won't." His head shook so hard he stumbled.

Kyp's voice sounded through our connection. "How the hell does he know we were planning something? We weren't even speaking out loud."

That was a damn good question. I tried to play innocent to gain the answer. "Hector, Lavinia's success is the Order's success. Why would you think anyone wants to see her fall?"

"You're teaching her Rituals," Hector said. His eyes grew wilder with every word. "You're up to something, Kyp. It wouldn't be the first time. And I want to protect you, I do. Lavinia didn't want a partner in raising you, so I didn't, but I want to help you. I just... not with this, son."

Kyp's chest rose and fell rapidly beneath my fingertips.

"Hector, please calm down," I said.

"No!" He grabbed me by my elbow and pulled me close. "Lavinia controls me." The words were choked out, like a half-chewed Heimlich by-product. "You need to listen closely. I don't have much time."

Kyp stepped forward, but I kept him back with the hand on his chest. "Okay, Hector. I'm listening."

"Girl, you better be. You can't begin to understand. Mind

Keys can control what you say, what you do, how you think. They keep your mouth shut when you want to fight. They know how you'll resist. They hold your sanity on a string. A Mind Key can perform mental torture, intellectual warfare. Do you understand?"

Not what I expected. My heart was leaden. Horror seeped through me. Horror for Hector and for me. Not only was I aligning myself with a Mind Key, but I was going against one. I needed to hear this, even if I wanted to clap my hands over my ears and tune every word out.

"Your father was the only person who ever stood strong against Lavinia. But whatever he did, it disappeared with him. If he has passed anything to you, anything at all, use it to your advantage. Mind Keys get what they want. You should always consider exactly what they are out for." He looked at Kyp. "What he wants from you."

"Raymond never gave me a thought when he left. Do you really think he told me anything?" Even now, knowing he was innocent, I didn't know the circumstances of him leaving us. Did he even consider what would happen to his family when he started a rebellion? But then... was I considering what it would do to mine? The thought twisted deeply in my stomach. Then I caught up to the rest of what Hector said. "What exactly are you trying to tell me about your son?"

Hector didn't blink. "He's not a bad kid, but he's *hers*." He looked at Kyp. "I'm sorry, kid. But it's true. A Mind Key's weakness is madness. Their unfading memories, it drives them mad. You can't trust him, Jacklyn. Hell, you can't trust me."

My stomach churned. He was right. I couldn't trust him, but I felt for him. Whatever awareness he still had, he focused it on helping me.

"Okay." I swallowed hard and took a deep breath. "I listened."

"Now erase me before she discovers what I know. I don't want any part of this." He looked at Kyp. "Please."

Kyp looked at me, then at my hand on his chest. Apparently, I hadn't been paying attention to my own strength. I was still pushing him back.

I dropped my hand. It trembled at my side.

Kyp placed a hand on Hector's shoulder. "Thank you." Then he cupped his head in his hands and pulled him forward until their foreheads were pressed together. For a moment, they were both silent. And then Kyp let him go. "Thank you so much, Hector. I really appreciate you mediating our disagreement. I'll try to be a more understanding teacher in the future."

"Anytime, son." Hector gave a sharp nod, and when his gaze met mine, all evidence of his previous panic had disappeared. He turned on his heel and left the room.

For a moment, all we did was breathe. Then Kyp groaned and motioned for me to follow him. He walked out his room and headed for Gana's.

"Gana and Cass are having an Aegis control training session," Kyp explained quietly. "We need to speak with them."

He knocked on the door. Cass answered.

"Kyp! She's meditating. You can't just interrupt a session!"

He put his hands on her shoulders and marched her backwards into the room. I followed.

"Um... what the hell?" Gana asked.

"I'm throwing up a thought barrier," he said. "Jacks, I need to use your Aegis for a moment. I need to do something only you can do, and once I've done it, you'll know how. It's another antithetical Aegis thing. We'll need it often in the future. May I?"

"What do you need to do?"

Kyp leaned forward, his voice strained. "I need you to create an auditory block around us. Normally, I would show you how, but I can't risk it failing this time. Can I please have your hand?" He paced his words evenly, pronouncing them as if he was talking to the five-year-old Jacklyn he remembered.

"Yeah, fine, as long as you stop talking to me like I'm an infant. I'm inexperienced, not stupid."

The words seemed to snap him out of whatever he'd worked himself up into. "Sorry. I didn't realize I was doing that." His eyebrows arched, his forehead creasing in the center. I'd bet he just realized how often he spoke to people that way.

I nodded and took his hand. He closed his eyes, and I felt the auditory block form around us like a glass case.

"Okay," Kyp said. "We need to talk. Hector has informed me that Mother and the adult Guardians patrol the grounds on a set schedule."

"Wait," Cass said, "we're trusting Hector now? He's a born

and raised part of the establishment!"

"No, we're definitely not trusting Hector," Kyp said. "He even told us not to. He warned us of the issue, then made me erase his memory of it."

When Cass and Gana just stared at us in confusion, we launched into the story. When we were finished, Cass and Gana shared worried glances.

"This is too much too soon," Cass said. "I never agreed *she* was trustworthy, and you're already adding people?" Cass thrust her finger in my direction like it was a knife she'd gladly stab me with.

I flinched. I didn't know Cass all that well yet, but I hadn't realized she didn't trust me.

"Jacklyn is trustworthy," Kyp said, his voice steady but his eyes blazing.

"Being a good kisser doesn't make her trustworthy, Kyp."

Just like that, the cat zoomed out of the bag.

"A good what?" Gana practically shrieked.

"Well, I suppose soundproofing the room was for the best," I said. Kyp and I exchanged weak smiles.

"Thank you, Cassandra," Kyp said. "It wasn't as though I told you about the kiss in confidence or anything."

Gana glanced between the two of us. "Explain. Now."

"It was..." I tried. "It was just..."

"It wasn't just a kiss," Kyp said.

"Maybe you shouldn't explain." Cass looked to Gana, whose

jaw was clenched hard enough to crack teeth.

"We're together," Kyp said firmly. "Jacklyn and I are... together." He shot a quick glance my way before taking my hand and standing his ground.

"Won't that put her at risk?" Gana eyed our joined hands, her nose wrinkling.

"I'll protect her," Kyp said. "Mother will never find out."

"Never? You must have big plans for this relationship if you'll never make it public. My sister isn't here for your amusement."

"I'm not using her for my amusement." Kyp's lip curled in disgust.

"He means she won't find out until action is taken against her," I said.

"It doesn't matter," Cass snapped. "This is an unnecessary risk."

"Enough," Kyp said. "Jacklyn and I don't need your blessing, only your discretion. Understood?"

They both grumbled.

"This is not why we're here, anyway," Kyp said. "Jacklyn and I met the other night so I could teach her some Arvokian Rituals. Hector found us."

Gana facepalmed. "When did Arvokian Rituals become code for making out?"

"You risked your own mission to make out? I seriously can't believe this." Cass dropped her face into her hands.

"We weren't making out," Kyp said.

"We weren't *just* making out," I said at the same time.

Kyp glowered at me. "That's not the point. I only came here to warn you both about Hector. We need to be careful around him."

Gana rolled her eyes. "Big shock. He's sleeping with the enemy."

"What if Lavinia already has this information?" Cass asked. "It's been hours."

"If we see evidence of that, we grab Jaina and run," Kyp said. "Screw the wards. We're not all ready for war, and I did not bring you here to die. In the meantime, I'd like to know what Gana was doing snooping around Mother's office."

Gana's jaw dropped, and she glared at Cass. "I was hiding from interdimensionals."

"Gana." I shot her a pointed look.

She sighed, then flashed Kyp a cocky grin. "Fine, I broke into Lavinia's computer and downloaded her files."

Kyp's head tilted slightly in what I was beginning to think of as his 'error in calculation' look. "What? Why? She wouldn't keep anything on there. She's not stupid."

"Hey, arrogance runs in the family." Gana smirked. "Or she wasn't raised in the computer age and never learned to password protect. She probably figured with only one other computer in the library, none of us would have much experience using them. You were all raised here. But I wasn't. And I can tell you, there are ways to find a lot of things you think you've removed from a computer."

A slow smile spread across Kyp's face. "Find anything interesting?"

"Not sure yet. Some of it is complete garbage, but other things may be worth analyzing. Chat logs, e-mails, bank account, and credit info. If we're going to find anything we can use against her, I think this is where we'll find it."

"Brilliant," Kyp said. "Great thinking."

Gana barely blinked at the praise. "It's gonna take time to get through it, but if we can split it up, it would move faster. I nabbed Mom's phone and yours to spread the information to as many locations as possible. We can swap the phones throughout the day as we have time to review so we each cover some ground."

Kyp looped an arm around my waist and rested his hand on my hip. "An effective plan. We should start tomorrow." He smiled. "Welcome to the team."

The timer Cass had set at the beginning of the session binged loudly, and we all jumped as though Lavinia had broken the door down with a tiny beeping sound. Guilt was a funny thing.

"Shit," Cass breathed. "Dinner time."

"Go ahead," Kyp said. "We'll be right behind you."

For a moment, Kyp struggled to speak, his mouth opening and closing in false starts. Finally, he managed. "I'd understand if you wanted no part in this. Gana is right. You'll have a target on your back. Mother is powerful, and we've already made mistakes." His brow furrowed. "A relationship with me will only make it worse. I know what I want. But if you… if you change your mind, no hard feelings. We'll go back to being friends. I'll understand."

I met his gaze head on and pressed a quick peck to his lips. "Dude. I'm a monster hunter, and now I've joined a rebellion against other powerful monster hunters. I'll be risking my life pretty much every day. Adding you to the mix won't kill me any faster."

"It could. If we slip up."

"Kyp, please. We're in this. That's that. Don't argue." I pressed a kiss to his cheek, then turned on my heel. I hoped he believed in my confidence more than I did. "I'm going for a jog. I need to clear my head."

I changed into my jogging clothes and headed out into the crisp fall air.

My feet skated over the grass, stepping over stray branches, crashing through crunchy leaves. My instincts were like an animal's, moving me through the forest without fear. My body wouldn't fail me. It was the most powerful weapon I had.

The wind whipped through my hair, tangling it around itself, throwing it back from my face. Its bite cut across my cheeks and my nose, but I was otherwise unaffected. The euphoria of the run warmed me.

This was freedom.

Visions flashed before my eyes, a flip book of my dreams. Running through the forest, leaping over tangled roots and darting between trees. Bright green eyes and a melodic laugh. A strong arm catching me when I tripped, scooping me up and twirling me through the leaves.

And all at once I understood what I had to do.

I looked up at the sun. We had only just formed a functional resistance, and already the leaves had fled the trees as though they sensed the revolt drawing nearer.

My father was the only person with the answers on how to stand against Lavinia. Raymond Madison had not passed on that insight to me when he was alive. But there was no reason he couldn't pass it on to me now.

Cass could channel spirits.

TWELVE

LOSING BATTLES, WAGING WARS

The following day, while Kyp and Gretchen worked with Lavinia on updating a medical training manual and Gana practiced hand-to-hand combat with Mom and Hector, I visited Cass.

I knocked on her door and shifted on my feet, waiting. I wasn't sure what to expect. She didn't seem happy about me and Kyp, and we hadn't spent enough time together to get to know each other on our own terms.

"Hey, what's up?" Cass happily bounced in the doorway until she saw me. Then her smile melted away.

I smirked. "You might as well say, *oh, it's you.* Can I come in?"

Cass stepped aside, and as soon as the door closed behind us, I got to the point. Small talk between us would be agony. "If I wanted to talk to my father, could you help me do that?"

She looked stricken. The butterflies in my stomach kicked up a notch.

"Have you talked to Kyp about this?"

"I haven't talked to anybody about this, and I'd rather you didn't either."

Her eyes widened. "So you want me to lie to Kyp."

I shook my head. "I just... I want you to wait to tell him. I'll tell him as soon as I get an answer. I can't have him standing over my shoulder while I do this."

I paced around the room, trying to gain a sense of her from a quick glimpse of her things. There wasn't much there, but little things gave me insight into who Cass was, the largest of which was her eclectic CD collection, which ran the gamut from jazz to hard rock. There was a bag full of yarn and a half-knitted project between the bookcase and dresser.

Two framed photos rested atop her dresser. One was of her and Kyp at an amusement park. It must have been taken off-mission. They looked like normal teen friends.

"What a great picture of you guys."

She smiled. I was about to turn away when my eyes drifted to the picture beside it.

Cass was a child, maybe eight or nine, wrapped up in a tight hug by a girl who had to be her older sister. She looked about fourteen in the picture, pretty with hair in tight black curls, skin a shade lighter than Cass' deep brown, and a radiant smile.

Cass' gaze was haunted. "That's Mariana. My sister."

I smiled. "I didn't know you have a sister."

"I don't. She's dead."

My throat tightened. "Oh my God, I'm so sorry."

She looked away.

"I was trying to think of something to talk to you about." I scrambled for an explanation. "Something that wasn't Kyp or the Order or whatever."

"You want my help and you're trying to convince me." She crossed her arms over her chest.

"Well, that too. But we should be able to talk. You're my boyfriend's best friend. But we're always so busy."

Cass stared for a moment longer. "My sister practically raised me. And she died protecting me."

Damn. "She looks nice. Not that you can tell that sort of thing from a picture, but she looks... you look happy with her."

She laughed. "You're awkward as hell sometimes."

I shrugged. "I don't know how to talk to you. I only know two things about you. You're a Guardian, and you don't want me dating Kyp."

She dropped onto the edge of her bed. "I just want to protect him."

"I won't hurt him."

She shook her head. "You didn't come to talk to me about this."

"Not quite. Hector said my father may have had a way of protecting himself from Mind Keys. I need to know if that's true. Yeah, sure, I want to meet him, but the truth is, I'm not sure I'd even like him. It's more important to discover what he can tell us, and how it can help us plan."

"Then why not tell Kyp?" she asked. "Why another secret?"

"Two reasons." I ticked them off on my fingers. "Kyp will take over the conversation. And Kyp will be more emotional dealing with him."

She nodded silently.

"Kyp would promise not to do either of those things, but he wouldn't be able to help himself."

She screwed up her lips. "We'd have to sneak out. And we'd need a fire."

I smiled. She was in.

"More importantly, you'll have to meditate."

I wasn't going to enjoy this.

Trying to speak to dead people was infuriating.

I couldn't meditate. For one thing, Cass was watching me, which made things wholly uncomfortable. For another, I was holding on to a branch of an Arvokian herb called Grachta Root that had thorns. Also, Cass held my hand on one side and whispered the Ritual Chant, and my palm was sweaty and gross. Oh, and the Grachta Root was on fire and the flame traveled along it like a lit fuse.

"Stop squirming, would you?" Cass hissed. "If you don't get into a meditative state soon, the Grachta Root is going to set us both on fire."

Cass used a mixture of her own abilities and an Arvokian Ritual that allowed me to funnel her abilities through me. Cass could only channel people she knew, so I would need to use her abilities to find Ray, using my dream memories as a guide. Dream memories that were very likely real memories. It seemed like a great plan—if it worked.

But I couldn't concentrate. Maybe because we were under the tree where Kyp and I had met—after I canceled on him with a bullshit excuse.

I fought to ignore my guilt, to focus my mind—on my breathing, the sharp breeze pushing the crackling leaves as they tumbled along the forest floor, the earthy scent of the cold soil beneath the picnic blanket we'd used to cover the ground. I allowed these things to center me, pushing thoughts of Kyp, of what I was trying to do, to the background.

Time passed. I wasn't sure how long, but at some point, my own breaths echoed through my mind. I had finally made it where I needed to be.

Tufts of smoke appeared behind my eyes and took vaguely human forms, just as Cass had described. There were many, no matter how far I allowed my brain to move forward, wandering as though walking through a city street and looking at the people around me.

Cass' hum floated to me through the ether. "Spirits will be drawn to you based on a sense of familiarity. The stronger the sense of familiarity, the more you'll know about them without contact. You'll recognize Ray because you'll sense the family link."

Three somewhat familiar presences surrounded me, but they were diaphanous, vaguely human-shaped beings I was sure I should know, but I didn't know how. I certainly didn't perceive any familial link. I reached for one, and its broad, dark cloud of an arm moved toward mine, smoky filament fingers reaching.

A feminine giggle followed by a deep moan made the wraith-like images disperse, and my eyes snapped open to meet with Cass' equally surprised gaze.

"Is someone hooking up out there?" I wasn't sure why I'd whispered. I had an auditory block up.

"Sounds like it." Cass made a face.

Another giggle, and I knew exactly who it was. "That's Kylie! Who would be..." A drumbeat in the back of my mind repeated *Kyp wouldn't do that to me*, accompanied by clashing cymbals that said things like *what if his mother finally got to him? Or what if canceling our date led him to move on to someone more immediately available? Or what if you don't know him as well as you think you do?*

I launched myself to my feet and marched toward the sound.

"Jacklyn!" Cass yelled, scrambling to follow me. "Jacks!"

I trust Kyp. I trust Kyp.

My heart kicked up to full speed. If I truly believed this was silly, I wouldn't be so afraid.

I don't trust Kyp. Not the way I should.

Kyp said everything public with Kylie was an act, but what if the only actual act was the way he was when we were alone together? What if Lavinia and Kyp were two sides of the same coin and Hector was right and I shouldn't trust either of them?

Cass walked up beside me, our camaraderie gone, and the anger returned to her gaze. I channeled my Aegis and created a fire in my palm for illumination, my steps careful and soft. Whoever this was, I wanted to catch them by surprise. "Well, hello there, lovebirds."

Kylie's eyes widened, and she punched the guy hovering over her hard in the shoulder. Blond hair, cut military-style. An exhalation somewhere between relief and horror at my previous thoughts rocketed from my mouth and Cass' gaze sharpened.

Ross looked back and swore. "Jacks!" Kylie was sprawled out on the forest floor in her bra, her jeans down around her calves. Ross straightened his clothes somewhat before stepping forward, shielding Kylie as though she had anything I hadn't seen before. "Jacks, please. You know how the rules are." Ross leaned in, his voice a whisper. "Liv wants Kylie with Kyp. We both know that's not happening, don't we?" He raised his eyebrows and looked behind me. "Is he out here with you?"

Apparently, Kyp and I were not nearly as discreet as we thought. "Why would he be?"

He held up a hand to stop my line of questioning as Kylie rushed up behind him, yanking her shirt down over her head.

"You guys aren't supposed to be out here," she scolded.

"You gonna tell?" I tried to sound cocky, but she was totally spiteful enough to do it, even if it bit her in the ass. She did it in the memory Kyp had unlocked. If either of us said a word, we were both in trouble, but she had less to lose than I did. She had Lavinia to piss off. I had Lavinia and Kyp.

Kylie's jaw tilted, her eyes hard with determination. "If you tell a single soul about this, I swear I will kick your ass, kill you, wait until you come back, and kick it some more."

"And what will you do to me?" Cass asked.

Her lip curled. "Quiet, the adults are speaking."

Cass stepped forward, but I held her back with one arm. "We're shaking in our boots, Big Mama. Your secret's safe with me, anyway. What would I gain?"

"Kyp." Her hands fell to her waist, and she smirked at me.

"But you've got Ross. You don't actually want..." I trailed off. Ross' attention was on the ground somewhere to his left. "Wow. You're one bottom-feeding bitch, aren't you?"

"Hey, don't judge me! I have *needs*, and just when I was getting close to having Kyp tend to those needs—"

Cass scoffed. "You were never anywhere near that."

"—you showed up and ruined everything. At least Ross doesn't take much coaxing."

Ross shrugged, but the look in his eyes was weighted.

"Wow," I said. "Dude, he's right there."

"I'm not your *dude*. Kyp and I are the future of this place. If you hadn't done the marriage rite when you were children, he would have moved on a long time ago. That's the only reason he looks twice at you. You needed an Arvokian Ritual to land a man."

"How do you even... What marriage rite?" I said, but I felt like a helium-filled balloon who'd just lost its anchor.

"I saw you. You were out in the forest, breaking the rules as usual You guys did a blood oath with a ceremonial knife designed for marriage, carved with Arvokian binding symbols and dipped in their herbs." Kylie rolled her eyes. "Wait. You didn't realize? God, you really are completely stupid."

My heart lurched, and then took off.

"When the hell did this happen?" Cass asked.

"We were five." My voice sounded tiny, and my stomach churned. Did Kyp know this? He had to, given how well he understood what our special connection was capable of.

Cass spun towards me, jaw dropped. "You two got toddler married?"

"Not on purpose!" This was unbelievable.

"Look, I won't tell him he can undo it if you leave me alone," Kylie said. "How's that? You keep your distance, and when Kyp decides he wants a playth—"

"Don't!" I held my finger up, my eyes blazing. "Do whatever you want with each other, but don't you dare finish that sentence. Good luck with her, Ross. She's all yours." I turned on my heel and marched towards the house, Cass dogging my steps.

"We have to tell Kyp," Cass said.

I leaned against the tree by the yard. "I will." I looked at her, willing my heart to slow down. "I promise. Just give me a minute to process the whole toddler married thing, okay?"

"Okay." Cass's eyebrows drew together.

I spent the rest of the walk back fighting against the fear that the blood oath influenced what Kyp and I felt for each other.

I lost.

Gana and I lay in bed side by side, reading through the data she'd downloaded onto her phone, when she stumbled across the motherload of information: a series of chat logs between Lavinia and a group of unknown contacts.

"Who are they?" I asked, leaning over to view the screen. The screen names were randomized jumbles of letters, numbers, and symbols.

"No clue," Gana said. "I can try to track them down, but that'll be hard without an untraceable internet connection. I'd basically be setting us up to be caught."

"They're probably dummy accounts." I shifted the pillow to prop up my neck. I still ached from the morning's training session, and I didn't want to use my Aegis to set it right. I was getting spoiled. "No point in even trying if they're not saying anything interesting."

But it didn't take long for Gana to find something interesting.

"Oh shit. Ohhhhhh shit."

"What is it?" I sat up.

"She's trying to make a baby!"

"What?!" I leaned over to read over her shoulder.

She was right. Lavinia wanted to bring these people the child of two Keys, the Skeleton Key. She believed it would help her retain her Aegis, even if the rifts were closed. The others suggested using Ross, because he'd be more cooperative. Lavinia shot them down. She wanted the child to be from her bloodline.

That tracked. She definitely had a superiority complex.

I needed to tell Kyp. But we hadn't spoken since I'd canceled with him the night before. It was difficult to judge how much of that had to do with our standard behavior, for appearance's sake, but it seemed like he was avoiding me. Or it could be my guilt...

So I tried to get his attention. All through lunch. All through weapons training, as I grew increasingly at ease with the bo staff. All through our free period, where we sat on the couch with the others playing board games. But he wouldn't meet my eyes, and at one point, when I tried to speak to him, he completely ignored me.

Cass shot me a look that was pure apology.

"Brr, there's a chill in the air." Kylie shouldered past me as we headed out of the room.

When Kyp did the same, I snapped. He had some damn nerve. Cass must've told him what I'd done without him. So I'd lied to him for an evening, and he'd lied to me for weeks now. And now he was pissed?

I just couldn't win.

"I'm sorry," Cass whispered. "I told him you intended to tell him the truth, but he's still... well, Kyp can be an ass when he feels slighted.”

Gana groaned. “You lied to him and had Cass back you up? Are you *trying* to become Mom or is this accidental?”

“Apparently I’m stupid.” I shot Cass some major side-eye.

“We’ve been besties for five years. I can’t B.S. him. He looks at my face and knows.”

Gana snorted. “Or he reads your mind.”

Cass gave her a light shove. “Such a cynic.”

“Ugh, Jacks! Kyp would have probably been totally on board with the whole thing if you hadn’t lied about it.” She facepalmed. “I just defended Kyp. What has become of me?”

I needed to fix this. I needed to make him listen to me, even if I had to get a little crazy.

I got more than a little crazy. Which was why I was balanced on the ledge outside Kyp’s window. Thank goodness for my agility. The last thing I wanted was to explain why I died the first time by splattering in the backyard.

I knocked on the window.

Kyp whipped open the blinds with a clatter. A glance into his room reminded me I’d never been inside before. His bedroom was empty, clinical. He had lived his entire life without amassing anything.

He threw the window open so hard the door frame shook. I stumbled and my heart tried to jump into my mouth.

“Crap!” He snagged my shoulders and half-dragged me

inside. I was still catching my breath as he muttered an apology, but he still wouldn't look at me.

"Jeez, Kyp. You nearly knocked me off the sill."

He met my eyes, and I found the chill Kylie mentioned earlier. "I said I was sorry."

"You're angry. I'm here to hash it out. It was hard enough for me to wait until everyone else was asleep. Planning on pouting about it all day tomorrow, too?"

Kyp glared at me and slammed the window closed. "What is it you want to say?"

"Well, for starters, stop slamming things or someone's gonna hear." I glared at him. "But, more importantly, I know. I know I should have told you what I was doing. But if I needed to talk to my father, I wanted to be the one doing the talking."

"I would have liked to be there. To support you. But I understand now that I wasn't wanted or needed." Kyp's tone was even, but there was a bite to his words, a cold snap. "Cass said you didn't reach him. Maybe you didn't do it right."

That made my hackles rise. "Of course not. How would I ever succeed without you?"

"Sarcasm isn't necessary."

"It's like you don't even know me."

He laughed, then backed away and pinched the bridge of his nose. "We could try again, together." He rested a hand on my hip.

I stepped back from him, smacking my back into the wall. "What? You think you can locate my father better than I can?" My stomach felt hollow and wrong.

Kyp's back went rigid, the look in his eyes frosty. "Oh, I understand now."

"Yeah? What do you understand?"

Kyp's mouth twisted into a sneer. "I assure you, there was never a competition between me and you. Please note which one of us grew up in the house of horrors and who got her content, oblivious life. In case you didn't notice, nobody rushed to my rescue."

"Oblivious? You mean defenseless," I corrected.

"But you got a family, Jacks. I don't think I've been quiet about how much I hate the way my life has gone, but don't you worry. I may remember your father, and I may have been close to him, but you were the priority. Want to know how I know?"

I didn't think I did, but I'd opened this wound, and I wasn't sure how to staunch the bleeding. I shook my head.

He leaned forward and smiled. It was fond, but there was a well of hurt deep in his eyes. "My mission is to always protect you, remember? What mission did he give you?"

My stomach clenched, tears welling in my eyes. "Okay. I'm a jerk. I get it. I do. I got out of this place with a super light sentence, and you're still being punished. I'm sorry, but there's nothing I can do to change that. The bottom line is, I didn't see my father, and I had a downright crappy time. I regret hurting you, but I hurt myself, too, so I think we're even." I slid out from where he had cornered me and plopped on the edge of his bed, exhausted.

His eyes shot to the wrinkles my butt made in his impeccable sheets, then back to me, puzzled. "You're upset because you couldn't reach Ray—"

"And other stuff I'm trying to figure out if I should tell you." That would mean admitting I wasn't sure about us, and I had already hurt him once today. But then, he had lied...

"You apologized for lying to me, but you're considering lying to me further." Kyp shook his head. "I can't believe you sometimes. I've never met a single person like you. How does someone manage to be so thoughtful one minute and so infuriating the next?"

I smiled weakly. "It's part of my charm?"

"What happened? What didn't Cass tell me?" Kyp leaned back against the wall, his arms crossed over his chest, his gaze razor sharp. "I'll try not to get upset."

"Try being the operative word here. You can't get mad at Cass either."

He cracked a smile. "I never would have guessed you'd defend Cass after she tipped me off. Still unpredictable." He shook his head. "She's safe. Don't worry."

I shook off my hesitations. "Kylie and Ross are together."

Kyp blinked, and some of the anger disappeared from his face. "Of course. That makes perfect sense. No wonder you're so upset!"

"Sarcasm isn't necessary."

"It's like you don't even know me."

I smiled to acknowledge the joke, but it felt tight on my face.

"Why, especially at a time like this, would I care?"

I rolled my eyes. "I'm getting there. I was out with Cass because it was required to contact Ray—"

"After lying to me, yes, go on." That smug face returned, just when my tears were drying on my cheeks.

"Can we put that aside for one damn minute?"

"I said *go on*."

I shook my head, but continued. "I heard Kylie, and it was obvious she was, well, you know, canoodling with someone."

"Taking away your stack of *People* magazines."

"Ha. Anyway, I went to go check it out."

"Why? Voyeurism your latest thing?"

I shrugged. "I found Ross and Kylie. We argued a bit. Kylie told me to leave it alone and as long as I keep my mouth shut, she graciously offered me a place as your Royal Girl-on-the-Side."

Kyp sighed. "She's a lovely girl, isn't she?"

"They should write songs about her," I said.

"I believe they already do. Just not the kind she'd like." A smile quivered at the edges of his lips, but didn't quite make it. "Kylie didn't get to you with an idiotic comment like that. Why are you so upset?"

"Well, when I called her on it, she said she'd have you to" —I grimaced— "fulfill her needs if I didn't get in the way. Then she said our blood oath was an Arvokian Marriage Rite, and that's the only reason you want me." My voice cracked.

His eyes widened, and he paled. "I must seem like a hypocrite to you."

"You might even be one."

His eyes fluttered shut, breathing so deeply it was as if his entire body was inhaling. "I wasn't aware at the time. When you asked about it, I realized the truth. I remembered the entire Ritual but had never realized what it was until I thought through the details. By then, I was worried I'd scare you the hell away if I explained I had married you. I was the more advanced child. I should have realized."

"And you didn't think I'd be scared away when I figured it out?" I placed my hands on my hips and turned the full force of my glare his way.

"I... hoped you wouldn't?" He winced. "I considered reversing it, but it provided us with an added connection and increased strength. It was a tactical advantage. And besides, I didn't..."

"You didn't?" I rolled my hand, urging him on.

"I didn't want to reverse it." His cheeks flushed. "Being connected to you... It's a comfort to me."

My voice shook as I blurted out, "What if the oath is the only reason we feel anything for each other?"

Kyp hissed a sigh. "That's not it, Jacklyn. Raymond and Jaina once performed the marriage rite. They separated. The bond caused by it can be broken and often is. You and I had thirteen years apart. If it lasted, it means we're still connecting."

I wanted to curl up in a ball and cry until my eyes burned.

"That's not all that's upsetting me."

"Tell me." Kyp knelt down in front of me, his hands on my knees. "I won't be an asshole. Promise."

I explained what Gana and I had discovered, and he dropped back onto his ass on the floor, his head in his hands.

"So she's decided that is my destiny. Why would it be normal?" Kyp shifted, but didn't look up. "My relationship with Mother has never been normal. After all, it's totally healthy to view your son as a breeding stud."

I lowered myself to the floor beside him and laid my head on his shoulder. "Do you know anything about this Skeleton Key?"

"No. But I'll figure it out." He turned his head, resting it on the tops of his knees. His fingers interlocked with mine. "We can't allow a baby to be brought into this madness."

"Agreed."

"Not only do I never want to do that with Kylie, ever, but it would make us too easily malleable to Mother's interests. She'd control me through that child, and I'd let her."

I let out a thoughtful hum. "I was thinking if Liv wants it, it's bad, but yeah, your explanation too."

He smiled, but it was weak. "You checked on Kylie to see if she was with me."

I flinched.

"You gave it away with your body language when I asked you why you would look."

"I'm an idiot." I slumped against him and wished I could

disappear into the floor.

"I'm not going anywhere, Jacks. You realize that, right? I never meant for this to happen." He took my face in his hands. "You could tear me to shreds and I'd be powerless to stop it."

My heart clenched. "I don't intend to."

"It seems you do it when you don't try." He laughed. "Are we okay?"

"Yeah, we're okay." I kissed him, sweetly at first, but things escalated. It wasn't long before my fingers were weaved in his hair, his hands sliding up under my shirt. I had to push him away when he leaned me back to lie on the floor. "Nope, not a good idea. Not ready to go there yet, and if we start, I'll do something stupid." I pushed myself upright, this time climbing to my feet.

He chuckled, shaking his head, a full grin on his face, the likes of which I rarely saw unless we were alone. "Unwise, maybe, but..."

It was tempting. Because he was gorgeous, but more because of the way he looked at me with awe.

"Another time," I said sternly.

"Ball's in your court." He nodded, smile still shining. "Your time clock. When the buzzer goes off, let me know and I'll lead the play."

I smacked him on his arm. "You done?"

He nodded, sitting up straight with his hands folded in his lap like a good boy. I rolled my eyes.

"I should head back." I moved to leave.

"Wait." He caught me by the arm, stopping me. "Ross and Kylie are together. Mother wants the child of two Keys."

"You want to discuss that now?"

He smirked. "Instead of more of this... Why don't we figure out how we can use what we've learned to our advantage? As a team."

I liked the sound of that.

# THIRTEEN

PERMISSION

Kyp spoke to me in my head as we marched through the hall, his fingers wrapped around my upper arm. *"Remember, we are your superiors. Be respectful, but don't be a weasel about it. You still need to sound like yourself, or it won't work. I'll keep you connected to me mentally so you can hear what goes on once you leave. Understood?"*

I nodded.

"Good. Remember, the best acts are rooted in truth. Now, no more talking."

We slowed to a stop in front of Lavinia's bedroom door. Kyp moved in front of me before knocking.

"Who is it?" A sharp reply.

"It's me, Mother."

A moment later, the door opened to Lavinia and her beaming smile. "Kyp, darling. What brings you here?"

He glanced over at me. "Um, I'm not sure. Jacklyn came to

see me right after breakfast and requested a meeting with us as soon as possible. It sounded important."

"It is. I promise I wouldn't have bothered either of you if it wasn't." I didn't have to try to look nervous. I was nearly quaking with nerves.

Lavinia's eyes narrowed as she stepped aside and allowed us to enter. Where Kyp seemed to have nothing of note lying around his bedroom, Lavinia's was an odd smattering of photos and memories, including a framed photo of an intense-looking newborn baby with dark hair.

"Kyp was an adorable baby." Lavinia laughed. "So serious all the time. He hasn't changed much. He makes an equally handsome adult, wouldn't you say, Jacklyn?"

I didn't have to fake the blush on my cheeks, either. "Yeah, sure, I guess."

"Mother, I'm fairly certain she's not here to discuss me."

"That's not entirely true. It's not about how handsome you are... I mean, how handsome someone might... I mean..."

"Stop talking." Kyp sighed. "What did I do now?"

"Nothing. You didn't do anything. I'm more concerned about what's being done to you." I wiped my hands on my jeans. The sweaty palms were real, too. There was a lot of authenticity in this fake out.

"Done to him?" To her credit, Lavinia looked genuinely concerned. "Have a seat. Both of you."

Kyp sat on the purple ottoman at the foot of her bed. He

motioned for me to sit beside him, but I moved to the other end. Lavinia lowered herself to the edge of her bed atop the ruffled, frilly purple duvet cover.

"Jacklyn, please start at the beginning. You are a whirlwind." Her mouth curved into a smile.

As Kyp predicted, coming to her for help did more to endear me to her than anything I could say. She knew me well enough by now to understand how little I wanted help from anyone, let alone someone that considered themselves an authority figure. With one action, she believed I had learned my place.

At this moment, with Lavinia being so sweet with me, it was hard to see her as a monster the way Kyp painted her. I almost wanted her to be innocent.

"I snuck out into the forest," I blurted.

Lavinia's brows raised. "Oh?"

No matter how much Kyp assured me she wouldn't punish me for the slight, I was nervous. "Not off the grounds. I'm a city girl, and nature gives me peace. I needed peace to meditate. I'm bad at it, and Hector said working on it would help me gain control over my Aegis. Cass spotted me and she followed me out. Please don't get angry at her. She wanted to keep me from doing the stupid thing I did."

"And you came here to confess this?" Kyp slid off the edge of the ottoman, knelt in front of me, and placed a hand on my knee. "You seemed so afraid when we spoke."

"No. I just understand there are consequences for the actions

I've taken. I'm sorry. I'm aware of how out of whack I've been since coming here. I'm lost. The rest of you have known each other almost your entire lives and then there's the Madisons, on our own. We haven't figured out our place here, and the pressure to find it can be crushing. I needed a walk, but I definitely learned my lesson after what I saw out there."

"You *have* been all over the place. I'm glad to see you've finally learned to trust your superiors." Kyp's mouth twitched with barely contained laughter. "But tell me, what did you see?"

The way he found fun in this ridiculous farce made me wonder how many psychopathic tendencies got passed down to him from his mother.

"Kylie was... well, you know... *with* Ross."

Kyp's head ticked back a notch, feigning surprise. He looked to Lavinia.

"You must be mistaken." She rose from her seat. "Kylie wouldn't dare."

"I swear, that's what I saw." I held my hands up in deference. "You can ask Cass! You think I'm a troublemaker, and I get that, but that's why you should investigate for yourself. I'm trying to protect you both from humiliation."

For a moment, we were silent.

"I don't want to believe she'd do that," Kyp said.

"I'm sorry," I said. "I didn't want to hurt you, but you're a good guy. She shouldn't treat you like that."

Kyp's eyes met mine, then sharply fled.

"Jacklyn, leave us," Lavinia commanded. "Kyp and I have things to discuss."

"Okay. Sorry to be the bearer of bad news." I moved to leave.

"I understand your reasons for leaving the grounds of the estate after hours, and Cass will not be punished for her quick thinking. However, I remain uncomfortable with how easily you break the rules," Lavinia said to my retreating back.

I turned to her with a shy smile. "You've met my mother, right? I'm trying. I'm used to making up my own rules for me and Gana. I'll kick that habit. If anything, this taught me that if I don't, I end up mixed up in trouble I don't want."

She smiled. "My rules are for a reason. I'm not simply trying to be a despot."

Now I grinned. "Despots don't fight the bad guys, do they?"

Her smile grew. "They are too busy *being* the bad guys, my child."

"Go on ahead, Jacks," Kyp said. "Thank you."

I left while Kyp spoke to Lavinia, all the while allowing me to listen in through our link. I sat against my bedroom door and tried to quell the shaking in my hands.

"Now what?" Lavinia's voice bounced around the walls of my mind.

I heard the smirk in Kyp's voice. "Now what? That's all you've got?"

"Don't take that tone with me. You act as if I expected this to happen."

"I know you didn't, Mother. But she was your idea. Maybe you put your money on the wrong horse?"

"We can't be sure of the veracity of Jacklyn's claims." A pause. "Oh, who am I kidding? Kylie and Ross have been attached at the hip since they were children. I should have anticipated this."

"Probably."

Lavinia laughed. "You don't even care, do you? She cheated on you and you're delighted."

"I'm not delighted."

"You lie well, but not that well."

"I care that if this gets out, we appear foolish."

"But you don't care that she betrayed you."

A laugh. "What do you want me to say, Mother? She was the love of my life and I'm heartbroken?"

"Preferably," Lavinia grumbled. "I haven't been fooling myself, sweetheart. I'm aware of your issues with her. But I worry about you. People need to be close to someone."

"Like you're close to Hector?"

"Don't be snide."

"You won't marry the guy."

"That *guy* is your father."

Kyp snorted. "In DNA only."

"I don't wish to bind myself to anyone," she said. "Marriage to the wrong person can weaken you."

"And yet you're pushing me to marry that vapid leech?"

"Nobody is asking you to marry. I want you to find a life

partner."

"Kylie is not the kind of person I want to be my partner," Kyp said. "I appreciate what you are trying to do, Mother, but—"

"Jacklyn, then."

My eyes snapped open.

"What?" Kyp's reaction mirrored my surprise.

"You believe Jacklyn is better suited to be your partner."

Silence. This wasn't part of the plan. We were supposed to plant the seed of possibility with this act. We were supposed to give Kyp a reason to break up with Kylie. We were not supposed to jump to the end game.

She must have already considered this as an option. She knew Kyp and Kylie didn't have a real relationship. The only option left, if she didn't want to use Ross, would be me.

"You look surprised." Lavinia laughed.

"I thought you had a problem with her."

"You decidedly do not. Besides, she has grown more compliant. That alleviates my concerns."

"Mother, I don't think... She doesn't see me that way."

Lavinia laughed. "She obviously does."

"You didn't read her, did you?" He groaned like a normal guy would, embarrassed his mother would try to set him up on a date.

"No. It's obvious. As are your affections for the girl."

"And you didn't feel the need to mention this sooner?" A pause. "No, of course not. You wanted me with Kylie."

"Kyp, look at me." Another pause. "Things may be difficult

between us, and I acknowledge our drastic ideological differences, but I still look out for what's best for you, as I trust you do for me. I genuinely believed I could trust Kylie with you. More than I ever would have trusted Jacklyn. But perhaps, for once, I was wrong."

Kyp snorted. "For once."

A second of silence, and then, "Do you think she is worth the risk?"

Kyp didn't respond right away. "I'd like to find out."

"I will consider the possibility."

"You will?" There was pure excitement in his voice. "Mother, I—"

"I said I'd consider it. Considering is not a decision. Considering is considering."

The ottoman creaked as Kyp stood. "Thank you, Mother." The muffled sound of a kiss pressed to a cheek.

"I love you, Kyp."

The connection cut out.

I didn't get to speak to Kyp again until post-lunch dish duty. I didn't try to use our connection when we weren't in the same room. The more we used our connection, the easier it was to maintain. But I needed to ask him this face-to-face.

"Are you sure about Lavinia? She seems to genuinely care for you."

"She was acting." His voice was cold and direct. "As I was with her. We play a game."

"Are you sure?"

Kyp's back went rigid. "You have no idea what you're talking about. You don't know how she punishes people, how she's punished me, for stepping out of line."

This was infuriating. "In case you didn't realize, I'm not the mind reader out of the two of us. You keep talking about these punishments, but what is the punishment?" I needed to know. I was walking on thin ice.

"She... I—" Kyp paled and his breath caught. His mouth moved, but no words came out. "I can't. I—I don't want to talk about it."

I wanted to argue, to shout at him, to shake him, because I deserved to know what I had gotten myself into, but the plate he held slipped through his fingers and crashed to the floor. Ceramic slivers exploded outward like fireworks. Kyp cursed and bent to pick them up, his hands shaking.

After that, we worked in silence.

The following morning, I gathered my things for a run, walked out of my room, and found a note plastered to my door. Another test today. Of course.

When I got to the basement, I took my place between Ross and Kylie and awaited the challenge.

"Don't tell Liv I said this." Ross glanced nervously between me and Kylie, as though somebody had untethered his eyeballs and let them roll free. "This is kinda pointless, isn't it?" He pulled his hands out of the pockets of his sweatpants and shoved them right back in. "I mean, what did we learn between this race and the last one?"

"Nothing," Kylie said. "This is about last night."

"What happened?" I feigned innocence.

Liv had sent the day's assigned perimeter guards, Mom and Hector, on a search for Kylie and Ross. And they found them exactly as I said they would.

"Oh, you don't know, Jacks?" Ross asked. "I figured Jaina would've told you. Gossip and all that."

"Know what?" Kyp joined us, nudging me playfully with his shoulder.

"That me and Kyl—" Ross said.

Kylie smacked him upside the head, hard. "Shut up, idiot!"

Ross' glare was deadly.

"Whoa! What the hell did I walk into?" Kyp asked.

"I think we're all just nervous." My voice was high and tight.

"Good afternoon, everyone." Lavinia strolled through the gym doors, her Guardians flanking her. "We are here to once again test the skills of our fledgling Keys. I am aware this seems accelerated, but after several discussions with the youth of our Order, we discovered they'd overcome many of their previous obstacles and are once again prepared to have their abilities analyzed. We have decided to go forward with the previous format."

I steeled myself. Whatever she handed down, I could handle.

"Can I do it?" Gretchen asked Lavinia.

Lavinia smiled. "I don't see why not."

Gretchen stepped forward. "Kylie, you will face off against..."

Oh, come on. Don't drag it out.

"Ross." She clapped with glee.

"Oh," Ross said quietly. Kylie said nothing.

I looked to Lavinia and tried to appear hopeful and secure, but I worried what this meant for me.

"As for you, Ms. Madison, I fear I may have been too hard on you during your first test. Pitting you against my son, the far superior Key, may not have been the epitome of fairness and welcome."

Far superior. Was she giving me a gift or trying to bait me?

"Therefore, if you can run the course within two minutes, you will achieve active Key status."

"What?" Kylie snapped. "That's too easy!"

Lavinia glared at her for a moment before continuing as though uninterrupted. "Are you ready, Jacklyn?"

Not only did she believe me, but she was taking me under her wing. This was more than Kyp and I could have hoped for. And much less than Kylie could ever want. That, of course, meant Lavinia had something up her sleeve. We needed to exercise caution.

"I'm ready."

A hundred feet of rubber mat rested between me and the first hurdle, then ten hurdles to jump before the next obstacle. I couldn't see beyond that before the race began.

"Go!" Lavinia shouted.

My feet pounded against the rubber in a line toward the first white hurdle. I leapt over one, two, before gasping for breath. *What the hell?* It wasn't even much of a run. I pushed through the sensation, but my legs were rubbery. Three, four, and five. Another sharp pull of air. I forced myself on to the second set.

"Kylie, what the hell are you doing?" Lavinia shouted.

"Kylie, stop!" Kyp's voice boomed.

I didn't have time to care. There was no time for distractions. Distractions lost races. I kept jumping hurdles. One, two, three, fo—

Something knocked into my side. My head smacked the floor, pain reverberating through my skull. Hurdles scattered around me. One snapped beneath my weight.

Kylie loomed over me. I swung a fist, but my head was still cloudy, so she batted it away easily. She countered with her own punch. Pain exploded behind my eye. She dropped both knees onto my stomach, and air punched out of me.

This was not the first fight I'd been in, nor was it the first punch I'd taken. I was bullied regularly in high school, and I'd learned to give as good as I got, whether I wanted to or not. I would not be defeated by Kylie.

I lunged at her, and her nose crunched under the force of my forehead. Blood sputtered free from it, but before I gained any momentum, her hand slipped around my throat and the air was sucked right out of my lungs, replaced by the leaden, unnatural pressure I'd felt when running. Colored lights exploded behind my eyes. I gasped, struggling to draw in air, but failed.

A commotion erupted by the finish line, but my vision dimmed. My next swing fell short. My nails scratched at her wrists, but I wasn't strong enough to push her away. She should be feather-light. I bucked under her but couldn't throw her.

She knocked my head back against the concrete. "You told!" I bucked again, but her face swam in front of my eyes. This was her power. She was pulling the air from my lungs, and I couldn't do anything to stop her. So much for treating her threats like a joke.

A forceful tug plucked her free from me. The airflow switched directions and my nose filled with the odor of burning flesh. I sat up, my eyes finally clearing as the oxygen returned to my brain. My head pounded.

"You okay?" Kyp dove to the ground, landing unsteadily enough that he nearly bashed into me. The skin on his forehead was bruised and bleeding, leaking blood into one of his eyes.

Gana dropped to the floor on my other side. Mom stood between me and Kylie, hands ablaze.

"What happened?" I croaked.

"Kylie tried to kill you," Gana said.

I glared at Kyp, rubbing my throat to soothe the burning sensation. My head throbbed with each shuddering breath.

"I tried to stop Kylie." Kyp winced as he spoke, his hand probing his forehead. "Then Ross tried to stop me." His eyes fell to my neck, and he swore. His fingers gently slid across the bruised skin.

I jumped at the contact. She may have been sucking the air from me in an unnatural way, but her hand around my neck hadn't exactly tickled. "My back's scratched up from the hurdles, too. And my head is pounding. Probably not as badly as yours."

"What the hell were you thinking?" Mom shouted, dragging Kylie to Lavinia. Beyond them, Ross lay on the floor.

"I'm not stupid," Kylie said. "I know she told. Why else would Lavinia reward her and punish me in the same breath?"

"I ordered you to lie low and behave yourself, and this is how you accomplish that?" Lavinia asked through gritted teeth. "I didn't reward her. We had an odd number of Keys. Somebody was going to get the easy route. After deliberately breaking the rules, did you think it would be you or Ross? Jacklyn got the gift by default." The lie came off smooth as velvet. "You are not in charge here, my dear. We can't make you a soldier without also making you a responsible adult. I would not approve of anybody sneaking out of my house in the middle of the night to congregate in the forest. It's not safe, and it's unbecoming behavior for a young girl." Lavinia leaned in even closer. "You publicly made a fool out of me and my son."

"Jacklyn's trying to get me out of the way so she has a shot with Kyp," Kylie protested, ignoring the true reason for Lavinia's fury.

All eyes went to me. Mom's looked particularly suspicious.

"Even if she did tell, did she make you sneak out with Ross?"

Kyp stood. "Is that somehow her fault, too? You should be far more concerned about what you did, rather than that you got caught doing it."

Kylie's eyes narrowed as they slid from Kyp to Lavinia. "I'm sorry for acting out of turn and attacking her, Liv. I shouldn't have done that." Her words were empty and cold, stilted.

Lavinia barely seemed to hear her. "Gana, run upstairs and bring down ice packs for Kyp and your sister."

She rushed to comply.

"Hector, Gretchen," Lavinia said. "Punish the lovebirds."

Gretchen grinned. "I thought you'd never ask!"

Kyp's eyes widened, and he forced his words out through a groan of pain. "Mother, I don't think that's ne—"

"You don't? Do you intend to question my authority as they have?"

The color leached from Kyp's skin, and his mouth snapped shut.

Hector seemed to drag himself toward Ross to collect him. Gretchen took Kylie's arm with a grin and tugged, but Kylie refused to move.

"Kylie, please. Just go," Kyp pleaded.

They shared a look, and Kylie nodded slowly. She followed Gretchen out in silence.

"Thank you, Kyp," Lavinia said, "for persuading her to follow orders."

"Of course, Mother." His shoulders drooped.

"Show's over, everyone. Out of the training room," Lavinia said. "Kyp, Jacklyn, may I speak with you for a moment."

Everyone began to file upstairs and Gana had to push past them to bring us our ice. Mom didn't budge.

Lavinia approached. "Gana, thank you for the ice. Please hand it to Kyp and go upstairs."

"Liv," Mom said.

"Relax." Lavinia placed a hand on Mom's shoulder. "They haven't done anything wrong. I only wish to make sure they're all right and to reassure them as their leader."

Mom hesitated. Under the circumstances, relaxing was a joke.

"I'll be fine, Mom. Go on ahead."

Kyp handed me half of the ice, then pressed the other half to his head. He looked miserable.

Mom looked from me to Kyp and Lavinia. Her jaw clenched. "Let's go, Gana. Jacklyn, I'll see you at lunch." She looked back to Lavinia, who nodded.

My family left, and I was alone with the potential root of all evil and her well-meaning son.

I pressed the ice to my eye and flinched from the chill.

"You okay?" Kyp asked.

"Yeah. Just a little unnerved. One minute it's hurdles, the next someone's choking the life out of me."

"That is how attacks come." Lavinia leaned against the wall, shaking her head. "You never expect them. We should choose to see it as a lesson."

Kyp moved to nod, then winced.

"I think it's time I healed that lump on your head."

"I don't need—" His volume raised, but he listed sideways, catching himself with his hand and righting his balance.

"Oh, stop it. Let me." I reached for him, but he caught my hand in his and squeezed.

"You first." That crooked grin. "That's an order."

Lavinia sighed and flipped her hair over her shoulder. "Don't listen to him. He's a fool."

"He's my superior." It wasn't the knee jerk response I pretended it was. The words stung as they exited.

Kyp coughed into his hand, but I caught a glimpse of a grin.

Lavinia looked pleased. "Kyp, you can stop being a martyr now. Your injuries are worse than hers."

I shook my hand free from his and pressed it to his forehead. "Can't ignore the chain of command, Kyp. She outranks you." I celebrated getting my way in a Lavinia-approved manner.

Once finished with his wound, I moved on to mine, but only got halfway through the wounds on my face before forcing my powers to sputter out for Liv's benefit. It was better if she was unsure of my capabilities.

"I apologize for Kylie's behavior," Lavinia said. "I should have anticipated her poor reaction to the circumstances."

"You didn't know she'd react that way," I said.

"Yes, I'm afraid even *I* make mistakes now and then." She smirked. "We may have argued in the past, but I believe we're beyond that now. I understand you haven't come by this under the best circumstances, and if you're going to be... close to my son, I expect us to become good friends."

"Yes, of course." I tried not to gape. "I would like that very much."

She smiled. "Congratulations, Jacklyn. You're officially cleared to go on missions."

"Does this mean I get to go to the temple to meet the Arvokian liaison?" I had an idea I wanted to test out.

"That is protocol," Lavinia said.

"She's a batty old witch," Kyp grumbled. "You sure you want to meet her?"

"I want to meet at least one interdimensional who doesn't want to eat my face off."

"Fair."

"Kyp, since you brought her into this world, I will consider you her mentor. You and Cass can introduce her. Gana, of course, will come with you." She sighed deeply. "But that can wait until tomorrow. For now, go eat." She smiled fondly at me, then walked away from the wall she was leaning on, moving toward the stairs. "I will miss lunch. I have work to do. After dinner, Kyp, I wish to speak with you."

"Yes, Mother."

She watched us for a moment before continuing to the stairs. The door clicked shut behind her.

Kyp sighed heavily, his eyes sliding closed, fists clenching.

"She's right. If she should have foreseen it, I *certainly* should have, since I pulled the damn strings. I should have known she would punish them."

I traced the angles of his face with my fingers, sliding across the smooth skin of his forehead, the sharp cut of his chin. "It would be risky, but we could stop her from punishing them."

His eyes snapped open. "No, we can't. We're not ready. I've made a mess of this."

"It isn't your fault."

"It is."

I passed Kyp a dish to dry. He took it. His silence and the mechanical movement of our assembly line was unnerving.
I washed another dish and looked up in time to catch Kyp watching me. The look in his eyes tightened my lungs.

A slight tap on the door frame broke the moment, and I turned off the water, my chore complete.

"Hey, Gana," Kyp greeted.

Gana's lips formed a tight line and her foot tapped impatiently. "Blocks."

Kyp and I shared a look, but did as she asked, erecting the thought barrier and auditory barrier. When we were done, I nodded and wiped my hands on the dishtowel.

She took that as her cue to march into the room and smack Kyp in the arm.

"What is with the women in your family hitting me or

threatening me?" He was only mildly outraged.

"What is with you?" Gana's eyes lit up, flames dancing on the edges of her fingertips.

"Whoa!" Kyp took a step toward me as though I would shield him. "What did I do this time?"

"You're playing Russian roulette with my sister's life! Kylie nearly killed her!"

"It's part of a plan." Kyp held his hands out in a plaintive gesture. "We're trying to get Mother to allow us to date."

Gana whirled on me. "That's an actual plan? That you're in on?"

"Yes, Gana, calm down."

"Don't tell me to calm down," Gana said. "He's painted an even bigger target on you."

Kyp spoke over us, his voice stern. "We're working on a plan to handle that. We will capitalize on Ross' anger with Mother to bring him in."

"Oh sure. And what happens when he *so obviously will not agree to do this?*"

"I can erase the memory if necessary. Also, I think it's time to pull Jaina in."

Gana groaned. "Yes, let's get more people killed."

Kyp crossed his arms over his chest. "You have very little faith."

"In you?" Gana snapped. "You think you're God? You're just a little boy."

"I'm bigger than you." Kyp smiled that crooked smile of his, and this time it was not so cute. "Your leader, if you've forgotten."

Gana's hands clenched into fire-encased fists.

"What is *with* you two?" I stepped between them. "You both need to cool down, now."

Gana shrugged. "Somebody's gotta pull him off his high horse since you won't." She returned her attention to Kyp. "You're a smug son of a bitch and I hope we're not caught in the crossfire when this blows up in your face."

"I was trying to protect your sister," Kyp said. "If we're to be together, isn't it safer if it's approved by Mother? Hell, as atrocious as it sounds, if she wants a baby and thinks we're working up to that, she'll leave Jacklyn alone. I saw an opportunity to keep her safe, and I took it. I apologize for not notifying everyone first, but there wasn't a lot of time to set things in motion."

"You thought you would keep her safe by promising to impregnate her? I don't think her safety was what you were looking after."

Kyp's mouth tightened. "Her safety is my priority. Protecting her and your family is more important than what I want, this mission, everything."

I struggled to ignore the way my heart clenched. I couldn't decide if I should interfere. They needed to hash this out, but they both teetered along the edge of a line I didn't want them to cross.

"I don't give a damn about the *mission*. I'm trying to make sure you don't get my sister killed." Gana turned to me, still all hellfire and rage. "You keep following him blindly and you'll follow him to your death."

"It's a shame," Kyp said. "The way you fiercely defend your sister makes you a great Guardian."

"I defend my sister because I love her. The rest of you can go to hell." Upon seeing Kyp's dissatisfied face, she added, "Oh, I'm sorry. Is that not what you wanted to hear, fearless leader? I love you all." She mock saluted. "Go team. See, I can lie, too." She leaned in and pressed her pointer finger to his chest. Her voice lowered to a threatening whisper. "To be clear, I'm not an idiot. You speak maybe one minute of truth a day. If I find out it isn't directed at my sister, I will end you."

"Watch it, kid," Kyp growled.

"Enough!" I turned to Gana. "Go upstairs." She opened her mouth to argue, but I cut her off. "Don't. I'm not only pissed at you. Go." She left in a huff and I whirled on Kyp.

"What the hell was that?"

Kyp's jaw clenched, and he nodded. "Gana has legitimate concerns and I shouldn't have reacted that way, but I don't appreciate—"

"Being challenged. By the lowly Guardians." Sometimes he wasn't that different from the people we wanted to change.

"That's not fair. Cass is my best friend. And I view Gana as an equal, despite her clear dislike of me."

"And threatening her helped, I'm sure."

"She threatened me first."

I smirked. "You haven't come far from calling Kylie a stupid head back in that tree all those years ago."

He placed his hands on my shoulders. "Please. I don't want to fight with you again." He took a calming breath. "I try to be progressive, but I can't help how I was raised. I don't even realize I'm doing it. I'm sorry I was nasty to Gana. I apologize for not controlling that immediately. I have an awful temper."

"You think warning me you can be an asshole excuses you from being one?" He made me want to scream sometimes. "Don't make me choose between you and my sister. You'll lose. Every time."

I left him there without another word. Gana waited at the base of the stairs, the same look on her face she'd worn when she was eight and she accidentally put Mom's ID card through the shredder. I turned a stern eye on her, but she spoke before I reached her.

"I'm sorry. You know how I am."

"Don't say you have a temper. That's what he said, and it doesn't excuse anything," I said. "I have a temper, too. Since coming here, I've used it a lot. See how it keeps me out of trouble?"

She made a face at me. "I'll go apologize."

"Maybe, if you speak calmly, you can come up with a compromise."

She rolled her eyes. "Yeah, yeah, chill, Elmo. You already gave me the feel-good lesson of the day." She headed for the kitchen.

"When's the last time you've heard Elmo use the word 'compromise'?" I called after her.

When she was in the kitchen for a few minutes without smoke billowing from the doorway, I figured it was safe to head upstairs, but I could barely lift my feet to climb.

It had been a long day. I couldn't use my Aegis to rejuvenate or I'd never get to sleep. At this time of day, it was like a shot of caffeine.

I practically rejoiced when my room was in sight. Then I pulled the door open.

"We need to talk." Mom leaned her behind on the edge of the vanity, taking her spot beside where Bulma, Elektra, and Wonder Woman lived in collector's edition display boxes. She looked as tired as I felt.

I closed the door with a sigh.

"Are you okay?" she asked.

"I didn't expect what happened with Kylie, but I'm okay."

She rolled her tongue over her teeth, a familiar gesture that indicated she was holding words back. "As we speak, Lavinia is telling Kyp that she has approved your courtship. She certainly didn't ask my opinion, but she *informed* me Kyp had chosen you." She paused, eyeing me. "Did you expect that?"

"If you're asking me if I'm surprised Kyp likes me, I'm not." I shrugged. "We have similar interests. There's a spark there. And I'm not exactly terrible to be around."

"Your self-esteem is wonderful. I guess I got one thing right."

Her smile was bitter. "But don't pretend you had no idea he asked her about you." Her eyes narrowed. "What's going on with you? Why won't you just tell me?"

What *was* going on with me? I hadn't solidified the thought yet, but the moment she asked, my heart raced. My throat ached with the truth of the words as they left, both terrified and liberated.

"I'm in love."

Mom's expression hardened. "Not with Kyp Franklin, you aren't."

I hadn't expected her to be so direct. "Gee, why wouldn't I come to you?"

She sighed and her body sagged. "Birdie, this is bad. You have no idea who he is. He can be cold and calculating."

"Yes, but he's much more." I sat on the bed, sinking into the soft mattress with relief. "I know him better than you think."

"You think you can change him? You can never change them, Jacks. That's the mistake I made with Carson."

"I don't need to change him. He's a good guy."

"Was he a good guy when he tricked you out of winning your first race?"

I didn't have the energy for this. "I'm tired, Mom."

She pushed off of my dresser with her hips and headed for the door, stopping with her hand on the knob. "I love you, baby. I can't stop you with Liv on your side, not here. But for your sake, I hope you understand what you're doing."

The door slammed behind her.

# FOURTEEN

BATTY OLD WITCH

"Come on." Kyp shuffled me along impatiently. "Gana and Cass are waiting."

"Okay, okay. I'm sleepy, shut up," I grumbled, stumbling down the stairs as I rubbed my eyes. "It's too early for this crap."

Kyp answered in my head. "We got permission to go, yes, but I don't want anyone pushing their way into our visit. Let's go so we can talk to the Arvokian liaison alone. I like your idea, and I want to get the chance to do it right." He grabbed a heavy wool coat that hung down to about mid-thigh and threw it on, pulled on a gray knitted hat and matching gloves, and knotted a scarf around his neck.

I slid my leather motorcycle jacket over my shoulders and waited with a smirk. It was nice to have a built-in heater.

"Very funny." He playfully shoved me out of the house. The screen door rattled shut behind us. He led me forward with the gentle pressure of his hand at the small of my back. The air was crisp and cold.

Cass and Gana waited for us in the clearing by our tree.

"Why hide when we have permission?" I asked.

"We're not hiding," Kyp said smoothly. "We're doing this perfectly Order-legal thing far away so nobody bothers us. And before we do that…" He leaned forward, pressing a sweet kiss to my lips. "That was also a perfectly Order-legal thing." He pressed his forehead to mine. "You my girl?"

I grinned. Well, that was one way to wake me. "Sure thing, boyfriend."

"Good. Now let's go get answers." He took my hand, swinging it in his as we moved toward our tree.

"Morning!" he greeted cheerily when Cass and Gana came into view.

Cass had climbed the tree to the second level of branches. Gana sat on the ground with her back to the tree, arms wrapped around her knees.

"Good morning." Cass flipped off of the tree and stuck the landing right in front of me.

"You guys are rather chipper today," Gana said, glancing up from her spot on the ground and not bothering to move.

Kyp shrugged, bouncing in place. "I'm hoping Cxarana has something to tell us."

"Cxa-what-now?" Gana asked.

"The current Arvokian liaison," Cass explained. "They switch out every hundred years. Cxarana became the liaison a couple of years before we started. Kyp was her first Key."

"We have a very special relationship." Kyp smirked. "Did you bring the herbs?"

"Yep," Cass said. "But we were lucky. We're low on Quipplin leaves. Pretty clear Lavinia hadn't been to the greenhouse in a while to pick up herbs. She definitely wasn't planning on making a temple visit for a while."

"Well, Kyp did kind of spring us on her," Gana pointed out.

Kyp pointed at her in acknowledgment.

Cass took the lead, settling on the floor and holding her hands out for us to take. We sat in a circle, and Cass mashed up the violet leaves using a mortar and pestle. She then soaked them in a vial of liquid.

"Ropslankin Tincture," Kyp explained. "It's an activator."

I made a face. "Yum. Smells like moldy asparagus pee."

"Join hands. I'll start the chant," Kyp ordered. "Ready?"

"As we'll ever be." Gana took Cass' hand in one of hers and mine in the other.

Kyp was between me and Cass, who lit the mixture in the bowl and placed it in the center of the circle.

The language of the Arvokians was strange. Parts of it were spoken in a sharp, staccato rhythm, like Star Trek's Klingon. Others were spoken in the smooth climbs, drops, and sways of Tolkien's Elvish. The words didn't resemble either, a smattering of vowel sounds strung together followed by clumps of consonants. They sloped and rose, then dove, Kyp's deep timbre adding bass to the musicality of the words. I'd heard parts of the language before. Cass had whispered it when we'd performed our Ritual together. But Kyp sang it out proudly, with no shame or concern, and I discovered this was a part of this world he enjoyed, the language and culture he got to experience.

The ground in the center of our circle shimmered and sparked to life. It undulated like a wave, then peeled back. I leaned forward and swore. The ground had disappeared, replaced by a dark tunnel and a rope ladder descending into its depths.

"The Arvokian Temple," Kyp said with a flourish.

Cass leapt to her feet. "I'll head down first. Then the Keys. Gana, bring up the rear."

The rope was coarse on my palms as I followed Kyp into the tunnel. It was like a cave, walled with craggy stone. The cold air outside the temple was sealed and amplified within the rock, and I had to be careful not to try to warm myself with my internal fire or I'd burn the rope. This Aegis thing had spoiled me. Weird how using it had become second nature to me in such a short amount of time.

The area at the bottom was dimly lit by wall torches, and the flickering lights caused by the breeze at the entrance cast eerie shadows along the unevenly textured walls.

"Jacklyn Kathryn Madison," a raspy voice spoke into my ear. I turned, but the voice's owner wasn't there, leaving behind only the slightest flicker of the flames in the torches on the wall.

"Stop playing games, Cxarana." Kyp's voice echoed along

the walls. He leaned forward, whispering in my ear. "She likes to mess with us because we rely on her. Also, she's the Arvokian equivalent of a rookie."

"Well, young Mr. Franklin," came that scratchy whisper. "I have to have fun somehow. However, anything involving you is no place to find it."

I opened my mouth to argue, but Kyp's voice in my mind stopped me before I had the chance. "Relax. You seem nervous."

"Well, there's a disembodied voice chattering at me, so..."

"Yeah, but you can't show weakness or defensiveness in front of her. She will capitalize on it."

"Our lost Key." The voice carried on a gust of wind that rippled through my hair. "And you must be the sister." Gana's hair fluttered in the wind. "Morgana Madison, you will be an accomplished Guardian for some time. Although, *some* time doesn't say *how much* time, does it?"

Gana's eyebrow raised, her eyes rolling. She was unimpressed.

"Keep trying to unnerve her, and I promise your life will be considerably shorter than you planned." Yeah. So much for not showing defensiveness.

Kyp sighed like he was exhaling everything he'd breathed in since he woke up this morning.

Yeah, yeah, I know.

"I would be frightened, but you need me, Key." The once-disembodied voice gained a face as she sauntered toward me from the shadows of the cave. She was tall, but appeared fragile and weak-boned, like a rodent. Her skin was a splotchy, bruised purple. She wore her hair wrapped around her head like a crown, and it was the kind of off-white color painted on walls in new apartments to make them more interesting.

She inclined her head and nodded slightly. "Cassandra."

"Cxarana." Cass returned the gesture, stone-faced. They stared at each other for a moment, neither moved by the other's silence.

Probably bored, Cxarana returned her attention to me. "Your sister has the heart of a warrior. That could get her into trouble. However, she's not much for dying for others. That could be trouble for *you*." She ran one finger, a skinless bone, spindly and tapered to a point, along my chin. I barely suppressed a shudder.

"She's the spitting image of her mother, with the hair like spun gold, the hazel eyes, the long, thin face. You are different. Dark curls and a rounded face—you may have your mother's eyes, but you favor your father quite a bit. You have inherited your mother's wicked tongue. Did you inherit your father's cowardice?"

"We're leaving." Kyp grabbed for my arm. Now, it was him messing up, showing defensiveness.

"I see I hit a nerve, although not the one I intended." She leaned in to whisper to me, and her breath carried the scent of rust and decay. "You ever wonder if lover boy sees anything in you but Raymond?"

I wrapped my hand around her throat, not squeezing, but holding it there as a warning. I needed to take control of this situation. So, I bluffed. Hard. "Should I take you apart to see how the pieces fit, or can we play nice and be friends?”

Cxarana didn’t have eyebrows, but the skin on her forehead wrinkled as though she was raising one. The humorous spark disappeared from her eyes, and she stepped free from my hold. She glanced at Kyp. “This one doesn’t understand the politics of our relationship. What have you been teaching her?”

Kyp smiled, but it was tense. “This one has been taught what she needs. She just doesn’t particularly care.”

She emitted an impatient clacking sound. “Wonderful. Follow me.”

We followed Cxarana around a corner and stopped at a rustic table that was more tree bark than wood. Atop it rested a gold bowl, and a matching serrated knife. “Ms. Madison, you are here to provide a blood sample. With this sample, you will gain access to Arvokian temples, which can be used to gather herbs for Rituals, for shelter, and for healing. You will also be able to bring Guardians here to pledge. Slice your hand with the knife, bleed into the bowl, and we will learn who you are.”

The knife had surprising heft. I pressed it against the palm of my other hand, preparing myself. My oversensitive pain sensors would ensure I felt every layer of skin I sliced through, every capillary damaged. Kyp said not to show weakness in front of Cxarana, so I focused on dulling the pain. I bit my lower lip and ran the knife’s harsh serrated edge over my skin fast, tearing through it and a couple of layers below. An awful burning sensation traveled in the knife’s wake, but it could have been much worse. Drops of blood oozed from the slice through the fingers of my fisted hand and dripped into the bowl. The vessel swallowed each drop up, not allowing time for the blood to pool.

"It shall be transferred directly into the sample system for my security Ritual," Cxarana said. "You are now a friend of the Arvokians, although *friend* is a weighted term." She wrapped a worn, leather-like hand around my wrist. She placed a finger over my wound. Blood welled, and she licked the blood off her fingertip.

I glanced at Gana, my nose screwing up. She smiled.

"A Key walks a path that cracks beneath her feet, my child. Alliances can be weakened, failed authority lost, fiercest defenders as dust. Those once joined by blood can be torn asunder. At times, one walks a path of loneliness beside the one person they would blindly consider to be the last they would follow." Her eyes opened again, meeting mine. "Every Key's journey is unpredictable, unique, eventful. If you wish to hold on to your innocence, you'd better hold on tight, Ms. Madison."

I shivered.

"Oddly specific for a speech that said absolutely nothing of value," Gana muttered.

"She's a batty old witch." Kyp shrugged.

Cxarana rolled her eyes, which was bizarre, as her eyes were better suited to a fish than a person. "Your arrogance, Mr. Franklin, is astounding, considering the powerful gifts my people have granted yours."

"My arrogance is merely an attempt to rival your own. Imitation is, after all, the sincerest form of flattery." Kyp smiled his genuine smile.

This wasn't a rivalry. This was how they did friendship.

But we didn't have time for this.

"I have a question, if I may, Cxarana."

"You may, Ms. Madison." She bowed her head.

"What is a Skeleton Key?"

Cxarana's head snapped up, creepy fish eyes going wide. "Where have you heard that term?"

"In one of the books in the estate library." I tried to make my eyes wide and innocent. I probably looked insane.

For a moment, Cxarana stared at me, her eyes blank. "Sure you did."

"So, you don't know?" Gana asked. "I suppose that makes sense. You *are* rather new here. Can we speak to your supervisor?"

"I do not have supervisors!" Cxarana gasped haughtily. "I am the Arvokian liaison. I suffered many trials, learned more about your people than your very own historians are likely to learn, built a life around human-Arvokian relations. And you dare question my knowledge?"

"I dare." Gana grinned.

Another blank stare. Then an eye twitch. Then a broad, frightening grin, teeth glinting in the firelight. She looked like a shark.

"She has learned our language rather easily, hasn't she, Mr.

Franklin?"

Kyp smiled. "She's rather clever."

Cass bumped Gana's shoulder.

The smile dropped from Cxarana's face. "A Skeleton Key is the child of two Keys. Keys do not make children together easily. The mother often dies after childbirth. The child only survived in one instance, and only then for a short time. Your blood can seal rifts. The blood of that child could open them as well. However, the child's power was volatile, and he wasn't able to survive very long. A Skeleton Key would be powerful, but not helpful to a Key's mission."

"Unless that mission was to control when and how long rifts stay open," I said, the pieces falling into place.

"Thus controlling who uses their Aegis and when," Kyp added.

"What are you suggesting, Key Guard?" Cxarana asked, her voice grave.

Cass looked between us. "We're doing this now?"

Kyp nodded. "We're doing this now. Aren't we, Jacklyn?"

"That's why we're here," I said. I'd been considering this plan since I'd first read about the Arvokians in the texts. I took a deep breath. "I would like to request that what we discuss from this point on remain under the strictest confidence."

Cxarana's eyes sank into her skin, flesh sealing over them as they shook within. When she reopened them, she nodded. "The Arvokian Council has put a system into place wherein they can choose to listen in to our conversation as necessary. Nobody in our world is free of surveillance, my friends. I have temporarily severed my connection from the Council so we may speak freely."

"Thank you," I said.

She paced the open space of the temple, gliding as though her feet were made of smoke. "You may speak."

Kyp opened his mouth, but I cut him off.

"Why don't we start with evidence? Have you been asked to take down the wards around the estate recently?"

"Yes," Cxarana said, her tone questioning.

"How many times?"

"Twice."

I glanced at Kyp.

"Once was to allow the Madisons through. The next time was a conscious choice to punish Jacklyn for questioning an order from Lavinia," Kyp said, his hands clenching at his sides. "She made a point out of drawing interdimensionals toward us and put the entirety of the Order on the line."

Cxarana stilled. "I see. Already causing trouble, Ms. Madison."

"Everywhere I go," I said, steeling myself for the possibility she would side with Lavinia.

Cxarana's browbone raised again. "There is hardly evidence of abuse of power as you're suggesting."

"I'm aware. There is further evidence. Had I been prepared to have this conversation," he said as he slid a sly smile my way, "I would have brought record of the conversation where Jacklyn truly learned the existence of the Skeleton Key."

Cxarana hummed. "I did not recall any mention of that in the texts."

"Because there aren't. Or else I would have known about it," he reminded her. "In written correspondence, she promises to supply some outside group made up of three unknown beings with a Skeleton Key. Lavinia and her followers are abusing the powers afforded to them by the rifts, and rather than fight to destroy those from the Dusk that would hunt the Arvokians, they are in deals with them. That would threaten you as well."

"It would," she acknowledged. "The Arvokian Council will not be able to act without proper evidence."

"We can continue to search for further evidence," Cass said. "We have some written evidence, but I'm sure there's more."

"Gather what you can find. I will speak with the Council. A trial is the likely outcome. It may get... ugly, Mr. Franklin. These are serious questions, and she is the one who reared you."

"She sired me, Cxarana," Kyp corrected. "Raymond Madison reared me."

For a moment, the two stared at each other, eye to creepy fish eye. Then Cxarana nodded.

"I will inform the Council. If there are any you believe are not compliant with Lavinia's plan, I would suggest you complete their transition to your side. The Council will not see shades of gray."

"But there's lots of gray shading," I argued. "It's as gray as a pencil sketch in that place! She is a Mind Key. People don't choose to work with her. They're forced. Made into puppets."

"Understood, Ms. Madison," Cxarana said. "We have ways to determine this. In the meantime, you must arm those you wish to save with knowledge of what is to come. Those that attempt to protect Lavinia when we come for her will be considered her ally. You'll do well to warn those you believe are ignorant to what she has done."

"Thank you for your assistance, Liaison." Kyp smiled, genuine and warm.

"Kyp." She pressed her hand to his arm, the motion seeming markedly more human. "I understand the risk you have taken in alerting me. I am uncertain of how long the Council will take to act, but I will do what I can to move things along as quickly as possible. In the meantime, be careful. Stay safe. If your suspicions are correct, these are the kind of accusations people kill to hide."

Kyp swallowed hard. "Noted."

"Stay safe, children."

Blinding white light bloomed from a space on the palm of her hand, expanding until it filled the entire cave. Pain spiked through my brain and I covered my eyes until I no longer saw the brightness behind my eyelids. When I pulled my hands from my eyes, I was back in the circle we'd started in.

"Holy shit," I said.

"Same." Gana's voice was distant.

Kyp and Cass shared a glance.

"We've got work to do," Kyp said. "If we're going to recruit

Ross and Jaina as planned, we'll have to do it immediately."

"And we'll have to do it carefully," I agreed. "Like Cxarana said, this is a matter of life or death."

I remembered when saying things were life or death was an exaggeration. It would be nice to exaggerate again.

PUNISHMENTS AND REWARDS

"I think I found something," Gana announced as she led the rest of the group into her room. She plopped onto the edge of her bed with triumphant glee, wrinkling her pink and brown bedsheets.

In two months, those sheets, a framed photo, and a few books were the only proof Gana even lived here. Her intention to escape was all but scrawled on the white, unpainted walls.

Kyp perched beside me on the edge of Gana's desk. With a shared nod, we performed our thought and auditory block.

"Let's hear it," Kyp said.

"There's a medical company the Order pays big bucks to monthly and—"

"Lifestone Pharmaceuticals," Cass said. "It's legitimate."

"But there's no record of it anywhere," Gana said.

She showed off the wrist brace she'd acquired on a tense mission two nights before. There was a logo on it—a green tree surrounded by several gray stones. "Courtesy of Lifestone Pharmaceuticals."

Kyp nodded. "It's a small business serving Keys, Guardians, and other people who avoid mainstream health care. They also sell to hospitals and clinics, but that's the front."

"But do we pay for their shipping?" Gana asked.

"Shipping and handling?" Cass asked. "I'm sure we do."

"No." Gana beamed. "Freight charges. Shipping crates. Why would we pay for that?"

"That bears investigation," Kyp said.

"I'll look further into it," Gana said. "Cass, can you help?"

Cass looked to Kyp.

Gana rolled her eyes, and Kyp ignored her. "Should be fine."

A commotion downstairs told me Ross and Jaina were back from their grocery run. We'd waited for a week for a moment when the two would be around while Lavinia, Kylie, and their Guardians would be on a mission. This was the only chance we'd be getting for a while.

"That's my cue," Cass said, leaving to retrieve them.

I couldn't breathe for the combined tension that filled the room. I bounced my leg to work through my nervous energy.

Kyp's fingers grazed my chin, turning my face to his. "You think I was certain you would join us? I bet everything on it, and you came through. Show only positivity. They *will* join us. They will see the truth because they must."

"You don't even believe that," I said, despite the way his

words soothed my nerves.

He flashed me his crooked smile before turning to face the door, his stone facade back in place. "Until they're here, signed and sealed, I have to believe it."

The doorknob jiggled, and I tensed.

Through the door, I heard Mom chatting amiably with Cass about her difficulties working with Gana and me on fire control. "You guys are really good with it, and I just want to make sure I'm leading them in the right direction."

Kyp's hand slid into mine and squeezed hard, fear shooting through our connection.

The door swung open.

"Please come in," Kyp's strong, seemingly confident voice greeted them. "We need to talk."

For a moment, Mom looked from face to face, and I could practically see the gears in her head moving as she drew a conclusion from the facts in front of her, the way we watched her. Her eyes went wide.

"Hell no! You are not doing this to my kids!" She lunged at Kyp and wrapped her hand around his neck, sending them both smacking into the wall behind us. Steam rose from her fingertips.

Despite her dislike of Kyp, I hadn't expected her to react like *this*. I grabbed her by the arms and ripped her away.

Mom yanked free from my grip, straightening her hair as though it was her only concern. Kyp poked at the blisters forming where Mom's fire-tipped fingers had squeezed. I held up a hand to ward her off, then healed his wounds.

He frowned. He didn't want to be coddled. I didn't care. That had to hurt.

"Who's doing what to your kids?" Ross asked, eyes circling the room. "What the hell is going on here?"

"It doesn't take a genius like you to figure out what you're up to, Kyp. You grew up listening to Ray's poison, and now you're spreading it as your own?" she snarled. "This idiot wants to form an army against Lavinia," Mom told Ross before turning back to Kyp. "You're an ass. It's been tried. It lost me my husband."

"I thought it was your relationship with Carson that lost you your husband. Cheaters never win," Kyp said. "You see, you can't fool me, Jaina." He tapped two fingers against his temple with a sneer. "Perfect memory."

There was that side of Kyp I didn't like rearing its head again.

"That's enough from both of you!" I dealt out scathing looks.

"Why are we fighting Lavinia?" Ross asked, still confused.

"I have reason to believe Mother has a deal with representatives of the Dusk through which she is alerted to certain interdimensional activities, while purposefully turning a blind eye to others." Kyp's tone was flat, as if he was reading from a history book. "The goal is to hoard power. She intends to use us Keys to create a new being. A child who can both open and close rifts, thus keeping her access to power. We also have reason to believe she killed Raymond Madison, as well as the other Keys and Guardians that were branded as traitors during the Great War within the Order."

"Is that what you're going with?" Mom's eyes locked onto his.

"Is there another version of events?" He didn't miss a beat.

Mom's nose twitched in disgust. "You're a sad little boy trying to get back at Mommy Dearest?"

Every ounce of light drained from Kyp's face. The picture frames on Gana's dresser began to rattle, though he didn't seem to notice. "*Mommy Dearest*, as you so eloquently put it, is a vile monster, a murderess, a sadistic, torturous villain."

I shuddered. I knew what he believed his mother was capable of, but I'd never heard him speak of it with such absolute, unarguable certainty. There was a virulent hatred in his eyes that stopped me from moving, stopped me from speaking, stopped me from quieting Mom before she said anything worse.

"Yes." Mom's head drooped, her shoulders sagging. "She isn't who I thought she was. I didn't find out until Ross told me about the punishment." She took a step toward Kyp again. "You were telling the truth about her when you were a kid. I should have listened to you. I may have even regretted it if you hadn't willfully dragged my daughters back into this. You're dangling them in front of her in some sick form of revenge."

"I needed help!" Kyp yelled, desperation in his tone like I'd never heard before. "It was me and Cass against the world. We're not enough against her. Ray wasn't enough, how can I be? But me and Jacklyn together? We can do this. Look what we did during the attack on the Estate."

Mom's head snapped up. "Yes. That. How did that happen?"

"We... um... may have done an Arvokian marriage rite as kids. Without realizing it." I shrugged.

Her eyes narrowed, and she glared at Kyp. "Right. It was an accident."

Kyp offered her a twisted smile. "Sorry for the surprise, *Mom*. I didn't mean to marry her, but staying that way was a choice. We need the combination of our abilities."

"Sure." She took another step toward Kyp. "You latched onto Raymond like he was yours. He never was. And now you're what? Trying to connect yourself to him? Still searching for his approval? Even after he left you behind?" I'd never seen Mom this angry. This purposefully cruel.

"You left me behind," Kyp said. "He was an idiot to trust you to take me with you as he asked. I'll give you that."

"Ray spent a lot of time doing careless, idiotic things."

"Perhaps, but you recognize Mother's behavior as wrong, and you bury your head in the sand to protect your own hide."

"Not my hide. Theirs. Always theirs." Mom jabbed a finger my way.

"Maybe, but now they are here," he countered, "which should tell you they don't want you to turn a blind eye to the suffering of others. They don't want you to stand by while innocent people are attacked and trafficked by the interdimensionals Mother chooses to ignore. You are aware of corruption in our ranks and you do nothing. There is something worse than being careless and idiotic, and that's being a coward."

Ross's eyes bounced between us like he was watching a ping pong match. "They're right about Liv. If anyone steps out of line, they're toast. Better if we all work together. She can't operate the Order without all of us. And after what she did to Kylie and me, I'm through with her punishments."

I'd had enough. "Okay, somebody explain the punishments, right now. No 'you don't need to know.' No 'I can't.' No excuses. I want answers."

Ross stepped forward, arms wrapped around himself as though warding off a chill. "There's a Ritual, usually used only for emergencies. Like if you're dead in a field of Talkers. Your Guardians can bring you back faster. But it hurts." He winced, as though reliving the pain. "Worse than the first time you come back. Worse than anything. 'Cause when a Key dies, its body takes time to prep before it returns. This Ritual skips that, but it can keep you from dying for good if someone's quick enough."

Kyp stared intently at the floor.

Ross shuddered. "What Liv does? She kills you in the worst way she can think of. Then she yanks you back. Then, sometimes, she does it again." He looked over my shoulder at Kyp, and his eyes darkened. "So, thanks for that."

My heart jammed in my throat so hard, I nearly choked. One look at Kyp's face, and it was clear he had been punished that way. To do that to anyone was sick, but doing that to your own son was beyond horrifying.

"I didn't realize she would do that." Kyp's skin went chalk white. "It was Kylie attacking Jacks that triggered her."

"I know," Ross said. "But you should have realized Kylie wouldn't go down easy."

Kyp nodded. "You're right. I take responsibility for my role in it."

"It's different for Guardians," Cass said. "They are tortured and healed by Gretchen, but the true damage is already done."

"How many times?" The words slipped from my mouth in a whisper.

"Once," Ross said. "Kylie got a second helping for her extra disobedience." He paused, staring meaningfully at Kyp. "But you're not asking me, are you?"

I looked at Kyp. He looked to the floor.

"Six times," Cass said hoarsely. "Six damn times."

He had lied to me during the estate attack. He'd said once.

"Cass!" Kyp's voice cracked as he shouted.

My heart ached for him.

"No, man, shut up," Cass said. "The people here—they mostly hate you. They don't want to follow you. Sure, me and Jacklyn are loyal, but the rest of them? Ross thinks you're a do-gooder idiot. Jaina thinks you're insane. And Gana hates you more than she hates Liv because she sees you as the more direct threat to everything she loves. But you guys tell me—after six incidents of torture—which one of you would have the brass balls to keep standing up? To keep fighting? You tell me one name, one person who has more courage. Who is more fit to lead this war?"

"Maybe someone who hasn't been caught six times?" Gana shrugged.

I love my sister. At that moment, I truly needed to remind myself.

Kyp smiled, but there was an edge to his voice when he spoke. "Fair enough, little sis. But I've learned from my errors."

"She's right," Mom said. "What makes you capable of leading a rebellion?"

Kyp's lip curled. "I'm highly intelligent. Well-versed in a myriad of strategic methods and comprehensive tactical—"

"You sound a lot like she did when she was younger."

"Don't say that." My response was shakier than I intended. Kyp's eyes narrowed. I opened my mouth to attempt to explain it away, but Kyp didn't give me the chance.

"Aunt Jainey, we can change this. We can do what Ray always wanted. I know it's easier to make things my fault, but the minute Jacklyn called Mother's methods into question, you were all skating on thin ice. And Jacklyn is approved for missions now. She's fiercely protective of her family. What will happen to her if someone gets hurt, and she blames Mother? How long before Jacklyn pushes the same button Ray did?"

"You knew he wasn't crazy, didn't you, Mom?" The pieces slid into place. "You let me believe my father was crazy."

Mom shook her head and reached for me, but I sidestepped her hand. "The truth was more dangerous than the lie, Jacklyn."

She glanced between me and Kyp. "Is your relationship part of the ruse?"

"Oh, for crying out loud!" Ross rolled his eyes. "It's the end of the frickin' world, but let's figure out who's taking who to the big dance."

"It was to protect Jacklyn." Gana winced, like it pained her to back Kyp. "We discovered Lavinia was looking for a dual Key heir and plugged Jacklyn into that plan to keep her safe long enough for Lavinia to believe the plan was well on its way to... accomplishment."

"Well, I guess that was a better word than completion," Cass said with a groan.

"But our relationship was not fabricated for the sake of the plan." Kyp's hands shook as he reached for mine.

"It's real, Mom. We're real."

"Well, there goes the only bright spot I thought I had." Mom sighed.

Kyp smirked. "Sorry to disappoint."

Mom looked between us, and the tension drained from her body. Her eyes were moist when she took my hand. "This is not a game or a comic book, Birdie." Her voice was gentle, like it was whenever I asked about my father as a child. "Heroes don't prevail through sheer force of will. Love isn't enough to overcome every trial. This is more dangerous than you could possibly understand."

"I'm not a foolish child, Mom."

"I know you're not, baby." She cupped my cheek. "But most

adults would be outmatched facing Liv."

"All the more reason I need you on my side." I placed my hand on hers.

She smiled. "I am always on your side." She looked to Gana. "And yours."

The words were a forklift pulling bricks from atop my chest.

"Except when you're against each other, at which point, I'm usually on Gana's side, because let's face it, she makes better choices." She stuck her tongue out at me.

"What? No!" I yelled, falling right into place. "I'm obviously the more responsible sister."

"Um... case in point." Gana pointed at Kyp. "Look at your boyfriend."

Kyp grumbled. "Anyway. What about you?" He motioned to Ross. "Are you in?" He squeezed my hand harder. If he kept that up, he'd break it.

Ross' mouth moved like he was chewing the facts. "We win, what happens to the others?"

We win.

"That depends on reactions to the new leadership," Kyp said. "I can, however, promise that not a single person will ever be subject to the punishment again."

A sense of doom planted itself like a seed in the pit of my stomach. "You're sure?"

Ross pulled a face. "About taking Liv down? Hell yes, I'm sure."

"Then let's start with information," Kyp said. "The Order is bleeding money into a shipping yard in Jersey. We need an excuse to visit and find out what's there. Anything we should be aware of?"

Ross hesitated. "Not about that, but something else. Kylie, Gretchen, and Hector are not going to turn against Lavinia. You can't amass any more troops."

"What if you have to fight Kylie?" I asked.

"What?" He clearly hadn't considered the possibility.

"If Kylie's loyalties are firmly against ours, it might be necessary," Kyp said.

Ross frowned. "Luckily, I can use my Aegis to induce a fever. I can knock her out without permanently harming her, if necessary."

"Yeah, but what happens once you've done that?" Gana asked. "She comes to, fever free, and you do what exactly?"

Ross smirked. "Won't have to do anything. Once she realizes which side is winning, she'll switch allegiances fast enough to make your head spin."

"Wonderful," Kyp deadpanned.

"That's my girl." Ross shrugged. "You can't trust her for shit, but she's a survivor."

Kyp nodded absently, eyes pointed skyward, considering. Then a more definitive nod, a confirmation of Ross' words. "Okay, our next move will be to learn more about that shipping yard. We'll keep digging and will be in touch. In the meantime, be ready. The time to act may come without prior notification. Think on your feet and stay safe."

Kyp leaned toward Cass and whispered something to her.

With a nod, she stepped forward and looped an arm through Ross'. "You and I are supposed to be working on weapons training. Let's get on that and leave Kyp to be torn apart by the Madisons." She grinned. "I mean, lovingly welcomed to the family." She waggled her fingers at him and pulled Ross out of the room.

Mom sighed and dropped onto the bedspread. Gana laughed. Kyp's eyes were wide, and his hand still gripped mine.

"Can I have the circulation in my fingers back, please?" I asked.

Blankly, he looked down at our hands, then back up at me, and released them. "Sorry."

I pressed my forehead to his. "It's okay. What's going on? You clearly wanted to talk to us."

"I guess I wanted to make it clear that I understand why you both don't trust me." He turned toward Jaina and Gana. "But Aunt Jainey, you remember how I was when she left."

Mom pressed her head back into the comforter, then sputtered a laugh. "You tore this place apart. And Jacklyn helped."

He pushed himself off the desk and walked to the center of the room. "She chases the dark away, makes me happier than I ever believed possible. Whatever is coming, I'll do anything to keep her safe. Anything. I need all three of you to know that."

My heart clenched violently. He sounded so determined.

"You're serious," Mom said, something like awe in her rounded eyes.

"I'm rarely anything but serious," he said.

Gana walked to me and leaned her head on my shoulder.

"I couldn't take you with me, but I should've listened. I didn't believe you about Liv." Mom swallowed hard. "For whatever it's worth, I'm truly sorry for that."

"Thank you, Aunt Jainey." His voice was clouded with grief.

The doors opened downstairs, and the rest of the Order flooded into the house. "We need healing! Gretchen's down!"

I swore and headed out, prepared for an exhausting evening. By the time I returned to my room, it was nearly two in the morning. I prepared for bed and crashed, bone tired.

For a moment, I'd pushed aside all that had happened earlier that day.

And then I heard Kyp's knuckles brush against our shared wall.

I drowsily pressed my palm there, my head still nestled on my pillow.

"Couldn't sleep. Thinking of you." Kyp's deep, rich voice filled my brain.

"Mmmm, which means I can't sleep either?" I teased.

"Sorry. I'll let you rest."

"You lied." The problem with speaking to someone within your mind is, if you think a thing, it's pretty much the same as saying it out loud. "Six times, Kyp?"

A tidal wave of anguish bounded through the connection. "I didn't want to talk about it, but you would've wanted me to."

"And you brought me here knowing what would happen? Why would you do that?"

"Seeing you again? Getting the opportunity to have this? The reward was absolutely worth the punishment. I would do it again in a heartbeat."

Speechless, I laid my head against the wall and let the warmth of our connection wash over me.

"Jacks?"

"Yeah?"

"Don't cut off the connection. Stay with me?"

I fell asleep with my hand pressed against the wall, my mind filled with the feeling of lying in Kyp's arms. For that moment, I could pretend nothing was wrong.

SIXTEEN

PUZZLE, PUZZLE

"Keys and Guardians," Lavinia greeted us, taking her place in the center of the study, where we waited for her to call my first official meeting to order. "I've gathered you here because a mission has come across my desk that I wish to discuss with the entire assemblage. Jacklyn, Gana—welcome."

I waved, and she smiled fondly. "Hector and Gana have discovered a possible lead. Please take the floor."

Kyp leaned over to whisper in my ear. "I hope she isn't too nervous. She's never presented in front of the Order before."

"Shut up back there!" Kylie snapped. "I'm trying to hear."

Kyp shrugged and spoke louder. "Fine, I won't speak. I'll trace whatever I want to say all the way up her leg." He skimmed his fingers up my thigh.

"Kyp!" Jaina shouted. "Want to lose that hand?"

"Sorry, ma'am." Kyp held his hands up in surrender and sank back into his seat. I fought down a grin.

"The area around Port Newark has filed a lot of reports lately," Gana said. "By cruising the police tip line and scanning news reports, we're getting hints of not only possible interdimensional activity, but odd weather conditions, indicating rift activity."

"Gana and I think someone is using regular deliveries to a shipping yard in the area to shield the transport of interdimensionals from the Dusk to our world," Hector said.

"We're thinking the Sirins probably own that shipping yard." Gana played the innocent so well. This was where we'd traced the Lifestone Pharmaceuticals payments.

This was where Lavinia got too arrogant. There was a damn good chance we'd find something if we explored that shipping yard. We'd have to be careful not to reveal we'd learned anything. We could leave that to the Arvokians once we'd passed the info on to them.

Lavinia processed the information, her eyes stuttering back and forth. A look I'd only seen on the subway when the person across from me was trying to read the posters outside as we sped past. When she finally spoke, it was slow, methodical. "Yes, we must pursue this lead. Assuming this place is run by Sirins, there will likely be many. These interdimensional reports?"

"The animal attacks are likely Gorvhans unable to wait for dinner time," Gana said. "The disappearances are well-planned, people from the fringes of society. Definitely Talkers." All true, but only discovered because we were searching for a reason.

"It's probably a large group," Lavinia said, as we hoped she would. "It is likely we will all be needed."

But she would have to keep us from finding any evidence of her involvement. Which meant our team would have to watch out for attacks from interdimensionals and Lavinia's side of the Order.

Beside her, Hector made a face. "At least Newark's a little closer to us than that godforsaken cesspool you came from." He flung a hand in my direction.

"Um... hey?" I argued.

"Be ready to head out after lunch tomorrow," Lavinia said. "Dismissed."

"I'm so glad you got permission for us to do this. This evening has been beautiful." I stared into the fire encircling us, orange flames flickering and leaping along the path I had created for them, just warm enough to make us comfortable. Nuzzling into Kyp's shoulder, I allowed my fingers to drift up and down his forearm, playing with the dusting of dark hair there.

He turned his head just slightly. "You're beautiful."

My eyes met his, and I remembered what I'd told Mom. What I hadn't told him yet. Tomorrow we'd head out on a mission that could blow the lid off of everything. Everything might change. But there was something I wanted to hold on to. Something that had been floating around in my head for a while now.

"I love you."

"What?" Astonishment was not the reaction I expected. Nor were the wide eyes, the double-take, or the way he stiffened as if a thousand volts of electricity rushed through his system.

"I—" My stomach lurched, and I looked away, studying the chipped bark on our tree. "Forget I said anything."

"Please." Desperation shone in his eyes. "Say it again."

The space around us was charged with tension. I was either about to be ecstatic or have my heart stomped to pieces beneath the soles of his hiking boots.

"Iloveyou." The words tumbled from my lips again, this time so fast they practically united to form a single word.

He caught my face in his hands and crushed his lips against mine with an overwhelming passion that sent me reeling. His hand against the small of my back pressed me flush against him. No matter how close he pulled me, it wasn't close enough; his desperation radiated through our kiss as his mouth explored mine. His touch slid over my hips. When he broke away, I prepared to hear his returned words of love.

"Thank you," he whispered against my lips, his voice rough with emotion. He caught his breath, then kissed me again with equal fervor.

Thank you. Thank you! At least he's polite! How did I let myself fall for a guy who says 'thank you' in response to a declaration of love?

He pulled back, continuing to press small kisses to my lips, my cheeks, nose, my eyelids, speaking between each kiss. "Sorry. Just... sorry. We need a distraction."

There was a firestorm behind his eyes. I yanked my gaze

away, despite myself. I wasn't angry at him for not saying it back. I knew how he felt.

Didn't I?

Or was it just that we were stronger together?

I cleared my throat. "We should practice. What Ritual should we work on next?"

He didn't seem to hear me at first. Then he shifted, pulled the Arvokian book from his back pocket, and tossed it onto the ground between us. I leaned forward to grab it, but he caught my hand. His eyes were sincere and sweet and no longer the equivalent of a match strike.

"I'm sorry. I just... I'm not good with... I don't even know how..." He sat back against the tree and rubbed roughly at his eyes with his palms. "Why did I start talking? Ritual?"

"There's no rush," I said, because I was trying hard to mean it. "You'll say it when you're ready to say it." I picked up the thin, leather-bound volume and flipped through it. It opened neatly to one page, the jagged remains of torn paper sticking up from the binding. "Kyp, just because you can read books, memorize them, and toss them, does not mean it's cool for you to tear out pages to jot down your cookie order for the food run."

He wrinkled his nose at me, leaning forward to look at what I was seeing. "What are you on about now?" He fingered the tiny bits of paper, the remains of a missing page, and his eyes narrowed. "Hasn't it always been this way?"

We'd been studying it for weeks now. I would have noticed a

ripped page. "Nope."

He scrutinized the book and gave no evidence he'd heard me.

"What?" I waited a beat, but he was still staring at the book blankly. "Kyp?" He looked out into the fire, his eyes darting around as if he was trying to pluck something from between the individual flames. "Kyp!"

"I've read this book from cover to cover," he finally said. "Puzzle, puzzle." He muttered it in a rhythm.

"Um, okay." My chest tightened with dread.

"It's a game Raymond and I played in my childhood." His eyes returned to the book, and he flipped back and forth through the pages. He pulled his lower lip between his teeth and bit down as he glanced over them, sometimes holding the book up to his face as though there was a clue hidden within it. "Raymond invented it with Mother, though I don't think she realized his motivation. Almalas, a rare breed of interdimensional, have mind control abilities. Mother believed he was preparing for all possibilities." He dropped the book onto the dirt in front of him. "Puzzle, puzzle, where is the puzzle? How do you know a game is being played in your mind if you can't remember the game?"

"Why do you think this is a puzzle?"

"Couple of things." He pointed to the page that was face-up beside the torn bits. "This is the Silencing Ritual, designed to quiet the Gorvhan screech." He flipped to the page before the tear. "This is the Mind Block Ritual. I can't remember what should go in between."

"But something must have been there."

"Of course. But I can't remember what. I can, however, remember speaking with Hector about the missing page, and he said the book has been this way for ages. It is believed the Sirins somehow got into the estate, or the Arvokian compound, and stole the Ritual. Can't recall anything else that happened that day. It's like Raymond used to say—you can't solve the puzzle until you know one is there." He was back to staring blankly at the page. "Do you have any idea how many times I've played that game?" His eyes were wild when they looked upon me again, and my heart pounded. I shrugged, and he continued. "Five times, all before you left. But I remember it. You know why?"

"Because you remember everything."

What must it be like to be in Kyp's head, surrounded by amateurs, including his girlfriend, with few people capable of meeting him on his level? Did he see it that way, or was it like me when I watched other people run and thought 'that's nice, normal running' instead of 'goodness, they are slow?'

"I can't remember anything else about that day. So, you see, the conversation can't be real. It was planted. I have perfect recall. And I can't remember the Ritual—"

"Because somebody removed the memory," I finished.

He dropped his head in his hands, his fingers flexing, as if trying to squeeze the answer free from his brain. "I almost missed it." He rocked in place. "I almost missed it."

The air was being sucked from my body, like when Kylie

attacked me, like when I was ten and Becky Canton kicked a soccer ball straight into my chest. I gaped at Kyp, struggling for a way to help and coming up with nothing but panic.

"Mother." His voice had that empty, emotionless quality it always had when he was looking at facts and figures and nothing else. "She got in. I can't tell you how or when." The emotion was seeping back into his tone, and with it, the terror I expected. "She took something out." He swore, jumped to his feet, and began to pace, like he was trying to tunnel a hole in the ground. I put out the surrounding fire just before he stepped into the flames. "God only knows what she saw in my head. Or what else she did." He grabbed me by my elbows and pulled me to my feet. "How can we find out which Ritual is missing? Wait. Don't tell me anything."

He grabbed my hand. "Share your Aegis with me for a second."

I did, hoping to enhance his own enough to block Lavinia.

"Clearly Mother has gotten the upper hand at some point and maybe she will again." His chest rose and fell with his rapid breaths. "I have another chess piece I can move. Maybe she hasn't gotten to it yet. We'll need it because it's too late to bail on the plan. I'll use you to reflect my Aegis back at me, so I can erase it from my brain for now. Cass is aware of it. Tell her to put it into play. And until I'm sure she is no longer in my mind..."

"What?" My breaths matched his.

"You're in charge."

"Me? I'm no leader."

"You'll do an amazing job. You'll do better than you think.

But I can't. I'm compromised." He kissed me, and his fear spread through me, a disturbance that made my skin crawl, despite the sweetness of his lips moving over mine. "I still feel like me. But I can't trust it. It would be dangerous to assume she didn't do anything more sinister while she was in my head." His fingers brushed my cheek. "If she realizes what I'm up to, she'll want nothing more than to make me bring harm to the person I care about most."

My heart leapt, then dropped to the pit of my stomach. I bit my lip to hide its quivering.

"Tomorrow, I need you to make sure you are never alone with Mother or with me. Make sure somebody else has your back. I can't be trusted."

"You'd protect me with your life." There was no doubt in my mind.

"Not if she has control," Kyp said. "I think I could wrestle her off if I tried, but I can't be sure. And I'm not risking it."

His hand tangled in one of my curls. "Be careful. Until I'm certain of what she was doing in my head, I need you in control. I will try to help when I see something happening, but I can't be involved with the plans. You understand? I trust you more than I trust myself. You can do this."

I swallowed, but my throat was desert dry. "What if I fail?"

"You won't. I know you won't."

I wished I had his confidence.

When I announced Kyp would not be joining us for our rebellion meeting, the others stared at me like they had that time I chewed my pen a bit too hard and it exploded on my face.

"He thinks he's been compromised because of one tiny memory hiccup?" Ross' lips twisted in a sneer.

"A paranoid Kyp is better than an arrogant one," Cass said. "Kyp talked to me this morning. It's missing from my book, too. As a matter of fact, I'd bet it's missing from the book of every adult Key and Guardian. She wants it completely out of circulation."

Gana was already looking through her phone. "Crap." Her shoulders slumped. "Lavinia's computer had several different copies of the Ritual Book. Each has the Rituals in different orders and combinations. I'll go through them, but it'll take a bit to come up with the missing one." Gana's eyes sparked with fear. I'd begun to believe she didn't experience fear anymore. "She probably knows. If she's in Kyp's head, she knows, right?"

"We don't know that she's in Kyp's head." Mom's protest came off as weak.

"More importantly, we can't assume she isn't," I said. After all, it was Mom who warned me not to assume everything was fine just because it was a nicer alternative to the truth.

"Cass, he says he has a chess piece. One move to checkmate. He erased it from his mind but said you'd know what to do?" I asked.

She nodded, but she quickly glanced away. "Yes. Did he tell you his checkmate move was unreliable as fuck?"

I took a deep breath. "No. Of course he didn't."

Why hadn't Kyp trusted me with the chess piece? It ate at the pit of my stomach because it meant Kyp had a secret from me, something that would help us he wasn't willing to tell me. It meant that despite everything, I was not an equal partner in this.

"Okay. I'll set it in motion," Cass said, "but I wouldn't make plans around it."

Or he just didn't believe in it enough and didn't want me to think we were out of options.

"Why aren't we leaving?" Gana asked. "I mean, why aren't we sneaking out in the middle of the night and getting the hell out of Dodge? Wouldn't that make sense?"

"Because Kyp has something to prove," Ross said. "He wants the estate. He's refusing to leave it, and that's why we're stuck here with the Queen Bitch."

"Wrong, dickhead," Cass said. "It's the wards."

"Wrong again." I stood in the center of the room, eyes meeting those of everyone surrounding me, every member of our rebellion. "We have a duty here. We need the estate and we need the Order. If we leave, who are we? Keys and Guardians on the run? Liv will be alerted by the wards. Do we leave Kyp? If she's in his head, she may be able to track him. We would have to abandon him here with her. We would need to abandon this place, this stronghold, our lives, our mission, the only home most of us have ever known. The remaining Order would be Lavinia and those loyal to her. What would that mean for the state of humanity?

"No, if we believe in the Order and what it's meant to do, we fight this battle because we protect humanity. We don't leave that to the bad guys. We keep that for the righteous. Heroes do not flee from danger. They fight for the institution. And they prevail." I stood a little taller, proud of myself for my declaration, and for a second, I thought I could do it. I could lead.

Ross laughed. Hard. "Wait, you're serious? You took that speech out of a movie, right?" Nobody else laughed, and Ross took the hint. "Look, I know we have a duty to uphold or whatever, but I still don't understand why we're taking orders from Kyp's piece of ass."

"Not okay to say," Gana growled.

"Is it okay to think?" Ross asked. "Dude, that's her only credential. She hasn't even been here long. There are better choices."

I was used to this. Guys in high school that considered me bangable because I was fit from track and disposable because I was a geek with passable grades who supposedly had nothing else to offer. Guys that never counted on my temper or bravado, or my ability to smart mouth people into oblivion.

I stepped forward, so I was face to face with Ross, my hazel eyes locked on his pale blue ones. My voice was low and calm. "Do not confuse my relationship with Kyp with your relationship with Kylie. Kyp and I are equals, and he chose me to stand in his stead. Would Kylie ever do that for you?"

Ross' eyes shifted from sparkling blue to burning orange. He wanted to tear me down. He didn't move a muscle, but that desire was why I'd never truly trust him. For now, we needed him in line. It was my job to keep him there. If that meant I needed to be as cruel to him as Kylie was, I would.

"The difference between how Kylie treats you and how Kyp treats me is all about respect. Rest assured, Kyp wouldn't put me in charge if he didn't trust me to lead."

Ross pursed his lips. "He's smarter than you."

I nodded. "That he is." I just hoped I was smart enough to keep us alive.

SEVENTEEN

GOING, GOING...
GONE

Lavinia rented a bus to get us to Newark. We parked it in the lot of a pharmacy that had closed hours ago and headed the rest of the way on foot.

"Hey, wait up, guys!" Gana rushed to keep up, hoisting her supply bag on her shoulders with an uncomfortable grimace.

I adjusted my pack onto one shoulder and held my hand out. Sighing, she handed me hers, which I threw onto my other shoulder without much struggle.

Kylie shoved at my back. "Pick up the pace, Madison. If you have to baby your Guardian, they aren't fit for guarding, are they?"

"Get bent," I muttered.

Kyp peered over his shoulder. "*Careful*," he spoke in my mind. Anxiety spiked through our connection.

I channeled my Aegis and used it to see more clearly in the night. "Guys, it's getting darker. I could be an asset in this situation. Maybe I should take the lead?"

"No," Kyp said through gritted teeth. "This is your first mission. You don't take the lead on anything."

"But I can—"

"I said no."

I stifled a growl. I knew he was nervous, but I didn't love the way he fell back on bossing me around when things got upsetting.

Lavinia turned back, a murderous look in her eyes, her finger covering her lips. She was right. If we wanted to draw the attention of Gorvhans, this was the way to do it.

We turned another corner and entered our destination, the warehouse district. The street was significantly dimmed, the only decent lighting coming from a generously sized loading dock over a block away. The rest of the buildings, a series of closed warehouses, were framed only by a few small reflectors. Lavinia waved her hand, leading us toward the loading dock.

We moved in relative silence, which made the harsh rustling sound stand out. It had to be Ross. He was always clomping around. Stealth had no meaning to him.

"Look out!" Ross' voice echoed off the buildings around us, and I whirled in time to see the source of the wet sucking sound that followed.

A clawed Gorvhan hand buried itself deeply in Kylie's chest. Her gray-green eyes rounded as she stared up at the creature before her in a mix of disbelief and awe. A bubble of blood erupted from her lips. The Gorvhan yanked its hand back out, and her heart came with it. She dropped to the floor like a marionette whose strings had been cut.

It couldn't have taken more than ten seconds, but it felt like minutes.

Ross barely had time to set the creature ablaze before the Guardians swallowed the Keys up inside a human wall. We stood back-to-back in the center. Several more Gorvhans rushed in to circle us. The one that had attacked Kylie had apparently jumped the gun, arriving seconds before the rest.

Kyp grabbed my forearm, startling me. "Stay close." Gorvhan screeches rang out around us. "Please, stay close to me."

I nodded numbly, replaying the look in Kylie's eyes.

"Please."

I shook my shock away and tore through my supply bag, yanking out two daggers. Beside me, Kyp drew a sword from the sheath on his back.

As I looked back to see if Mom, Cass, and Hector were covered, my eyes caught on a creature hiding on the low roof of a nearby building, about to leap down and join the fray. A warning flew from my mouth. "Liv!"

Her hand rose in connection with a mental push, and the Sirin flew off the roof to a splotchy death on the ground. "Thanks." Her eyes sparkled with genuine gratitude.

Kyp's eyes were on me, but I ignored him as more creatures streamed out from between the buildings. The primary enemies were the interdimensionals. Whatever Lavinia's involvement in this warehouse, the interdimensionals saw a chance to wipe out the Order in its entirety, and they were taking it.

The Guardians fought in front of us, and I itched to join, adrenaline firing through my veins. At first, the Keys were backed up into a tight circle, but as the Guardians fought outward, they provided us with more space to maneuver.

My eyes found a mass on the ground beside me. Kylie. I couldn't do this. I tore my gaze away and slid through the wall of Guardians, worming my way into the battle. I refused to just wait to die.

I fought by rote. *Sidestep Gorvhan claw coming at my throat, curl under, slam dagger between Gorvhan ribs, pull upward, slam other dagger into soft, meaty part under Gorvhan jaw, kick Gorvhan down, free daggers, next contestant.* I moved through a few of them this way, but the picture behind my eyes was Kylie's dead, blank stare.

I didn't even like her.

I'd never seen anybody die before.

Claws bit into my back, dragging me up, and then back to the ground with force. Snapping back into action, I caught myself and rolled to my feet. I whirled on the interdimensional that threw me, but Gana had already lit him up, whirling toward another and throwing him into the flames.

Kyp ran a Sirin through with his sword. Without looking down, he grabbed me by my arm and hoisted me back to my feet. "I understand, but you have to stay focused." The Sirin still dangled from his weapon.

When I glanced his way, I spotted Gana grappling with a four-legged beast with gray fur, red eyes, and fangs. The scent of burnt hair permeated the chilled night air. Her fingers burned it, but it didn't react.

Kyp grabbed me by the elbow. I whirled on him, but he calmly snatched my daggers away and shoved his sword into my hands.

"Tralsk skin isn't affected by fire. Take off the head." He nudged my back slightly, and I took his cue. I dove forward, knocking the Tralsk from Gana with a full body tackle, ignoring the way its weight stole my breath. Grabbing hold of its coarse fur, I pulled us both into a roll, punching at its snout with my free hand before continuing to roll right off of it.

"Jacklyn!" Hector called after me. "Get behind the line!"

Ignoring him, I leapt to my feet in time to see it charge me again, foul-smelling vapor pouring from its snout with each puff of breath. I spun, hitting it with a roundhouse kick, then caught the wall and redirected myself so I could swivel the other way. I swung the sword, cutting cleanly through its neck in a spray of green blood. Its head rolled across the ground and my eyes followed it to where a Sirin slammed a blade into Cass's leg. She screamed, stabbing her sai into both of its eyes.

"They have weapons!" Ross shouted. "They aren't supposed to have weapons."

"Yeah, well, it's a brave new world." Hector cut through a Tralsk headed for Gretchen. "Adapt."

I helped Gana to her feet. Her arm hung limply at her side,

blood dripping from a gash in her shoulder. I wrapped my arm around her waist until she steadied.

She shrugged me off, readying a fireball with her good hand and firing it at a nearby Gorvhan. "Jacks, in case we don't make it..." She trailed off; her eyes focused somewhere over my shoulder. I followed her gaze to where a Sirin swept Mom's legs out from under her and she tumbled to the ground, knocking her head on the pavement.

"We'll make it." I snatched a discarded knife from the floor, focused my vision to ensure perfect aim, and threw it. It sank into the Sirin's throat before it did any damage to Mom.

Gana pulled me close and whispered in my ear. "The missing Ritual can nullify an Aegis." She limped to where Mom lay, standing over her while she regained her bearings.

I'd deal with the implications of that later. In the meantime, I searched for my next opponent, my eyes scanning the crowd for an unoccupied enemy. A Sirin with a silly hat and glasses perched on the edge of his nose stood on the roof above Kyp's head. I remembered him from the attack on the estate. I reached for Kyp, but he was focused on diverting Gorvhans from Cass as she wound a strip of material around her leg as a tourniquet.

"Gana!" Mom screamed.

I twisted toward where I'd just seen them. A Gorvan bore down on Gana, but she was busy protecting Ross of all people and hadn't seen it coming.

I screamed for her, taking off toward her as a claw swiped for her neck.

Mom was closer. She shoved Gana aside.

Balance teetering, she managed to strike the Gorvhan with a flaming palm, but it was too close. The thing sank its teeth into her throat and thrashed its head from side to side, swinging her around like a rag doll.

"Mom!" Her name tore from me as if there were hooks on the end, my throat raw and bruised. This couldn't be happening.

Gana shrieked, a horrible sound that echoed in my ears as everything else seemed to go silent around us.

Ross hacked into the creature, killing it, and it released Mom from its jaws. She spilled onto the floor, blood dribbling from the side of her mouth, slicking along her throat. Her eyes were blank, but her mouth was moving, horrible gasping sounds escaping her.

This was what I was here for. To heal. To keep our people from dying.

The sword slipped from my hands, and I leapt over several downed Gorvhans to get to her.

I didn't feel the sword stab through my back. I simply watched as the tip erupted from my chest, metal glinting in the moonlight, a crimson substance coating the tip. I jerked upright.

My fault. I had allowed myself to be distracted. I dropped my sword to heal Mom and all but handed it to an enemy. *Stupid. So stupid.*

But I didn't care. I didn't care how stupid it was. Because the worst part was that Mom was too far away from me to heal her now.

Cass screamed for Kyp. The edges of my vision blackened as the sword disappeared from my view.

I couldn't feel the ground beneath my knees. I was drowning, but there was no water.

A choked cry sounded somewhere beyond the ocean rushing in my ears.

"Ross! Send Gretchen! Get the others to cover for us. Lead the battle away." Kyp's voice sounded strange, garbled.

When I was a child, I went to the beach, and there was sand and water, and a little boy playing with me—Kyp? We built sandcastles and there was this guy with us, and I think he was my father and—

The pavement rushed at my face, but something halted my fall, redirecting me so I saw the moon's white light far above the crest of the tallest building. A face swam into view, with chocolate brown eyes that spoke of their fear. They, too, were filled with water.

"Jacks!" Kyp held me, his lips moving, but the sound was muffled—too far away to be so close to me. "Give me your hand. Share your Aegis with me and I can heal you." His breath came fast, his eyes wide and pleading.

Mom. I had to heal her. I didn't have strength for both of us. I tried once, twice, to tell Kyp, to *breathe*, but they were half-breaths, ragged, racking things, and my words wouldn't come, and my arm wouldn't move and... *Oh God*. My eyes blurred with tears. I was dying.

We had discussed how I couldn't die, so I thought I would handle death well. But everything was cloudy or muffled, and my lungs were too full to grab any more air. Everything was the wrong color and it should hurt but didn't, and I was pretty sure that meant I was in shock. My body should be screaming.

Kyp wiped at my tears. "Jacks, come on, I need you to listen to me." His voice was jittery, and he pulled my hand up in front of my face. I gazed at it in surprise, and that was when he understood. "C-can you... can you move anything?"

"No," I finally managed through shuddering gasps.

"Okay, okay, we can fix this." He looked at where our hands joined and squeezed mine as though he could pump the healing free from it. "Come on, come on! I need more. We're stronger together."

Kyp examined my wound and his face went a sickly shade of pale. One tear escaped, making a track over his nose and dropping off onto my cheek. I felt it, the only blessed thing I could feel.

"S-sorry," I whispered. Something thick dribbled from the side of my mouth. Blood. My blood.

"What?" Kyp leaned closer, his forehead pressed to mine. He stroked a hand over my hair.

"I screwed up. I couldn't heal her."

"What? No. You didn't. And I need you to listen to me." His hand slid over my jaw, his fingers tightening to insure eye contact. "I need you to listen to me. This is important."

I nodded between gasps.

"I need you to come back to me." His voice cracked. "You need to fight to protect who you are, okay?"

Kyp shook me. I didn't remember losing consciousness, but I came crashing back. Time blurred and crawled, then raced and zinged. "You can't go. Not yet. I'm the one who should be sorry. I'm the biggest asshole." He pressed a kiss to my forehead, gazing at me with fierce intensity. "I love you."

Now? Of all times?

He laughed, but it was damp and shaky. "Hey, don't look at me that way. I know, I know. I can't believe you can be so filled with attitude even when you're dy—" He cut himself off. "Love never seemed an adequate description for what I feel for you. Come back to me, okay? Not empty, not different. You. I need you."

I nodded again, the only communication I was capable of at this point. Kyp smiled crookedly.

The world darkened and my vision narrowed to slits. I should be terrified but staying alive was a struggle. I needed to let go.

I turned my head to where Mom lay. Gana sobbed into her chest.

"It's okay, my little Birdie." Mom's voice was always a source of comfort, even now, when it was all in my head.

She was gone. My mom was gone. She'd never comfort me again.

I stopped struggling for air.

SACRIFICE

Keys return from the dead. I'd heard it a million times, and it still sounded impossible. If I died with a huge gaping sword wound, drowning in my own blood, there was no coming back from that.

Kyp would laugh at the idea that I'd looked Sirins in their buggy little eyes, healed a compound fracture with my hands, but couldn't accept that there were some things that were beyond the reach of conventional science.

And wait a minute—I'm thinking. So, not quite dead.

I couldn't see, feel, or move, but I was there. I was filling my body, senses returning to me. First, my hearing—muffled sounds from familiar voices, but one rang through.

"... don't understand why you would." It was Gana. I relaxed into my body at the sound of her voice. She was home for me.

"I swore to protect Keys as a Guardian of the Order." It was Hector. "My fealty is to all Keys and to the Order's principles."

"In other words, Mother's attention was on me and not on controlling you." Kyp.

A shiver rocked through my body. I convulsed with it, shooting up into a sitting position. It was like I'd taken an hour-long bath in ice water. I tried to use my Aegis to warm myself, but came up empty.

"Jacks! Are you okay?" Kyp and then Gana shouted, one beat behind the other like a musical round.

I coughed and sputtered for air, clutching the sheets of the bed I was lying on. My vision returned in spots of brightness and shade. I was in my room, surrounded by blurry figures. There was no evidence of my wounds. Somebody had changed me into fresh clothing. As I took stock of my surroundings, my vision cleared, bringing with it a throbbing pain in my head. My fingers were blue. I shuddered so hard I nearly tilted right off the side of the bed. Strong hands clasped onto my shoulders, and I flinched.

I couldn't. No! I needed to escape.

"Jacks." Kyp's eyes were red-rimmed, but they lit up the way they always did when he first saw me.

An image flashed in my mind—Kyp's hands coated to the wrist in crimson. I flinched again, pulling back from his grasp, my eyes going to his hands. "Y-y-y-you have blood on your hands." I shook my head, unable to place the source of the image in my head. "S-sorry. I thought..."

Kyp's mouth moved silently for a moment before saying, "I do, Jacklyn. I do."

Hector nervously listened through the door for approaching enemies. When had he joined our side? Gana watched me cautiously from the foot of the bed, as though she expected me to start hungering for brains. Neither of us had any idea what to expect from a Key's first death.

"Where's Mom?" I asked. And the minute I said it, the image flashed through my brain. Mom bleeding on the ground in Gana's arms. Mom telling me it was okay to let go.

The sob left me on a prayer, and I couldn't sit up anymore, couldn't breathe, just curled in on myself and cried.

I called for my sister, my voice hoarse and wet, something unrecognizable. She rushed past Kyp, taking me into her arms like I was her baby sister, rocked me as I cried.

Jaina Madison wasn't a perfect person. She was a screw-up by a lot of metrics. She'd regularly bitten off more than she could chew. She struggled with men. She was exactly the type of woman who kept her married name when she moved in with another dude. She had a tattoo of my father's name on her hip and regularly wore clothes that revealed it, even though she had moved on long ago. She lost job after job, scrambled on unemployment, and never quite figured out how to help us with our homework or give us even the slightest bit of structure. She was mostly awkward when we needed discipline, and she was easily frustrated.

But Jaina Madison was warm. She loved us. She came into our bedrooms after she thought we were asleep and tucked us in, even as teenagers. If we needed something, she went without. She wanted to know the details of our lives, even when work made her miss the big stuff, even when we tried to hide things from her. She lauded our good parts. She scowled at our bad.

We were just starting to understand each other, had only just gotten the truth out on the table before us so we could start working past it. And now we never would.

The best thing about Mom? She always hugged us when we cried.

Gana and I clinging to each other as the world fell out around us could never be a fitting replacement.

I missed her powdery scent. I missed the home we had made with each other, the dynamic this detour into Keys and Aegis' had destroyed.

I wanted to go home and find her there, waiting for me.

I wanted out.

And I was going to make that happen.

I needed to see this through and get me and my sister to safety. For Mom.

I straightened, Gana still clinging to me.

"We need to finish this," I said, my eyes meeting Kyp's.

Gana sat back and away from me, and Kyp scooted forward. They moved like this was planned. A choreographed dance.

"Jacks." This time when he moved to touch me, he showed me his hands first, proving they were clean. Then he returned them to my shoulders, cautiously, like I was a wounded animal. "You came back to me." The half-whispered words gave voice to the longing in his eyes.

"I-I think so." My vision swerved in odd directions as I searched the room. "Where's Cass? Did she make it?" My voice cracked.

His shoulders slumped. "She's downstairs meeting with Mother before—" He caught Gana's eyes over my shoulder and stopped mid-sentence. "It doesn't matter." He pulled me to him until my cheek was pressed to his and I was fully curled up in his lap. "I've never been more afraid in my life." He pressed a kiss to my forehead and squeezed me tightly. "I'm sorry. I'm so, so sorry. I know we were always fighting... but..."

"I understand." Another chill ran through me and Gana rose, returning with blankets and wrapping all three of us up in a cocoon of warmth. She rested her cheek on Kyp's back.

Gana was comforting both of us. Why was Gana comforting both of us?

"What did you do?"

Kyp hesitated. "Why would you think—"

"Something's wrong." My voice was still shaky, my body ice cold. "Why is Cass with Lavinia? And Gana barely likes you. Why is she hugging you?"

Gana blushed, jumping back. "I'm not."

Kyp glanced at Hector before offering me a wry smile. "Don't hate me, okay?"

My eyebrows drew together. I ran my fingers over the plush blanket, searching for comfort in its softness until I found my words. "Why would I hate you?"

"Because I did something you would consider galactically stupid. But I promise you, it was worth it."

A knock sounded on the door. "Hector," Gretchen said. "C'mon. It's time for the trial."

Trial? "Kyp..."

He answered within my mind. "If anyone asks, I controlled you the entire time. All of you." He met my gaze with watery, frightened eyes. "I finally understand it. What love is. I understand. What Jaina did for Gana, what I should have done for you from the beginning."

The door clicked open.

"Love is sacrifice."

"No!" I didn't even know what he was sacrificing. I just knew I couldn't bear to lose any more.

"Kyp," Hector warned from the door, the solemnity in his stance a sharp contrast from Gretchen, who now stood beside him, looking utterly thrilled. "Your trial awaits."

I was too weak to stop this, and bile rose in my throat as Kyp let go of my hand.

"No!" Gana rushed at Gretchen, right past Kyp's hand as he tried to stop her. "I'm not gonna let you do this."

I must have missed a lot while I was dead.

I tried to get out of bed, but took a wobbly, undignified spill back to the mattress. Gretchen swung her fist, knocking Gana to the floor with a jarring crack.

Gana's feet scrambled beneath her but didn't find purchase. A lump was already rising along her jaw, but when her eyes locked onto Gretchen, they contained an inferno. "I *will* kill you."

"If I don't get there first," I promised. "You're lucky I've been weakened. But I won't be weak for long."

Gretchen took a threatening step forward, but Kyp stopped her, raising one hand.

"Gretchen, enough. I'm coming. Willingly. Just give me a moment."

Gretchen looked impatient, but Hector placed a hand on her arm, and she fell in line.

Kyp dropped to his knees before Gana. "Please, don't get up."

"I can't allow this. It isn't right." Tears filled her eyes, and my stomach lurched. "I won't let her take you, too."

Kyp's voice shook. "Thank you, little sister. But I need you here, doing your job." He tilted his head toward me. "I'll be fine, as long as I can trust you're looking out for her. You're damn good at this, kid." He tucked a strand of hair behind her ear. "Now, please, don't get up." He rose, pressed a kiss to his fingers, and held them out to me. "I love you. I'll come back to you."

He seemed resigned to whatever was to come, but as he walked away, the room began to shake, trinkets on bookshelves tumbling to the floor, perfume bottles on my dresser clinking as they smacked into each other, the furniture groaning. He was not calm; he was terrified and unquestionably pissed.

"I love you, too!" I croaked, but the door slammed between

us. "What the hell happened?" My heart ran like a frightened deer, another shudder wrenching through me. "Why is it so damn cold in here?"

Gana gripped the edge of the mattress and pulled herself onto it. "How can I help?"

"I want Gretchen to bring Kyp back here, now, before I tear out her tongue and wear it as jewelry." Maybe I did come back different.

Gana didn't react, so maybe my outburst wasn't as strange as I thought. "It's not cold. It's basic biology. You were dead. Your blood is just starting to warm again."

"Yeah." My voice wobbled. "Basic biology."

"When you... died... I was with... well, Cass said..." Gana looked away and started picking at a cuticle. "Hector suggested he and Cass take you and Kylie aside, somewhere away from the battle, so you were safe from Talkers. But Kyp spotted a vial of Dreviara on his belt."

"What's that for again?" I tried to remember, but my brain whined like a broken engine.

"The Death-Bringer Ritual for one," Gana said. "But it's part of many other Rituals. It was just Hector's turn to be supply guy for this trip, but Kyp freaked. He saw the Dreviara and assumed it was meant to harm you, even though doing the Ritual then would have meant killing Kylie too."

"Finding out Lavinia had gotten to him set him on edge. He's been off ever since."

"Hector tried to tell Kyp he was wrong." Gana nodded. "He wouldn't listen."

"What did he do?" I knew what I would have done. It wouldn't have been good.

"He telekinetically lifted the weapons on the battlefield and took out the remaining interdimensionals," Gana said. "Which would have been awesome if it wasn't terrifying to have a half dozen sharp weapons zinging through the air. Then he pulled a dagger on Hector."

The doorknob jiggled. Gana leapt from the bed, but it was Cass, looking somewhere between vomiting and passing out. She limped her way into the room.

"I'm so glad you're okay," I said.

Cass looked grim. "More okay than others."

"I wish I could heal you. Maybe later?" Right now, I was completely spent. Being dead was exhausting.

Add that to the list of sentences I never thought I'd think.

"What did they decide?" Gana pulled up a chair for Cass. "I guess Kyp not being here answers that."

"The trial barely took a minute," Cass said briskly. "They're calling it an assassination attempt. Kyp aimed a sword at Lavinia. There's no getting out of that."

An image of Ross literally stabbing Kyp in the back flickered in front of my eyes, unbidden. "Ross ratted us out?"

"You saw it coming?" Gana asked.

I shook my head. "It's not that. I mean, yeah, I trusted him the least, but I swear I saw it, somewhere..."

"Some Keys have residual memories from their deaths. They claim to have experienced things that never happened," Cass said. "Nobody knows what happens to Keys when they're gone, because they only remember fragments, and what they do remember rarely makes any sense."

"Great." I really needed another layer of bizarre on my weird sandwich. "So when exactly did Ross betray us? Before or during the mission?"

"After," Gana said.

"As soon as Kyp acted and failed, Ross was prepared to tell Lavinia everything for immunity," Cass said, "but Kyp didn't let him."

"He shut him down, erased everything about the revolt," Gana said, eyebrows furrowing. "I don't think he was going to stop there."

I dropped my head into my hands, my fingers pushing into my hair as I rocked forward. A stream of foul language cut through all coherent thought.

"Gretchen stopped him," Gana said, "and Kyp turned himself in. He said he controlled all of us and made us help. He wouldn't let us take responsibility."

"We were all supposed to be at the trial, but I invoked our rights according to the Order's laws," Gana said. "You have the right to have your Guardian watching over you until you return. If she didn't follow that law, none of the Keys would feel safe."

"Smart move," I said. "How was Kyp allowed in here?"

"Gretchen stayed with Kylie on Hector's request. He agreed to guard him and bring him to Lavinia for the trial once you woke up, and Lavinia, well... He's still her son," Cass said. "Gretchen having to come and get them probably doesn't bode well for Hector."

"If she controls him, how did he even get that far?" I asked.

"Kyp says the only way to break through control is singular focus," Gana said. "You draw a line you refuse to cross; your brain won't let you take that leap. Mind control requires some level of obedience. It's easier to listen than fight."

"Protecting you was Kyp's line. His emotions were running high, and they feed his Aegis," Cass said softly. "And Lavinia was fighting him so hard, she temporarily lost control of Hector. Not sure how long that will last."

"In the meantime, we should worry about the trial," Cass said. "Kyp was found guilty. Technically, they tried all of us, but they found us to be his innocent victims. Probably only because they believe they've neutered us by hurting Kyp and realize they can't operate effectively as an Order without us."

"If we'd been found guilty, we'd be dead," Gana said. "That soft spot I mentioned? Kyp was banking on that."

"To save us, he... love is sacrifice." I could collapse under the weight of what Kyp had done for me. For us. For all of us.

Cass sighed, her face grim. "The punishment is the usual one. For each person under his control."

Kyp. Me. Mom. Gana. Cass. Ross. Six counts. Six.

Anxiety bubbled within me, crushing my lungs. "Why would you let him do this?"

"We tried to stop him, Jacks," Gana said. "He kept saying it was his sacrifice to make. That he owed it to us."

"He's being a good leader," Cass added.

"I don't care! We can't let him do this! What if he comes back wrong? Five or six times in a row? What's the most he's ever done?"

Cass sniffled. "Three. And it was bad. The more he experiences, the more damaged he is when he returns." She shook her head. "He's not supposed to protect us. We're supposed to protect him."

My father had directed him to protect me. That was a ten-ton weight on a toddler's shoulders. If ghosts were stabbable, Ray would be the first one I'd track down, father or not.

"We have to do something. Now." *I* had to do something. I couldn't help Mom, but I could save Kyp, stop him from enduring the macabre vignette of torture that was playing in my mind. I scooted off the bed, but the minute my feet touched the floor, everything tilted.

Gana caught me before I dropped. "You can't go anywhere. Everyone is too busted up. We need rest."

This was the kid I grew up beside. This girl with the stubborn set to her shoulders, the bruised jaw, and a grim curve to her mouth. She looked so much older than she had before this started.

Everyone would be better off if we'd never come here.

Mom would still be here. She would tell me what to do. Her advice would probably be awful.

Tears pricked my eyes again.

"I need to stop Lavinia."

"I get that." Gana rubbed my back gently. "But it's too dangerous right now."

"Right now? There isn't anything else but now. After this, what? We go back to normal and continue to be pawns in her quest for power and we sit back and take it?" I was building toward an explosion.

"We don't have a choice," Cass said.

"Guys, no. We have to—ow!" A needle pricked my arm.

A syringe dangled from Gana's fingers. "Sorry, but you can't do anything for him."

What the hell? I couldn't make my brain think of anything more helpful than that. Why would Gana do that? What had she given me?

I looked to Cass in a panic, but she took hold of my shoulders and pushed me back onto the bed. "You need to rest if you expect to rebuild your energy and there's no way you'll sleep while Kyp is in trouble."

My view began to narrow, and it felt like dying again. My chest seized, and I bucked up, but my muscles were loose and unwieldy. Cass and Gana held me down easily.

Gana brushed her fingers through my hair. "Sssshhh, it's okay. It was Kyp's idea. He was scared you would get hurt trying to protect him."

"Why?" The inside of my mouth turned to cotton.

Gana snorted a humorless laugh. "Because he just got himself hurt trying to protect you."

I blinked and when my eyes opened again, Gana had disappeared and Cass loomed over me. The room was otherwise empty. The drug had clearly worked, but something had changed. Liquid energy flooded my veins. I shoved Cass, and she tumbled right off the bed.

"Ow, what the hell?"

"You drugged me! Do you think we're on good terms?"

"Hey, that was your boyfriend's idea." Cass hoisted herself up from the floor with some struggle. "I gave you a shot of adrenaline to wake you up, so you can thank me."

That tracked. It certainly explained the weird energy I felt.

She perched on the edge of the bed. "I followed through with Kyp's plan because he ordered me to, and Gana didn't trust you to stay put without it. It's her job to protect you above all others. But it's *my* job to protect *him*. So I woke you up. A lot."

My Aegis zipped through my blood like electricity through power lines. "It's definitely having an effect. What now?"

Cass stood with a sigh. "Now, you hit me."

"Um... why?"

"I know this day has been awful, but if we're going to make it to tomorrow, you need to put your thinking cap on. Lavinia is testing us. She assigned me to guard you here to prove I can't be trusted. I need to look like I tried to stop you or the next time you go for a romp through the woods, you'll be breathing my ashes."

"How long has he been down there?"

"A couple of hours. Not sure what that means. Kyp's mind can do terrible things to itself, especially when it comes to Liv. He's got an active imagination, and the anticipation will be worse than the punishment. She probably let him drive himself crazy for a while. That is, if he didn't pull the whole zen *I am justified and thus fear nothing* crap he pulled at the trial." Cass groaned. "If he did, she probably didn't waste any time."

Hope soared through me. "Is there a chance they haven't started yet?"

"No."

Hope crashed on its ass. "How do you—"

"We *heard* him." Cass massaged her temples. "That's when I decided to directly disobey Kyp's order."

"How can I stop this without putting the rest of us in danger?" I got out of bed and dressed myself in loose, comfortable clothing. Clothes for a fight.

"You can't win. If you get involved, you're endangering all of us. But what kind of rebellion would we be if we allowed our leader to be taken and tortured without recourse?" Her voice shook with passion.

I brushed my rat's nest of hair into something resembling a ponytail. "I need to negotiate for our leader. Where are they?"

"Basement," she said. "There's a window behind the parking

area on the side of the house. Only Lavinia has the keys to the door."

I straightened my ponytail in the mirror. "I see you've cased the place."

Cass smiled weakly. "Long ago. Even with all this, you still have to look pretty for him, huh?"

"A hero makes an entrance."

"If you walked in there coated in swamp water, you'd still be making an entrance."

"Or maybe I'm distracting you." I grabbed her head and knocked it into the nearest wall. She slumped to the floor. "Sorry. I couldn't do it if you were expecting it. I owe you a healing."

It was bizarre how unafraid I was. Not at all like any comic book or movie heroine I enjoyed. I was about to challenge my greatest foe, and I couldn't muster up a single ounce of give a fuck. It disappeared the minute I woke up and realized Mom had really died and I had come back. Maybe I came back wrong, after all.

NINETEEN

HEALING

Two swift kicks made a hole in the window large enough to jump through. I landed in a crouch, the broken glass crunching beneath my sneakers. Here I was, in the belly of the beast. I picked up a particularly sharp shard of glass as I stood, just in case.

Lavinia turned toward me, eyes wide and mouth tight. I ignored her and turned my attention to Hector, whose hand was wrapped around Kyp's throat, pinning him to one of the support beams. His expression was vacant, but his hold loosened at the sight of me.

Whatever we'd seen before was gone. Lavinia had regained control.

Kyp gasped for breath, his eyes half-lidded. He blinked once, twice, as though he was trying to blink away a mirage, and then he seemed to wake up, alarm overtaking his expression as he realized what I'd done.

Love is sacrifice, baby. And it goes both ways.

"Liv, I think things just got interesting," Gretchen said.

Lavinia glared at her. "That is because you are an idiot. Jacklyn, how can I help you?"

I'd thought about killing or hurting to protect myself or someone I loved, but I'd never *wanted* to kill someone before. The idea of killing interdimensionals still made me squeamish. But seeing Lavinia's business-like manner in the midst of torturing her son cemented it for me. I wanted to be the one to take her out. Though that would make me a killer, I was strangely at peace with the thought.

"Sorry about the entrance." I ran my finger along the edge of the glass shard. "It could have been better, but I was pressed for time. Cass got in my way. That window would be the..." I pretended to think. "...second thing I've had to hit since I woke up from my little nap. Who wants to be the third?"

In any other situation, Kyp's glare would have been comical.

I expected Lavinia to be outraged. Instead, I received a patient smile. "Jacklyn, you don't belong in the middle of this. You were hurt and you can't possibly understand what occurred when you were gone." Her shoulders straightened, her chin jutting forward. "This punishment was earned, and it simply must be carried out. It's for the good of the Order that Kyp understands what he did was wrong."

"I was informed," I acknowledged. "It was a misunderstanding. He thought Hector planned to kill me."

"He was plotting a rebellion, Jacklyn." Lavinia stepped closer. "You love him. So do I, but as I've explained before, I must create *soldiers*. Though Kyp is meant to be a general, he can't fulfill his destiny until he understands how to be a good subordinate. Understands what it takes to follow rules."

"Nobody follows rules here." My eyes were on her so I wouldn't look at Kyp, see him in pain, lose my steady hand. "What Kyp says you do isn't following rules."

Something in my mind tugged sharply, but I shook it off. Was she trying to control me? It didn't matter, because whatever had just happened hadn't broken my single-minded focus.

Lavinia's eyes darkened, and I tensed. "Leave now, Jacklyn. This is none of your business. It is my job to maintain this army, and how I do it—"

"—is not your choice, actually. It's under Arvokian jurisdiction, isn't it?" I'd come untethered from my fear, from all conventions holding me back, from anything that ever told me I had to respect these people and fall in line. And it felt damn good. If death had done that to me, then I hadn't come back wrong. I'd come back better.

"Jacklyn, stop!" Kyp shouted, his voice hoarse. "Mother, she's mourning. She doesn't understand—" Hector kicked him in the ribs and Kyp curled in on himself.

"Stop that." I hurled the glass shard into Hector's leg with enough force to bury it there. A stream of curses erupted from him.

Lavinia shook her head, but remained mostly unmoved by his

pain. "What do you hope to accomplish?"

"I'm here to negotiate," I said. "What purpose does this serve? You gain nothing by doing this to him."

"I gain obedience!" she shouted.

Kyp's headshake was nearly imperceptible. His white t-shirt was caked with dried blood, but aside from some bruises, I didn't see any fresh wounds. He must have made a return trip very recently.

"You gain nothing," I said. "This is why he hates you."

Gretchen plunged the knife toward Kyp's chest. I was at Kyp's side in a second, relishing the energy the adrenaline shot had provided. Catching Gretchen's knife hand mid-plunge, I pulled strength from her until she dropped to her knees.

I glanced over my shoulder at Kyp, who looked like he didn't know if he should kiss me or kill me.

"Well done." Lavinia sneered. "But it is of no consequence. You will not interfere with the affairs of my Order."

I reached behind me, my hand open, and whispered so only Kyp could hear. "Stronger together, remember?" His hand clasped mine. His Aegis was far too weak, which only increased my anger.

"I'm not here to fool around, Lavinia. And I don't *want* to square off against you. But things need to change. We still have a few more surprises up our sleeves."

Her head tilted. "My dear, you have had *no* surprises. If you are alluding to the way you kept your relationship with Kyp a secret, I will inform you I would have needed to gouge my eyes out with kitchen implements, and I often wanted to, to not see the way you two latched on to each other."

I smiled, meeting her gaze. "I think I understand you. You want the power that comes with keeping the rifts open, but you also believe in the cause. You don't want the interdimensionals overrunning things either. You've been maintaining a balance, keeping the rifts open and the interdimensionals at bay. But war has casualties." My voice cracked. "People die. And they'll keep dying. You blame the numbers you have left on the previous rebellion. But you're wrong. The Order is dying because it wasn't meant to last forever. Like any other race, it had a finish line. And you've ignored that. But you can't afford to keep losing soldiers. And you can't afford to lose me. Think of what we'd be capable of if we worked together instead of against each other."

Kyp pulled his hand from mine. "What are you doing?" His head hung forward, his hair dropping in his eyes, his breath coming a little too quick. Bruises dotted the entire path from his right eye to his shoulder.

"Do you think I want to do this?" Lavinia asked. "That I enjoy this? He's my son. What I want is for him to follow me without question, as he should. I have tried again and again, and I have exhausted all other forms of discipline with him long ago. So, unfortunately, regrettably, I had to move forward with progressive disciplinary measures. Had this been a regular army, a soldier would have been removed from service for less than what he has done, but we Keys are so few, we must continue to attempt rehabilitation. By any means. You see, there is no choice."

"There is," I said. "We can keep everyone in line. Keep *Kyp* in line. You don't have to do this."

"No," Kyp growled.

"Enough! Your way hasn't done you any good." I didn't look back at him, lest I lose my nerve. "Stop torturing your people, and let's turn our attention toward the real problem. Your fellow Order soldiers aren't your enemies. If what my father believed, if what Kyp believes is true, you're making deals with the interdimensionals. That has to end. In return, you will have us, loyally standing at your side, patrolling the rifts and keeping them safe without the expenditure of human lives. If we close all but one, we can monitor that one and handle anything that comes through it. It can be done. You have such great talents at your disposal. But only if you stop this."

Lavinia's lips quirked. "I do enjoy your unique way of thinking, Jacklyn. I always have. But there is one thing you can provide to sweeten the deal."

I huffed a laugh. "Sweeten it more than allowing you to walk out of this room alive?"

"You don't have murder in your heart, darling." Lavinia barely blinked. "Do you want a child, Ms. Madison? I do."

"You have one. You've tortured him so much he can barely sit up. So, no. I will not be giving you this baby I've heard you're so desperate to obtain. I wouldn't trust you with a guinea pig. If you live to be one hundred and five, I will speak the Death Bringer

Ritual over your bed with not a single grandchild in sight." I shrugged. "But that's not what we're discussing."

"No, we're discussing the insane idea that you want me to lead with Kyp." She looked amused.

"What? No. He panicked for no reason during the battle. He's not cool under pressure."

Kyp's head shot up so fast, the air around him whistled. I ignored him.

"Do you see me panicking?"

Lavinia looked at me as if she could appraise my soul with a glance. "This isn't a war."

"Isn't it?" My eyes met hers in a challenge.

Shockingly, she balked first. "Was this entire drama a power play? Do you even care about him?"

"Of course I do. I love him. But he wants to seal all the rifts," I said. "All of them. It's dangerous, and frankly, I like my Aegis. No way am I gonna have this power and close the rifts just to die in a robbery at 7-11 or something even more pedestrian. There has to be a better way. I'm not willing to put us on the line for his silly ideals. He'll come around."

Lavinia eyed me for a long time. "And all I must do is stop this method of punishment and dissolve the deal with the interdimensionals, and you'll do—what? Keep him from rebelling? How do you intend to do that?"

"I'll talk to him. He's angry, but the issues between the two of you go way back," I said. "He's more likely to listen to me. We don't have the baggage between us you do. Still, he's not the one you need to please. I am. You should be glad I'm willing to work with you."

Lavinia watched me, likely rolling the deal around in her mind, looking for a way to double-cross me. I was under no delusions. I fully expected this to blow up in my face. I just hoped to buy us time.

Her eyes ticked to Gretchen, then Hector, then back to me.

"I'm going to let you in on a secret, Ms. Madison," she said. "It was your grandfather, Julian, who originally forged the deal we now have with the interdimensionals, the very deal your father so despised. It leads me to question who you are most like, your grandfather or your father?"

"Neither," I said. "I'm my own woman. And I'm done sitting back and watching you mishandle this Order."

Lavinia's jaw clenched, and for a moment, she was silent. When she finally spoke, she'd regained control of her temper. "Let's make a deal."

I smiled. "Let's."

"My rise to second-in-command was a hostile takeover, so I will ignore your insubordination, because I have been in your shoes before. I will give you one month to work with me to decide the future of this Order. If your plan succeeds, you will ascend to your rightful place at my side. If it fails, you'll take Kyp's full sentence on yourself."

My fists clenched at my sides. "My plan will work."

Lavinia smiled icily. "Good." She knelt before Kyp and cupped his chin in her hand. He met her gaze with defiance. "I am truly sorry, darling. Parenting requires discipline. I am determined to make you into a powerful leader."

Kyp's mouth worked, and I slapped my hand over it before he spat. I grimaced at the slimy wad of saliva likely mixed with blood on the palm of my hand.

"No," I scolded. His eyes blazed with anger.

"It appears you have your work cut out for you." Lavinia motioned at Hector, who struggled to his feet. Gretchen used the wall to pull herself upward.

"May you both be torn apart and eaten by Tralsks," Kyp growled.

I shrugged, wiping my hand on my sweatpants. "He'll come around."

"He better." She turned and headed up the stairs, and Gretchen and Hector limped closely behind. The door slammed behind them.

They left. They really did. I couldn't believe it.

I put up an auditory block before I cautiously knelt before Kyp. His eyes sparked with anger and his teeth were bared.

"Kyp."

"Get away from me." He soared to his feet, only to drop back against the beam. Grumbling in frustration, he tried again, but his legs gave out and he sank to his knees. I grabbed for his arm and he avoided me, latching onto my other arm and pulling me down onto my knees, my eyes looking straight into his terror-filled gaze. "Mother was a good person. Ray said she died and came back wrong. I've allowed the same to happen to you. No, dammit. No! There's gotta be a way to fix this. There's gotta... you came back wrong. That's what happened. You came back wrong." He looked away.

My blood ran cold. "Kyp, I'm fine. I'm still me." I attempted to wrap my arms around him but came up with air as he tipped over onto his side, losing his balance again.

"Dammit! Why won't anything work?" He punched the floor to punctuate each word.

"How many times did they..."

Confusion flashed in his eyes. He gritted his teeth. "Five. They were on the way to six when you burst in here and used me as a bargaining chip."

The anxiety I had been pushing down shot from my chest in something between a sob and a hitch. "No, please. Kyp, just..." I grabbed his hand in mine. "Just look."

His eyes narrowed, searching mine. Focusing seemed to bring him back to Earth, and he shuddered, as if trying to shake off his confusion. "I don't understand."

I took his hands and placed them on either side of my head. "Read me."

"Why?"

"So you don't need to doubt anymore." I met his eyes, nodding.

His eyes slid closed, and I allowed him to pull from my Aegis, allowed him to use that to roam my mind freely.

After a moment, a tear tracked down his face. He rested his forehead against mine. "I was terrified." He expelled the last word on a whistle of a breath. A shudder ran through him. He tried to fight it down, his voice coming out as a groan. "I can't. I c-c-can't do this. I don't want to. I'm not weak. I'm stronger than this. I have to be strong." It was a plea. "I'm always strong."

"You don't have to be." I threw my leg over his hips, settling myself onto his lap and wrapping my arms around him. "Not with me."

I died once. He watched his mother order his death eleven times. The loss of my mother made his mother so much more monstrous to me. I didn't want to imagine how I'd feel in his situation. He was stronger than he understood.

He buried his face into my shoulder, shaking, and my t-shirt grew damp, but for his sake, I would pretend it was the cold making him shake, sweat soaking my shirt.

The shaking slowed, and he murmured against my sleeve. "Can we go for a walk? Get out of here? I need to not be here."

"Of course. We'll go to our tree, if you want. But it's cold out there."

He snuggled in closer to me. "You're warm."

"Feeling better, I see." I laughed. "I could make a fire."

He offered me a weak smile. "That would be nice."

I helped him to his feet, and we made the slow trek up the stairs.

"Jacks," Cass whispered as we crested the stairs. "What are you doing? Kyp, are you okay?"

"We're fine. Come here." I waited until she was close. "Wake Gana. Lavinia and I have reached a ceasefire, but in case it can't be trusted, I'd like to create a sleep schedule, so nobody rests unguarded."

"You think she'll try something?" Cass' eyes widened. "What should I do about it?"

"Defend." Kyp twitched his fingers, then pressed them to her forehead. "That's an alarm. Anything happens, I'll be alerted."

"Hey, next time you put something in my head, warn me." It was a half-hearted argument. She wasn't about to fight with Kyp right now.

"I just want you to be safe."

Cass looked away. "I should have protected you."

Kyp stepped away from me and straightened to his full height. "I'm glad you didn't. I wouldn't have wanted you to get hurt."

"But I'm your Guardian."

"But you aren't expendable." He squeezed her shoulder.

She smiled at him. "Where were you two headed?"

"Going for a walk," I said. "I need air."

Cass eyed me for a moment before nodding. "Of course. Be safe."

"You, too."

She headed up the stairs, cut across the hall, and knocked on Gana's door.

I waited until Gana opened the door for her. Once she was inside her room, I led Kyp to the door.

His eyes were distant, and he barely participated as I bundled him up and led him through the backyard, out into the forest, and to our tree. When we arrived, he seemed more present. He stripped off his coat, hat, scarf, and gloves as I surrounded us in a circle of warming fire. I retrieved the blanket from the picnic basket we kept hidden in an intersection of branches. Once it was down, he slid along the trunk, breathing a sigh of relief when he rested on the ground.

"What?"

"I love you so much." He chuckled. "I wasn't aware that I was capable of feeling this way. Whenever I've come back after something like this, I've struggled. I think what you did, bringing me into your mind, I think it stabilized me. I don't understand how you do it. Everything has always been so..." He snatched me by a shirt sleeve and drew me to him, guiding me into a long, slow, breathtaking kiss. When I pulled back, his gaze was warm. "We need to decide how we're going to survive this mess I've created."

I sighed. "Back to business." I moved to sit back, but Kyp held me against his chest and pressed a kiss into my hair.

"I'm not sure Mother will be able to work with you for long. She will now see you as a potential challenger, even if she temporarily acknowledges your benefit as an ally. Things have gotten more complicated, more perilous." His voice cracked and he shook his head, fighting down another emotional outburst.

"I'm sorry. All those back-and-forth trips throw my emotions out of whack."

I nodded. "You don't have to excuse it."

He was quiet for a moment. "You were incredible."

"I had no idea what I was doing. I just wanted to convince her there was a better way. She may not even *want* that."

"You bought us time. Mother wants to be seen as a successful leader, but she believes the only path involves everyone's unwavering allegiance. Maybe she'll appreciate your idea and use it to emulate a successful *and* magnanimous leader. But it's far more likely she won't." He cleared his throat. "I endangered everyone with my rash overreaction."

"You did it to save me." I smiled up at him.

"Yes, I did."

"I'm sorry, Jacks," he said. "About Jaina. I—"

"I can't. Please. I can't."

"Okay. I get that."

My mind worked through what I could handle—the scene I'd walked in on in the basement and everything that had happened afterward. Just thinking about it made my blood run cold all over again. Lavinia had been so calm, even as she tortured her own son. "You said Liv came back wrong? The first time she died, she changed?"

"She used to be different. When I was younger. Better. Kinder. When I asked Ray why she changed, he said sometimes it happened—a Key died and came back with something... off. And every time it happened to her, it got worse. It may not be true. Ray may have just been trying to assure me it wasn't *me* that made her so cruel."

I thought for a moment. "Yeah, I don't buy it. You've died eleven times in terrible ways. If you aren't a complete asshole, either you were an actual angel when you were born, or what Lavinia became was already there."

"That may be. But it doesn't change anything." He leaned back so I could see him. As he spoke, desperation leaked into his tone and his eyes developed a manic glaze. "Jacklyn, I need to be sure you're safe. I need you to promise me you'll stop endangering yourself. We just need time. As soon as I can be sure she's out of my head, we'll go. We'll take Cass and Gana, and we'll run, and she'll never be able to hurt us again, never again. I—"

I kissed him as if it could heal his wounds, take away his pain, make him whole again. And all the while, my heart clenched. Because the idea of waiting for Kyp to be able to make a clean break was agonizing. Every minute I was here was another minute that threatened Gana's life. And I couldn't do it. I owed it to Mom to keep the two of us safe.

"Promise," he whispered against my lips.

"Okay, okay. I promise." If I left him here, he would hate me.

"I don't want you to say it because you pity me. Or to shut me up. I'm serious. I know how hard it is for you to listen to me when I'm telling you to do something that will keep you safe."

"Funny."

"I'm only partially joking. You need to lie low from now on. No matter what it means for me."

The idea made my heart stutter. "Kyp... whatever happened to stronger together?"

"Whatever happened to not arguing?"

I grinned. "Every superhero needs a catchphrase."

"We can't be stronger together if we don't survive. Please, Jacklyn. I can't lose you." His fingers slid up my arm, over my neck to my cheek, and he pulled me in for another kiss.

His lips met mine, tenderly, slowly, and the spark of his love for me, like a warm glow, passed through the kiss. If emotions made his Aegis stronger, then he was acting in overdrive, feeling so much it transferred to me. The kiss deepened, the sweep of his tongue against mine showing me more: his fear for my safety, his anger at our situation, his determination to keep us together, to keep us safe. I pulled back slightly, my eyes meeting his, and found every bit of what I felt reflected in his eyes. My chest tightened, my heart hurting for him and loving him, and I wished I could save him, bring him what he so desperately needed. Peace, for once.

I kissed him again, and using the tree for support, straddled his hips. His breath hitched a little, and his hands clamped down on my waist, held me against him. I pressed my lips to the discoloration beside his eye, healing moving through the connection, making the bruise fade beneath my lips. I moved down his cheek, to the stubble along his jaw, over his neck, never only healing the bruise, but feeding him energy, bringing him back to me. I allowed myself to be a little more adventurous, tasting his skin, salty with sweat. His body came to life beneath mine as I moved to his collarbone, sucking and nipping from there to his shoulder.

His hands slid under my shirt, and I flinched at the coldness of his fingertips. All went silent except for the crackling fire around us. I increased its heat, another attempt to return him to his usual self, to erase the scars.

"Sorry," he whispered into the crook of my neck, his nose brushing a sensitive spot, eliciting a gasp from me. "I'm a mess."

"I get it. I was just dead." I tried to keep my voice steady as he continued exploring. "Well, not as often as you, so maybe I don't *get* it, but I understand it."

I wasn't sure he heard me. "We should probably... slow" —his lips moved to my ear— "down." He nipped at my earlobe.

I pulled back reluctantly. The look of desire in his eyes made my throat sandpaper, but that desire was mingled with an open well of adoration, something he'd never truly expressed before.

I was going to leave him behind.

The realization pushed me over the edge of a line I had already considered crossing. I raised an eyebrow, a smirk crossing my face. "You want to stop?"

Kyp mirrored my expression. "I don't *want* to stop, but—"

I yanked my t-shirt off and whipped it somewhere off to the right. He stared down at my black lacy bra.

"You were saying?" I asked.

His eyes flicked up to mine, then back to my breasts. "Um, having trouble remembering at the moment."

"Ha. You don't forget anything."

"I won't forget this." His lips crashed against mine, a messy kiss that was all lips and teeth and tongue and ended in him catching my lower lip between his teeth.

I could still smell the iron tang of blood on his skin. The bad things were not as far away as we'd like.

I reached for his sweater, yanking it up over his head, and when it joined my t-shirt wherever it landed, I pressed my hand to his heart and reveled in the way it beat beneath my fingertips. "You're warm again."

He did the same. "You too," he whispered. He leaned forward to kiss me again.

And for that moment, at least, we were healed.

TWENTY

A knock on the door shocked me out of sleep. It had been a long night. When Kyp and I had returned to the estate, we were immediately drafted into our night watch shifts. Sleep hadn't come easily, even when we were actually trying to fall asleep. Which, admittedly, we did less often than we should have. At this point it was nearing evening, but neither of us had wanted to bother leaving the room, even to eat.

Neither of us could stomach food, anyway.

The sound of a chair sliding over the carpeting heralded the jiggle of the doorknob. I allowed my eyes to crack open, just enough to watch the back of Kyp's head as he peeked out the door.

"Good afternoon, darling."

My blood ran cold. For a moment, as I'd lay in Kyp's arms, I'd been able to sleep at peace, to forget the horrors of the night before. Her voice made it come flooding back. My mom was dead, Kyp had been tortured, and the first chance I got I would have to leave him to his torturer, if I had any chance of getting Gana to safety.

"Mother," Kyp drawled. "What a wonderful surprise."

She sighed. "May I come in?"

"Do I have a choice?" he asked. "Or will you just slit my throat and bring me back if I say no?"

Her tone sharpened. "Kyp. It's not like that."

"Is there a reason you're here?"

"Yes." She sighed. "I simply wanted to see how you were faring after yesterday."

That she had been the one to harm him to begin with made the caring tone she used infuriating.

"Awful. Your punishment has succeeded. I'll never do it again. Is that what you want to hear?"

I nearly groaned. Wasn't he supposed to be lying low?

"Kyp." She sounded so sincere that it stabbed at something deep inside. All at once, I understood why Kyp had been so insistent when I'd asked him if he was sure about Lavinia. Because it was easy to fall into her good side, just to be backhanded by the dark truth.

"Better. Not perfect, but better."

"That is a start. Jacklyn, I suppose you helped with this?"

I jolted up in the bed, yanking the sheet up around me. "I... Yes."

I barely made out her silhouette around Kyp, who moved to block her as she tried to look around him.

There was laughter in her tone when she spoke again. "Well, that wasn't the solution I had imagined for Kyp's sour mood, but it seems to have helped."

My cheeks reddened.

"Unfortunately, rest time is over. We need you both in the sitting room for a meeting in twenty minutes. And Jacklyn? Do get dressed before you grace us with your presence."

I yanked the sheet around me even tighter, even as the door slammed shut.

Kyp scratched the back of his neck as he turned toward me. "Sorry. I should have just let her knock, but I didn't want to wake you."

"It's fine," I said, but my voice was too quiet. In the harsh light of day, I realized I'd made a mistake. As great as my night with Kyp had been, I shouldn't have left Gana alone. Not after what happened to Mom.

"Hey." Kyp sat on the edge of the bed and tilted my chin towards him, pressing a gentle kiss to my lips. "We'll be okay."

I wanted so badly for that to be true.

Lavinia barely waited for the remaining members of the Order to gather in the sitting room before calling the meeting to order.

"Yesterday was an extremely difficult day. We have lost one of our own. And while I truly wish there was time for us to mourn, our duty does not give us that luxury. There are clearly differences among us, but we all agree we cannot allow interdimensionals to harm humans. A Gorvhan nest was discovered behind the bleachers of Bennett High. The school janitor found it and took the eggs to the science lab."

Ross swore.

"One of our contacts is an employee of the school. He recognized the eggs and was intelligent enough to reach out to us. Cass was manning the phones when the call came in. We must send a team, immediately. Our interested party says the Gorvhans are attempting to claw their way into the school to get their babies."

I looked to Cass, who nodded. The intel was legit.

"Good thing it's a Sunday," Ross said, his voice raw. "Nobody will be at the school."

"Let's hope nobody driving by has spotted it," Cass said. "That's a huge exposure risk."

"Agreed," Lavinia said. "As per protocol, I must visit with the Arvokian Council to report the tragic loss of Jaina Madison. She was one of the best of us, protecting a Key and a Guardian for years without the benefit of the rest of the Order. We will sorely miss her."

Gana sniffled. I laid my head on her shoulder. Kyp wrapped his arms around both of us, drawing us close.

"I must also report the Key deaths of Kylie and Jacklyn."

I opened my mouth to ask if she would report the many deaths and rebirths Kyp had suffered. Kyp may have been reading my mind. He may have just known me that well. He squeezed my arm before I spoke, his eyes wide with rebuke.

Right. I was supposed to lie low.

"Gretchen and Hector will accompany me. Kylie, you will take the lead on the mission. Go with Ross, Kyp, and Cassandra. Destroy the Gorvhans, the eggs, and make sure you find any witnesses and wipe them."

"But we just got back from a slaughter," Ross whined. I wanted to punch him in the face.

"Emergencies happen when they happen," Lavinia replied. "Not on your schedule. Any other questions?"

"There are three Keys and one Guardian on this mission. Why aren't Jacklyn and Gana coming?" Kylie asked.

"Jacklyn and Gana are mourning their mother!" Lavinia smacked her hands down hard on the table in front of her. I flinched. "Jacklyn and I have a sort of deal worked out. I am attempting her formation method for this fight." She locked eyes with me. "Perhaps there is something to this that we do not see. I wish to work with her to move toward a more equitable future for the Order."

"That's ridiculous," Kylie said with a sneer.

"That's enough!" Her eyes burned, and Kylie shrank in her seat. When she turned her attention to me, her eyes softened. "Jacklyn, Gana, get some rest. Once you have rested, I would like you to draw up the plan we discussed yesterday."

"Yes, ma'am." Surprise leaked into my tone. I glanced at Kyp, who looked perplexed.

"Good." She clapped her hands. "Make your preparations for

battle quickly, people. We have lives to save." She turned on her heel and left the room, Hector and Gretchen following closely behind her.

Kylie headed for the door after. Ross followed but stopped to cast a long look back at us. Probably wondering what we were sticking around for.

I shot him the finger. His eyes narrowed, and he left.

Once they were clear, I glanced at Kyp. "What?"

"She does this," Cass said. "She's feeling guilty, so she's overcompensating."

"It won't last long," Kyp added.

"Then I guess we should take advantage of it while we can," Gana said. "Jacks, let's not bother resting. Let's think up a great plan for this shithole."

This was why I loved her so much.

"Look at me. I'm an army wife, waiting for her husband to come back from battle," I said and immediately regretted it.

"You aren't far off, are you?" Kyp winked. He zipped up the leather jacket he wore to conceal the weapons strapped to his chest and hips.

I handed him his supply pack.

"That's not my supply pack. It's yours." He reached under the bed and pulled out his actual bag.

"My supply..." I opened the bag. There was money stacked inside. Two fake passports for me and Gana. A list of trustworthy contacts that would help us. Several other forms of forged identification for the both of us.

"I would be able to hear how much you want to run even if I wasn't connected to you." He knelt in front of me. He stared up at me, eyes glistening with tears. "Through the mind link? I can taste it."

"Kyp, I—"

"You don't have to explain." His voice was thick. "When I brought you here, I wanted to protect you. But I think protecting you meant staying the hell away from you in the first place."

"You saved me. You showed me who I could be." I didn't sound much better. My eyes ached from the tears I'd shed in the last two days.

"I got Jaina killed. And if I'm not careful, I'll get you and Gana killed, too." He cleared his throat. "I should have found another way to protect you. I was selfish. But I won't be now." He leaned up, cupping my face in his hands. "It's up to you. If you need to go, I'll understand. I won't blame you. I'll honestly be relieved. I want you to be safe. I want you to take Gana somewhere and start a new life. You've learned to hide your Aegis. It will be okay. I contacted a friend of mine. Zane. She's a tech whiz. She got me the paperwork and the money a while ago. There were passports and stuff for me, Cass, and Jaina, too, but..."

"I don't want to leave you." My heart ached, tears streaming down my face, blurring my vision. "I want us to be together. Isn't there a way we can run together?"

He shook his head, the movement jerky. "She'll let you go. You're more trouble than you're worth. I'm... for whatever reason, she'll see me leaving as an act of war. She'll chase you down." He pressed his forehead to mine. "Listen, I operate on the assumption that no matter how far we are from each other, it's still you and me. We're still a team. Unless you inform me otherwise."

"Sound logic." I smiled. Despite everything, he still made me smile. Probably always would.

"As soon as we settle things, I'll find you, but until then..." His fingers smoothed along my cheeks, wiping at the tracks of tears.

"So this is goodbye?" I shuddered.

"Hey, don't do that." He kissed me sweetly, his nose brushing mine. "This isn't goodbye. We'll say *see you soon* and we'll mean that, right?"

"Right," I choked out.

He firmly pressed his fingertips to my forehead. "That is a gift. I'm not sure if you'll need it, but if the right trigger occurs, it will open. I can't begin to explain what's in it. There isn't enough time. But you'll know it when you see it."

I laughed. "I don't understand what you're talking about." More tears.

Kyp leaned back, an odd look of disbelief on his face. "You really do love me, don't you?"

"Is that still a question?"

"I still can't believe it." He kissed me again, this time slow and sweet and filled with emotion. We kissed like it would be the last time, in case it was, and it was proof Kyp's confidence was fabricated.

He pulled back from me and wiped a hand over his face. "I love you." Another kiss, this one a quick tap. "I love you."

"I love you, too."

He threw the strap of his supply bag over his shoulder. "I *will* see you. Soon, right?" He stopped with his hand on the doorknob, still facing me.

I was not ready, but I mustered as much confidence as I could. "Careful, okay? I love you. I'll see you soon."

He nodded firmly, as if trying to shake off any notion of staying.

And then he left me to my decision.

TWENTY ONE

"Are you kidding?" Gana asked once the house was empty, and I'd filled her in on my plans.

"What do you mean? You've been itching to get out of here from the beginning!"

"Well, yeah, but you weren't. Not really. You said you were, but you've been totally invested since day two." She shrugged, her gaze dropping to her socked feet. "Besides, Mom wanted us here."

"Mom is..." I couldn't say it. Not yet. "She can't make that decision for us anymore. And I'm gonna choose your safety. Every time."

"What about Kyp?"

There it was. The deep ache that had set in when we'd said goodbye throbbed. "He'll catch up once he and Cass are sure he won't lead any trouble to us."

Gana made a face. Then she threw her arms around me and

buried her face in the crook of my neck. "Are you sure, Jacks?" Her words came out slightly muffled, and I grinned.

I pulled back, putting my hands on her shoulders and locking eyes with hers. Both of our eyes were just like our mom's. We were night and day, in so many ways. But Mom's eyes linked us. That and love. So much love.

"I'm sure." I kissed her cheek. "Go. Get packed. But pack light. We've got a hike ahead of us."

She lingered for another moment before rushing off to her room with a skip in her step.

I changed into clothing better suited for an hour-long hike through the forest. I stuffed a couple of changes of clothes into a backpack. I reviewed the map Kyp had left me in the case he'd packed.

I sat on my bed and picked up the teddy bear I kept on my bedside table, the one dressed up as Robin. I buried my face in its soft fur and fought the tears that wanted to shed.

There was no space to pack any of my things. All my geeky fandom stuff would have to stay there.

It turned out no magic switch flipped at the age of eighteen where you left childish things behind.

It was ridiculous. I was upset, seriously upset, about not having space to pack my toys. For so many years, those things had been the only way I'd escaped the heavy responsibility I'd faced at home caring for Gana. A responsibility I was about to willingly take on again.

I dropped the stuffed bear and instead wrapped my embattled pink ceramic bear in a towel and zipped the backpack. There was no way I was leaving that behind.

A bang echoed off the wall on the far side of my room, the one that connected my room to Gana's. I tensed.

"Hi there, baby girl. Where do you think you're going?"

Gretchen. Shit. What was she doing back so early?

I leapt from my bed and raced for Gana's room.

"Hey," Gana squeaked. "Um... I'm just..."

She had nothing. There was no excuse. We were caught red-handed.

"I'm curious." Gretchen strutted towards Gana, playing with something in her hands. I couldn't see what it was from my position. "How did you think this would go?"

Gana watched her hands with wide eyes.

Gretchen lunged forward, but I caught her arms and wrenched them behind her. Gana shot off the bed but looked at me.

"Get to my room," I said. "Barricade yourself in."

She didn't move.

Gretchen wriggled free, nailing me hard in the ribs with her elbow. It was then, as she was whirling toward me, I noticed the knife in her hand. The blade was jagged and worn, but sharp.

Gretchen made another lunge, this time in my direction, but I darted to the side, kicking her in the stomach and bringing my elbow down hard on her knife hand. The knife hit the floor with a thump, and I wrapped my fingers in her bouncy white-blonde ringlets, yanking her by her hair away from the weapon.

I tossed Gretchen aside and rolled, grabbing the knife on the way back to my feet.

She watched me with a wide, feral grin, inching her way toward Gana, who wouldn't leave my side, but was reluctant to join the fight.

"Do you remember what I told you when you first came here?" Gretchen asked, hands landing on her hips. "Back when you were nothing but a little girl with a big mouth and not a damn thing to back it up?"

"You told me to focus," I said. "I'm focused now." I punched her in the jaw, the way I had when we'd first met. But she didn't fall to the floor. Not like she had that day.

I took her second of distraction to check on Gana. She was staring at her hands near the doorway, flexing them in confusion.

Gretchen ducked down, running at me and tackling me. I reacted. I should have reacted sooner. Something was wrong. I was... slow. My head smacked into the bedframe, hard enough to make me see stars.

"We've been nullified," Gana cried. "Jacks! The missing Ritual!"

The panic that had been building in my chest the moment I heard Gretchen spiked. Gretchen took advantage of the way my vision was swimming, jumping to her feet and running after Gana, who took off toward the stairs at the end of the hall. I hooked Gretchen's ankle with mine, sending her stumbling on the way out of the room, but it wasn't enough to slow her down.

I rolled to my feet, taking off after them just in time to watch Gretchen grab hold of Gana around her waist. Gana kicked and screamed and twisted, but without her Aegis, Gana didn't have her main line of defense. Put on the same level, Gretchen, with her arms corded in lean muscle and her tall frame, outweighed her. Gretchen swung her around, so they were both facing me as I caught up with them.

Gretchen sighed. "Oh, honey. It would be easier for everyone if you quit."

"Never," I growled. "Get the hell away from my sister."

"But Jacklyn." She ran a hand down Gana's cheek, and she glared in response. "She's so young and small and malleable." Gana snapped her teeth when her fingers got close, chomping down hard enough on the offending digits to draw blood. Gretchen hissed in pain. "Oh-oh-oh, and fierce. Who knows who she would grow up to be without you here to twist her pretty little head? She could be the best of us."

"She already is." I inched forward. I had to get Gana away from Gretchen. She was dangerous and sadistic, and terror shook my limbs as I watched her manhandle Gana.

"It's really too bad we'll never find out."

It happened so quickly, I barely saw Gretchen move. She just tossed Gana over her shoulder, like she was a weightless doll. Over her shoulder, which was leaned up against the third-floor balcony.

I screamed and rushed forward, throwing myself towards the ledge, desperate to catch her, but my fingers came up empty.

For the second time in my life, I wasn't fast enough.

Gana's scream echoed in my ears. Before I could see how badly she'd landed, Gretchen crashed into my side, throwing me away from the overlook and any chance I had of saving Gana.

I turned and sliced the blade I'd taken across her cheek, drawing blood. Her hand came up to her face, and she whirled on me, wild-eyed. She grabbed for me, but I narrowly avoided her, hopping out of her way before she could take me down again.

I may not have been as quick on my feet as usual, or as strong, but I still had moves. I was trained for this. Hell, I was partially trained *by Gretchen* for this.

I jumped forward again, kicking at her lower leg as a distraction as I slashed at her arm. Her other arm careened my way.

Pain exploded through my jaw. Blood pooled in my mouth. Darkness, then the floor flew up at my face.

I threw my hands out to catch myself, the knife dropping to the floor, carpet fibers tearing at my palms. I had to get the knife back. I reached forward. A weight landed on my back and held me still. I shouted, frustration tearing from my throat. Forceful hands flipped me over and Gretchen's weight pinned my arms to my sides. She leaned toward me.

I needed to get to Gana and help her. She had to be okay.

She had to be okay.

"You wanna know something kind of funny?" She giggled.

"I could have healed Jaina if I'd wanted. I got to her just in time. But I was so sick of her sniveling, her attempts to protect you. Before she left, she was a damn good Guardian. But having you kids made her soft. And softness and weakness don't have a place in the Order. She had to die."

She had to die.

A scream tore from my throat and I bucked under her, getting her off-balance just enough to push her off and crash her head into the wall. I shoved her away. I needed to get distance between us before I'd be able to regain any leverage.

I scrambled to my feet, but before I could approach Gretchen or run past her to get to Gana, I discovered I didn't have to.

Gana climbed over the railing she'd flown over earlier. With a primal scream, she propelled herself into a clumsy roll, almost a flop. I didn't even notice her grab the knife until she slammed it into Gretchen's throat.

Blood spurted from the wound, splashing onto Gana, mingling with the blood that dripped from her own nose. She twisted the knife, leaning in, taking in Gretchen's face as she gasped, struggling for air, her face whitening.

"I told you that night I'd kill you. I wasn't playing."

She held the knife in place as Gretchen's eyes went wide and then glazed over, empty. With the knife still in place, Gretchen couldn't heal, and the wound was bad enough she wouldn't have had a lot of time to manage it, anyway.

Once it was clear Gretchen was dead and wouldn't heal, Gana

let out a ragged breath and yanked the knife free.

"Holy shit!" I shouted, unable to get out any other words.

"I know," Gana said, her voice wobbly, tears mingling with the blood on her cheeks. "I know. You probably didn't want me to kill her, but she was going to kill you. I had to—"

I interrupted her, pulling her into my arms. "You're okay. You're okay."

She grabbed on to me, one of her hands grasping the back of my shirt, while the other hung loosely at her side. "I almost wasn't. I grabbed the lower-level balcony and once I got my feet in place, I could climb back, but I think I dislocated my shoulder."

"You spider monkey! I'll grab our stuff. Hopefully Gretchen just went rogue."

"Gretchen left with Hector and Liv." Gana followed me. "Where else would they be?"

She was right. I didn't want her to be right. I scooped up the backpack I'd packed and grabbed the two daggers left for me by my father. I had practiced with them often and was accustomed to wielding them. Then I retrieved Gana's bag.

"We have to get out of here." I handed Gana an axe from my supply bag. "And we have to do it fast. If we can get to the forest, we'll be okay. Once we're free and clear, Kyp left me the name of a doctor I can go to, no questions asked. We'll patch up your arm."

"Sounds like a plan," Gana said, her brows drawn together. "We'll have to be careful."

I led the way, Gana following closely behind. We crept along the hall and down the stairs, eyes everywhere, vigilant against ambush. When we arrived in the foyer, I froze. This wasn't smart. Too many possible doorways, too many places for people to hide.

I turned to her, a warning on my lips, when I spotted the glint of a blade.

"Gana!"

Her name had barely left my lips before a thin red line formed along Gana's neck and the axe she carried clattered against the hardwood floor.

Gana clutched at her wound as if in the absurd hope of keeping the blood in.

My mouth moved in a soundless whisper of denial, my head shaking, my arms gripping my stomach, a vain attempt at comfort I would never receive. I stepped back, drawing the daggers from my belt loops, but I barely stilled my shaking fingers enough to grasp them.

Hector had been hidden just inside the coat closet. He stepped around Gana like she was nothing, wiping the razor blade on his shirt carelessly.

Hector. I had felt bad for Hector. I hated that Lavinia had such complete control of him that he seemed tortured. But everyone had a line they wouldn't cross. Kyp had told me as much. And Hector's line wasn't killing fifteen-year-old girls.

Hector's line wasn't killing my sister.

Desperation mixed with fury in my blood.

I hurled my bag at Hector's face with all my strength and leapt at him as he caught it. I jammed my dagger between his ribs, right where his heart should be. I yanked it back out, and it was just like that first night, pulling the rebar free from the Gorvhan. The same squelching sound. Except there was horror on this monster's face when the bag toppled to the floor. I stabbed him again with a cry, leaning all my weight into the motion, slamming him into the wall. His blood coated my knife hand. I pulled my dagger free one last time and let him fall.

I stepped over him like he was nothing and rushed to Gana's side.

My legs gave out. Pain shot up my thighs as my knees hit the floor with a loud thump. My chest tightened, and I fought for air.

I killed.

I killed a man.

A real person, not a monster.

A monster, not a man. Not all monsters are interdimensionals.

He hurt Gana.

I killed someone who deserved it.

Gana's skin was paper-white, fountains of crimson jetting from the gash across her neck, but somehow, her eyes still held life.

I knew it wouldn't work, but I still tried to fire up my Aegis. Nothing happened. Of course nothing happened. I tried again anyway, channeling everything I could into the heal. Once again, I got nothing. No energy. No Aegis. Nothing. Just me, with my hands pressed over a bleeding open wound, doing absolutely fuck all to close it.

A sob bubbled up in my throat. "No. No. No."

My brain grasped to make sense of it, but failed. This was a nightmare. I needed to shake myself awake in my bedroom in the city, whining about school. None of this, not even Kyp, would have ever happened. I was okay with that; I would give up every moment of being a superhero, every minute of falling in love, if it meant Mom and Gana would stay with me.

I pulled Gana into my arms. I wanted to break down, but Gana wasn't one for big emotions. She was about function. So I asked her a function-related question.

"What can I do for you?" I sobbed. "How can I help?"

She shook, and her blood soaked into the fabric of my jeans, creeping up my thighs. She tried to speak, but only a strange whistling noise came out. Instead, frustrated, she dipped her pointer finger into the fresh blood pooling on the hardwood floor, found a clean space, and drew out a word in her own blood, letter by letter.

She looked back up at me when she finished.

"I'll do my best. I'm so sorry." I held her close, my heart aching. She was so much stronger than me in all the ways that counted, a dynamo, steely and resolved. If this was the one thing she wanted from me, I would do everything in my power to accomplish it.

She clung to me in return, her fingers cutting into my shoulders, her nails nearly drawing blood. When she relaxed against me, I knew it was over. I lowered her to the floor, pressed a kiss to her forehead, and tried not to remember all the times I'd tucked her into bed and kissed her goodnight. Her eyes stared up at me, but they were empty, and that was so much like a knife buried deep in my gut. I rushed to slide the lids down, to cover that emptiness.

Staring down at my sister's body, I had to remind myself there was proof of an afterlife, that Cass' Aegis was proof Gana would be okay.

But my family was dead.

Kyp was right. Gana hadn't wanted to be a Guardian, but her very nature made her the best. I asked her if there was anything I could do for her, and her answer was scribbled sloppily on the floor.

L-I-V-E

Everything in me rebelled. I wanted to curl up in a ball beside her and go to sleep and stop fighting. Just stop. Stop. And never fight again.

Instead, I gathered my daggers and rose with newfound determination, my heart hardened, my resolve fortified, a righteous fury filling my soul. I looked straight ahead to the doorway, ready to destroy.

"My darling." Lavinia leaned against the wall, as though bored, arms crossed over her chest, mouth a twisted smile. "You're quite the mess. Is everything all right?"

I rushed her, slamming a dagger into her shoulder before she even flinched. With a wave of her hand, she shoved me through the kitchen doorway. My back collided with the counter. Pain shot up my spine. Glasses tumbled to the floor around me, shattering. My other dagger flew from my hand and straight into Liv's and she removed the one from the wound in her shoulder.

She still had her Aegis.

I moved to stand, but she knocked me back with invisible force. I wasn't getting up until she lost concentration.

"Thirteen years. *Thirteen years* since Raymond staged his little coup. And never, not once, did Kyp request an investigation by the Arvokian Council. Not once in thirteen years, Jacklyn." Lavinia laughed. "Did you really think you could come here and ruin everything?" She stepped toward me slowly, methodically. "You, Jacklyn Madison, are exactly what I thought you were. Like your father, you are a negative influence on my son, and as your father did, you will pay for that with your life."

How did she find out? Had Cxarana told?

I tried to remember what made me who I was, what made me ballsy, what made me strong, but it trickled through my fingers like sand.

I spotted Gana's sign on the floor.

LIVE.

Live, Jacklyn, live.

My hand wrapped around the sharpest piece of glass beside me. "And what did my sister do to deserve being murdered? What will Kyp do when he sees what you've done, what you wish to do?" I needed to keep her talking.

"If he wanted to harm me, child, he would have done it by now. He's had so much time, and he's never pulled the trigger. Do you think he ever will? Perhaps the only reason he recruited you to go up against me was because he realized he couldn't do it. He knows who deserves respect, but he's still young and young people rebel. For him, in his position of responsibility, at his level of intelligence, it is only natural." She advanced. "There comes a time when a mother must take away her child's toys to teach him a lesson." Another laugh. "He believed he was fooling me, but I suspected something the moment you arrived. He lost sight of how similar we are."

I allowed myself a bitter laugh. "Kyp is nothing like you."

"Neither of us forget. Just as Raymond's betrayal still stings, the way it always did, the way Kyp felt about you when you were children never changed as he got older. The two of you tore a car to bits when we tried to separate you the first time. Ripped it apart piece by piece when your Aegis mixed with his. I wasn't stupid enough to interfere again without a plan. So, I planned, as a leader should. A contingency for every contingency. Like a game of chess. I outmaneuvered him until he ran out of pieces. Kylie and Ross have orders to return with only Kyp alive. You will die." She leaned in until her face was inches from mine. "Once Kyp is out of toys to play with, he'll either learn how to fall in line... or I'll get more creative with my punishments."

This wasn't even about me. Lavinia was doing all of this because of my influence on Kyp. This was a game, and if Lavinia designed the game, Kyp was Player One, and I was little more than the avatar.

I reared my head back and smashed it into hers. Something in her nose made a satisfying crunching noise, and her hold lifted. I slashed up with the glass, going for her throat, but she dove forward, and I got her face instead. My knee rammed into her chin, and she sprawled out on her ass, my dagger sliding from her hands. I stomped my foot down on it, kicked it away, and hoped that eliminated the chances of her regaining access to it.

I launched myself to my feet. "You think taking everything away from Kyp will make him a good little soldier?"

For a moment, she looked vulnerable. Then she opened her mouth. "All I want is my Aegis, my attentive son, and my leadership. Anything else is superfluous. I can create a new Order. If I must remove all other obstacles to get what I want, then so be it."

I lunged forward and wrapped my hands around her neck. Her veins strained beneath my fingertips as I squeezed, her pulse a beat against them that made me clutch tighter. I had to do this fast. She gasped for breath. The floor quaked beneath my feet. I nearly stumbled. There was a *clack-clack-clack* before pain burst in the back of my head.

I woke beside hunks of a glass vase, seconds after a drop I didn't remember. Purple edged my vision. I adjusted in time to watch Lavinia swing a knife down at me.

It seemed she recovered that dagger, after all.

I rolled out of the way, kicking her hard in the stomach. The floor swerved below me, and I tried to gain purchase, to get to my feet and to gain distance and time to plan. Snatching the other dagger, I fought to rise. The world tilted dangerously sideways, and I tumbled to the floor again, slipping in Gana's blood.

A sob escaped my throat, and I scrambled back up to my hands and knees, but a sharp, burning pain shot through my leg. A glance over my shoulder revealed my other dagger sticking out of my calf. I bit back a scream. My pain sensors were not as sensitive as they usually were, and that was the only upside to Lavinia nullifying my Aegis.

Lavinia tugged the dagger back out.

Live! Live! Live!

I found my way back to my feet, pushing past the pain in my leg. A wave of dizziness crashed over me. I refused to let it slow me down. Instead, I let the tilt carry my momentum.

Somehow, I made it to the back door.

I threw it open and a wall of cold hit me, bringing memories of evenings with Kyp flashing through my mind. I limped through the doorway. Freedom was our tree, our spot. If I made it to the woods, I could hide and find a way to protect myself.

A force hit me in the side and sent me sailing into a bush, sharpness tearing along my arms and poking the back of my neck. I threw Lavinia off me, pulling my dagger, only to watch it sail from my hands and into the pool. I got up to go after it and was thrown again, Lavinia's powers smashing me into the brick wall of the house face-first.

Blood erupted from my nose. My eyes ached.

Keep fighting. Live. Live.

I threw an elbow back and connected with her chest. She grabbed me by my hair and cracked my head into the brick.

Once.

Stars erupted behind my eyes.

Twice.

My legs gave out on me.

Three times.

My body colliding with the pavement woke me up.

Live. You promised.

I wrapped my legs around Lavinia's feet and yanked them out from under her. She tumbled to the floor and her shout pinballed around my head. Her arm twisted beneath her at an odd angle, probably broken, but I would not stick around to find out. I ran, tripping on my way toward the forest.

I had to get away. I had to live.

I tried to catalog my wounds and failed. Couldn't remember. My world was tilted. Multi-colored bursts, like bruises, rippled through my vision.

My legs were yanked out from under me and I hit the ground, the air punching out of my lungs. I turned onto my back and she held me still with her mind.

I couldn't get up again. It hurt so badly.

"Don't worry, darling." She leaned forward and looked me in

the eye. "He'll be hurt for a while. But he'll move on."

My mind betrayed me, offering images of how Kyp would fare if he returned home to find our bodies scattered around his home.

Why make Kyp come home to this? Because it is brutal and horrible. Because he will never step out of line again with this memory burned into his brain.

"He won't forget me," I said. "Or what you did. He'll never forget."

Lavinia tugged a vial of Dreviara from her belt, prepping the Death Bringer Ritual. She drew a circle around my body with herbs, but my eyes remained focused on the space on her belt beside the vial of Dreviara, where my dagger swayed with every movement.

A sound, a crackle of brush, caught my attention, but somehow escaped Lavinia's notice. Behind her, someone crept toward the house. I coughed and moaned, hoping to get his attention, but he was already heading inside.

Something was familiar about his gait, about his profile in the dark, and it was as if a box opened in my mind. A box Kyp put there. My gift.

It started with the glimmer of a smile. A voice, deep and musical. An Irish brogue. Dashing through the woods, laughing. Being a generally bad influence, with me on one hip and Kyp on the other. Dancing through the house with me, Mom, and Kyp as Lavinia glared on. Yelling on a megaphone to wake the adults up for morning exercises, blasting music through the house at five in the morning. Dark curly hair, sparkling, engaging green eyes, a rounded face with a mischievous grin.

Daddy.

In a blink, I remembered it all. My time in the estate, and mostly, him. My father. I remembered him saying goodbye to me as the salt water stung my eyes, the fishy smell of the beachfront filling my nose. I sat on a rotted old bench on the beach and fiddled with a seashell as my father told us he wouldn't be coming back for a while, and Kyp cried on his shoulder and I pretended not to hear. I remembered how much my father loved me and how much Kyp loved me, and I remembered clinging to Kyp, joining hands because we were stronger together, and using our powers to tear a car apart in a show of strength meant to keep our mothers from separating us. A show of strength that only ensured they would fear us remaining together.

My father had loved me. He hadn't abandoned me, he had protected me, done his best to keep me safe from a world he feared. All the years I believed he didn't care...

My heart swelled with the feeling, my throat tightening as I thought of Kyp, the special little boy who would have done anything to keep me with him, who clung to me like I was a shelter in the storm, and it was almost too much to take.

And then another memory arrived. One that wasn't mine.

"But I found you!" I saw through Kyp's eyes as he looked upon an older, weary version of my father. "I worked my ass off, risked everything!"

"Because you're foolish, boy, and you always will be." Time had dulled the accent my father had in my own memories. "You could have led her right to me. If that wasn't what you intended, you shoulda thought cleaner."

"Your daughter believes you're dead, and she is completely unaware of who she is. It's a travesty and we need to correct it. You need to come back and then—"

"And then what, Kyp? You think I can beat her? That I haven't tried? I need an army. She's got powerful allies. More than you realize. I'm not gonna take her on and risk everyone. I already lost Arcad that way."

"Keep trying. You must—"

"You still miss her, yeah?"

"What?"

"Jacklyn." My father reached out, taking Kyp's chin in his hand. "Eleven years and you still miss her. My, she had a hold over you."

Kyp looked away. "That is not how time works for me. Every day is forever and no time at all. Every bad thing remains, all good continues. Mother tortures me every day, and Jacklyn... every day she tells me I'm not a freak, like she did when she was here. Like you used to tell me."

"You been to see Jacks?"

Kyp took in a shuddering breath. "We're in the city to recruit Guardians. We got a decent one. A preacher for Janice."

A smile flickered across my father's lips.

"Mother and Gretchen left me alone in the hotel and I snuck out and followed a lead I had. She was running track and saw me watching and smiled at me like I was a stranger. Raymond, she needs to remember who she is. She needs—"

"You?" He made the word a little rounder, more American. "That's the last thing she needs. That's what *you* need."

"It's the same thing. We're stronger together."

"It isn't the same!" He took hold of Kyp's shoulders and shook him, a hard jarring. "Boy, I need you to listen. My girl? I need you to keep this as far away from her as possible. You promised you'd protect her. She's never to learn what she is, and she's never to learn I'm alive. If she does, she'll be in danger because she's my daughter. If you tell her, Lavinia's Order had better be in its damn death throes, you understand?"

Kyp nodded because he thought he could make it happen.

"Oh, don't go doing that. I see that look. I'm telling you to do the impossible first 'cause you'll never manage it."

Forget "thought he could make it happen." Kyp *knew* he could make it happen. For me.

I snapped back to the present to find Lavinia leaning over me, lighter in hand, preparing to light the herbs. She would kill me, she would recite the invocation, and I would be gone.

"You better make it permanent. If I come back, if you have to fight me when I'm in control of my Aegis, I will tear you apart for what you did to my family." I wanted to sound brave, but I was shaking. Tears dripped into my ears, my hair.

I didn't want to die.

The back door rattled open, catching the moonlight in the distance. Lavinia moved to look. I reached up and yanked on the front of her silk shirt, now spotted with my blood, and pulled her close. With my last bit of strength, I grabbed the dagger from her belt loop and plunged it into a spot high on her thigh I'd learned about from watching way too many slasher flicks. The femoral artery. Blood gushed from the wound.

She may kill me but taking her down with me almost made it worth it.

"He outmaneuvered you, bitch. There was one more chess piece on the board. Checkmate."

Lavinia wrapped her hands around my head, and I saw a rush of movement, the face of my father careening toward us, horror written upon his expression as Lavinia snapped my neck with a twist.

TWENTY TWO

Darkness. Cold wetness seeped into me, into my clothes. Grainy dirt covered me.

Buried underground.

The realization brought a frenzied panic. I sucked in a large gulp of air. No air, only soil. Dirt filled my mouth and pressed down on my chest. There, in my grave, I died again.

And again. And again. With each resurrection, I lost a little more of myself, became more desperate, more frenzied.

Survival was all there was. I needed to get out. I needed to move faster.

Dig. Dig. Dig.

Live. Live.

My hands pushed through the soil, swimming through it until I couldn't hold my breath any longer. Soil filled my mouth and lungs.

Dead again. Again.

I could keep dying like this. Digging to the top was too hard, too slow. I could inhale myself to the top—*inhale dirt, die, inhale dirt, die,* until there was nothing left to inhale. Then I would be free.

My hand broke through the soil. I clawed through to the surface, pulling in huge gulps of oxygen-rich night air. My mouth still tasted of dirt, my nose filled with gravel.

Cold. So cold. I quaked with it, collapsed to the ground, my fingers raw and bleeding.

Everything was gone. L-I-V-E written in Gana's blood. I had nothing. Nothing at all here anymore.

Empty.

I glanced up at the sky.

The tree.

Our tree.

Uncle Ray says I'm supposed to keep you safe. Protect you, no matter what.

I love you so much, Jacks.

Kyp's voice, as a child and as a man. And with his voice, the memories of what had occurred came crashing back, my body jerking with their arrival, pain burning through me.

If I was buried beneath our tree, it was he who buried me. He must have believed I had died permanently. Or she made him do it.

I had to tell him somehow. If Kyp buried me, then at the very least, he was alive. Still, he would never be safe. Not here.

Everyone was gone. I was not strong enough to go to war to rescue Kyp alone. My Aegis surged along my fingertips.

"I love you," he had said. "I swear I'll find you."

Keep playing the game, Kyp. I will get a message to you. We'll find each other.

I shivered, jerking on the ground. It wasn't only mourning but also the weather that had me slamming my bones into rocks and tree trunks as I shook.

I struggled to my feet. I ran. As fast as I could, every bit as fast as I was able, through the forest, leaping over corpses of trees, dashing through the brush until my jeans tore to the point of being unusable, dots of my blood speckling the dried blood already on them.

Gana's. My own.

The blanket of my grief overwhelmed me at the sight, weighing me down. I slumped onto the ground on the edge of a road I had once been heading for, too frail to hold myself upright. I heard the sob before I understood it was me, and then I was crying until my throat was hoarse and my head ached. I tried to stop, tried to envision myself in Mom's arms, or Gana's, or Kyp's, but it only made me long for them.

Never again. Once I got through this, nothing would ever tear me down this way again. Never.

I swiped tears and mucus from my face, cleaning myself off with my sleeve. I forced myself to my feet, shaking off the tragedy, determined to survive.

I needed to find a safe place to recover, to plan.

"Jacklyn?" Shrouded in the shadows of the forest around us, barely highlighted by the headlights of a passing car, a figure approached.

I jolted and opened my mouth to scream, but he rushed forward and clapped a hand over my mouth. It tasted like dirt, and I gagged, clamping a fiery hand around his forearm.

"Fucking bollocks!" I looked up into emerald green eyes. Raymond Madison. "Fine!" He removed his hand from my mouth. "Just don't scream."

"I *should* scream." Because to hell with him for leaving me in the ground. For abandoning me yet again.

He rubbed at the arm I burned. A faded tattoo on the inside of his wrist was peppered with scars. A shield with a Key lying across it. Keys and Guardians.

And then, as I had back in my room when I saw blood on Kyp's hands, I heard Ray's voice in my ears, accompanying an image of him, hands on my shoulders.

"It will be grand. Fecked as it seems now, one day you wake and there's a little light beside the darkness. Then a little more, and a little more, and before you know it, you're not living in a world without hope anymore. It will happen slowly, but it will happen."

It had to be a vision from when I was dead, but it brought warmth despite the chill. I understood the other part better now. Kyp *did* have blood on his hands.

"You can trust me. I was part of the Order."

"Raymond Madison. I'm aware." I shook with rage. "Where is Lavinia?"

My bluntness seemed to catch him off guard. "Well, um, you killed each other. I couldn't do the Ritual. If you do it when more than one Key is dead, they'll both go... permanently. Plan B was to take her as far from you as possible, which I did. And don't worry. It took some doing, but it will take a while for her to pull herself together again." He smiled. "I came back as soon as I could, but found you buried. Dug you out a bit until the soil moved, but I figured you didn't want a stranger leaning over you, so I gave you space. Then I followed you here."

"Did you go back to the house? See who survived?"

"No. I was worried for you." He smiled, and it lit his eyes. "My little cailín."

"Stop." I couldn't. Not now. "I'm thinking. So Kyp found me surrounded by Dreviara—"

"Burnt Dreviara," Ray corrected. "She dropped her lighter onto the ring before she died."

If I had found Kyp that way, I'd be devastated. "So Kyp found me lying there in a circle of burnt Dreviara and buried me under the assumption I was dead." I glanced back in the direction of the estate, now miles away.

"Can't go back there," Raymond said. "No way to be sure what awaits. Liv has contacts in the wider world. Someone will probably help her out of her predicament, but that'll take time.

She won't just twiddle her thumbs waiting to kill you, but I can't be sure what her contacts have planned. I can take you with me. Train you so you're better able to take her. Even by herself, she's a feckin' force."

"She used a Ritual to nullify my Aegis. That's how she beat me." I took a deep breath to push the panic from my lungs. "I have to get word to Kyp. To tell him I'm alive."

"Aye," Raymond said. "We have a lad to save, yeah?"

"And a lass. If Kyp's Guardian is still alive."

"So, what do you want to do? I go where you go."

"I want—" I started, but I had to clear my throat before I tried again. "I want revenge. A feasible plan for revenge."

He nodded. "Come with me, Birdie, and I'll prepare you."

Birdie. I nearly choked. It was like my childhood had a sound. I thought it was Mom's nickname for me, but my new memories told me it was his. She had kept it around in honor of him.

"We're going to my car." He waved for me to follow and I fell into step beside him. "Do you still like superheroes?"

I didn't really even know anymore. Did it matter?

"Consider this your origin story. There's so much more to come."

That made me want to punch him. Origin stories always began with tragedy.

"Hey, listen." He stopped walking. "Do you know how to fire a handgun?"

I stopped short. "No." Another phantom memory from my

death. Cold steel in my hand.

"I'll teach ya. A knife then?" He pulled a dagger from his coat, one not so different from the daggers I'd left with Lavinia, and handed it to me. When my hand wrapped around it, he leaned forward, looking me in the eye. "It's okay that you don't trust me. I haven't earned it, yet. So, a weapon to defend yourself."

"Thanks?"

"I owe you. For leaving. You and Kyp. This is me starting to pay it back, yeah?"

He wanted to help, and I needed help.

Everything I was told made me hate him. Everything I remembered made me love him. I wasn't sure anything could make me trust him, but there was no doubt that since discovering the Order, this was what I was looking for. If only I hadn't lost so much on my way.

"Let's go save our people, yeah?" Raymond asked.

"And then what?"

"Who knows? It's better not to plan." He shrugged.

I took one more long look back at the estate. There was no other option. I couldn't go back. I flipped the dagger and stuck it into my belt loop.

"Let's go."

As a child, I used to go running with my father. Now, after all this time, I was running with him again.

I wouldn't run far.

Continue the Story with

Book 2:

The Skeleton Key

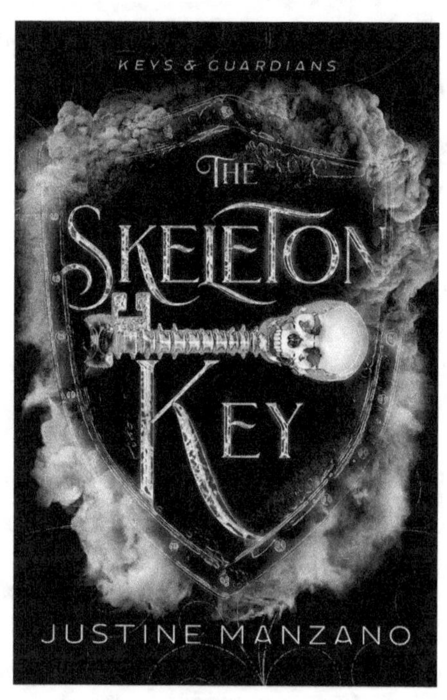

Kyp Franklin can't move on. One year after his mother officially declared war against him, Kyp is still struggling to find his feet as the Order of the Key's new leader. He's far too concerned about tracking her down before she causes even more damage than she already has. In fact, that's all he's been doing. Until one day, after a particularly reckless mission, he returns to find a surprising visitor on his doorstep...

Jacklyn Madison can't move on. One year after she left the Order, she has a new team, and a new mission. She's determined to close all the interdimensional rifts between our world and the Dusk, before more people die trying to stop the creatures that pass through them. But a vision she had while on the edge of death leads her to the one place she never intended to return …

Forced to work together, Jacklyn, Kyp, and their respective teams uncover Lavinia's next plan: an alarming mix of magic and science the likes of which has never been seen before. Jacklyn and Kyp must learn to work together again and confront the demons of their past if they're going to stop Lavinia and those assisting her before their larger plan is put into action—a plan that could bring the monsters of the Dusk to our world...forever.

About Justine Manzano

Justine Manzano is the geeky author of the geeky YA series Keys & Guardians, and geeky YA novel Never Say Never. Known as a Professional-Life-Ruiner-By-Antagonist, Justine's fiction is tough on the outside and sweet on the inside, like an M&M or a hard candy with a gooey center, delivered with sass and snark.

Also a freelance editor, Justine also serves as an Editor-in-Residence at WriteHive, a role which includes co-hosting the Word Nerd Cafe podcast and has also led to her serving on the board of the non-profit organization.

Justine lives in Bronx, NY with her husband, teenage son, and beloved puppy. She can usually be found at her website, www.justinemanzano.com. If you can't find her, she's probably off reading fanfiction. She'll be back soon.

instagram.com/justine_manzano

goodreads.com/justine_manzano

pinterest.com/justinehmanzano

ACKNOWLEDGEMENTS:

It takes a village to make a dream come true. I have been very lucky to have an incredible village. I apologize in advance for my tendency to wax poetic about all the amazing folks in my life. I tried to be funny, for your sake.

First and foremost, thank you to MB and Laynie from Sword & Silk Books for discovering and encouraging my writing. Though this is a new edition of the book, I will always owe you a debt of gratitude. Thank you Kristin, your blog and promotion work is eternally phenomenal. Thank you to Nicole, Jenna, and E.M. for the bountiful support and boosts you've given to me and my work.

Jennia, my editor, thank you for your wise edits and your consistent fangirl-ness. I am so happy to have made a friend and a fan out of you. Thank you to Celin Chen for your gorgeous cover art. I'm lucky to have you.

To my day job peeps, thank you for not getting angry in those moments of downtime when you walked by and saw my computer open to Google Docs. You are all champs. To the 24 crew old and new—you know who you are.

To the Manzano and Minners families at large. I have greatly appreciated your endless support and well-wishes. To the Manzanos—Thank you, thank you, THANK YOU, for raising my loving husband. He is a good man because you made it so.

To the Minners folks—We may all be crazy but we make being crazy fun. Thank you for raising me in an environment that cherished books and that fostered creativity. A special thank you to Grandma Helen and Uncle Bobby. We miss you now and forever.

To my siblings, Melissa and Jon, and their wives Dorothy and Kristy—you have always been my friends as much as you are my siblings. Thank you for being my sounding board and my backbone. You guys rock. Mel, Jon—here's to fight choreography (attack with claw and fang!), war games, invented wrestling federations (CGJW forever) and angry debates about media. You helped mold a geek, is what you did.

Thank you to my mother, Doris Minners, for your endless belief that I was made for big things and your refusal to allow me to stop believing. I wouldn't be who I am today without you.

To the kiddos I've acquired over the years—Millie, Wynnie, Moira, Little Wynnie, Genaro, Kaitlyn, and Chloe. Thank you for letting me be silly with you. It keeps the creativity flowing.

To friends who are family—Allegra, Fruh, Jennine, Anthony, Julian, Liz, Heather, J'vania, Christopher, and Victor—Thank you for being there, always, for basic life support, and for being giving, caring, loving people to myself and my family. Thank you for the belly laughs and the shoulder cries.

To Joy Garcia, my sistah from another mistah. Thank you for listening to me rattle on about all of my crazy ideas even when I can see the question marks circling your head. You have spent the last twenty some-odd years of friendship reminding me to remain unequivocally me. I promise to always understand. I would not still be standing, FOR CERTAIN, without you. Always remember—you are unstoppable.

To the Twitter Writing Community in general, and the Writer In Motion group in particular for the support.

To Casie Bazay and the rest of my Pitch to Publication 2016 crew. Because I am a jerk and forgot to mention your fantastic support in Never Say Never, particularly to Casie, who beta read for me. I am a dingus. Please accept my love.

To the groups at WriteHive and Teacup Dragons for your endless support. To KJ Harrowick for constantly answering my crazy internet questions and for designing my gorgeous website and to Jerusha Marie, Kota Rayne, and S Kaeth for being my biggest fans. You like me more than I do, I swear.

To the Sisterhood of the Traveling Pantsers and the CraftQuest Crew—Maria Tureaud, Ari Augustine, Megan Manzano, R. Miotto, Jeni Chapelle. You are my writing tribe. I don't know where I'd be without you. Probably sitting at a bar, lonely with my vodka and cranberry.

To my personal editors Jeni Chapelle, Maria Tureaud, Kaitlyn Johnson, Megan Manzano, and Ismael Manzano for their important insights and for having faith in this book, some of you since its very inception. You have seen this book in various stages, some stages that never should have been seen by eyes. You each taught me so much about writing, particularly Jeni who pulled a Hail Mary play in the final minutes of the game. You are each amazing.

A separate thank you to Megan Manzano, for being my sister, one of my best friends, and my writing mentor/mentee. Thank you for Tonka Trucks and Tumblr, for YA novels and absurdity. I always knew you were bound for great things. It's crazy how far you've come. I can't wait to see how much farther you'll go.

To Ismael—forget being a knight in shining armor. We've spent our lives rescuing each other. I am a crazy person and you take it and turn it into something beautiful. My partner in all things, my source of encouragement, my pat on the head, the fire under my ass, the smile on my face, the beat of my heart. There is not a single chapter of this book that wasn't read and reread and marked by your loving hands (PINK HIGHLIGHTS!). Thank you for believing in me. There is nobody in this world like you.

To Logan—I started this incarnation of this book while home with you in your first weeks of life because having you, raising you, taught me I could have my dreams in the palm of my hand. You are, always, my inspiration and my greatest adventure. I love you.

And lastly, but most importantly, to my readers—for taking a chance on the story I've been telling myself in my head for so many years. Thank you, and please remember that I would love to hear your thoughts and your opinions on this book and anything else. You are the reason I do this.

Like I said, I've been very lucky. We are all stronger together. Remember.

Also By This Author

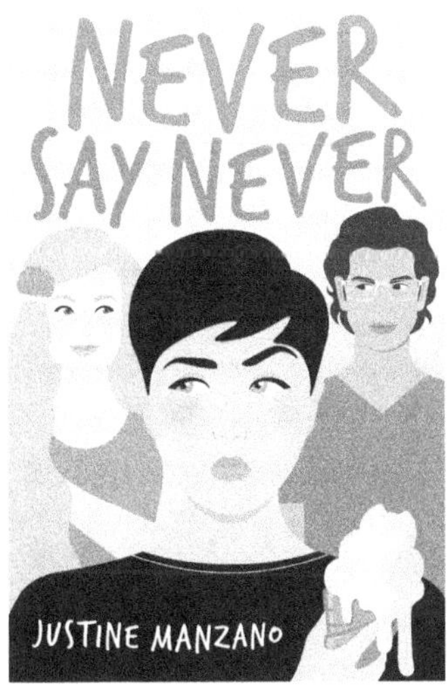

After she walks in on her mom doing the horizontal mambo with a man that's decidedly not her dad, Brynn Stark swears to NEVER fall in love. One of her friends--Val-- reveals her true identity--Aphrodite, goddess of love, and promises to show Brynn why she shouldn't lose faith.

But when Brynn realizes she's beginning to fall for Adam, Aphrodite's boyfriend, Brynn's forced to decide if she'll choose her goddess-given fate, or risk it all for the wrong-but-right guy.

One thing's for sure. Love sucks. And it's all about to blow up in their faces.